"There's r … said.

His tor … cling to a strut, the on … et that kept the view of the ground below at her back. Anxiety seemed to seep up from the empty air beneath them, stealing strength from her legs. "Let's go down."

Meredith's terrified plea spoke to the tender place within Archer that he sometimes feared had calcified. Acting purely on impulse, he held his arms open. Meredith fled into their safety, burying her head against the solidness of his chest.

"It's all right. We'll take the balloon down." He stroked the silken fineness of Meredith's hair. "Don't worry, baby." The endearment slipped out before he had time to censor it.

As he stretched up to reach the line that would deflate the balloon, his sheltering torso swung away. Meredith found herself looking over the edge to the earth hundreds of feet below. It wasn't the stomach-wrenching vision she had expected, but like an illustration out of an airborne *Alice's Adventures in Wonderland.* Her fear dissipated like a wisp of dark smoke.

She reached up to halt Archer's arm. "I think I'd like to stay up."

"Why don't you look around? I'll hang on to you."

Meredith pivoted within the comforting confines of Archer's one-armed embrace, then dared to look down again. The world lay at her feet.

"Only birds and angels have any right to this view," she breathed softly.

ALSO BY TORY CATES

A High, Hard Land

Different Dreams

Where Aspens Quake

Handful of Sky

CLOUD WALTZER

TORY CATES

POCKET BOOKS
New York London Toronto Sydney New Delhi

Pocket Books
A Division of Simon & Schuster, Inc.
1230 Avenue of the Americas
New York, NY 10020

Previously published in 1984 by Silhouette Books.

First Pocket Books paperback edition January 2014

Designed by Lewelin Polanco
Cover illustration by Craig White

Manufactured in the United States of America

10 9 8 7 6 5 4 3 2 1

ISBN 978-1-4767-3256-5
ISBN 978-1-4767-3261-9 (ebook)

Chapter 1

M*eredith Tolliver searched through her* closet, passing long, slender fingers over a variety of silks and delicate woolens. The fabrics, all in subdued shades of brown, khaki, and gray, were fashioned into exquisitely tailored suits and blouses, skirts and blazers. They sported labels and designs that subtly whispered messages of restrained elegance and unrestrained price tags. As she flipped faster and faster through them, the colors blended into one monotonous beige muddle of man-tailored blouses and vested suits. Meredith despised every one of them.

Seemingly without her willing them to, her hands and eyes reached out toward the more recent purchases in her closet. She felt for the nubby cotton of the blouse she'd bought in Santa Fe last week, where she'd met the woman who had handwoven the simple top of eye-dazzling pinks and oranges. She yearned to wear the blouse with her corduroy wraparound skirt of periwinkle blue.

Reluctantly, Meredith banished the idea of wearing the gaily colored clothes. This was most assuredly not the day for indulging her rainbow-hued fancies. She returned to the sober garments she'd rejected.

The trappings of my past life, she reflected, holding out the sleeve of a gray raw-silk suit. It was a life she'd struggled valiantly to lay to rest, but still had to resurrect at times like these to sustain the new life she was in the process of building. She decided that the gray silk was as good a choice as any.

She tugged it out of the closet. It was still encased in the plastic bag from the cleaners in Chicago where she used to take everything except her underwear to be laundered. As an investment banker who could make tens of thousands of dollars for her clients with a couple minutes of phone calls, Meredith's time was far too valuable for her to spend it washing blue jeans. She ripped the bag off her suit and took it into the bathroom with her. The steam from her shower should unkink whatever wrinkles a half a year of disuse had crimped into it.

Half an hour later she was fumbling in front of the bathroom mirror with a scarf as she attempted to knot it about her neck. Damn, she hissed under her breath as the slinky material refused to transform itself into the rosette bow she desired. She was out of practice. Cursing under her breath, Meredith wondered why she was even bothering. Then she reminded herself that if she was going to convince Archer Hanson to agree to an interview with her, she would have to look the part of the successful financial writer she was trying to become.

Worse, though, than the recalcitrant scarf, the long stay in the steamy bathroom had yanked out every bit of the hot-rollered curl she had labored to apply to her stick-straight blond hair and it fell in a straight line to just below the curve of her chin.

She'd always worn it long in Chicago because that was the way Chad had liked it. Each morning she'd spun the pale rope into a chignon before going to work. Then, on those nights when she wasn't too exhausted and he wasn't too busy, Chad had unpinned the bun with a kind of ritualistic zeal, freeing the long, corn-silk blond strands.

As soon as she'd moved to New Mexico, Meredith had chopped off the blond extravagance of her hair, ordering the hairdresser to shape it into a blunt cut that would require no maintenance whatsoever. She ended up with a style reminiscent of the little Dutch boy on paint cans, but she loved the weightless, free feel of it anyway.

"At last," she sighed as the scarf finally obeyed, flopping into an acceptable shape on her shirt front. With the triumphant breath that Meredith sucked in, however, the button on her skirt popped off, ricocheting across the tiled floor. Her annoyance at the lost fastener was short-lived. All she had to do to restore her spirits was to remember those hideous days when she'd had to pin up the back of this very same skirt so that it wouldn't slide right off her. The memory caused Meredith to become inordinately pleased by this latest testimony to her recent weight gains.

In any event, she didn't have the time now to deal with a missing button. She dashed out, picking up her jacket on the way. She simply wouldn't take it off, and no one would ever need to know about the popped button.

As she stepped out the front door, she was surprise-attacked by a rush of emotion that she should have become accustomed to by now. But each time she stepped outside, she fell in love with New Mexíco all over again. Even in the long line of spectacular days which had preceded it, Meredith knew that this particular day would be a standout. October the third. She engraved the date in her memory along with the image of a lustrous black raven winging its way across a crystalline blue sky. As she followed the bird's flight it led her to an even more extraordinary sight: a gigantic striped orb wobbling up through the cool morning air. For a fleeting instant she couldn't imagine what it was, until she suddenly remembered—the Albuquerque International Balloon Fiesta was starting tomorrow. She'd simply been too busy researching Archer Hanson to take any more than a perfunctory interest in the event.

She interpreted her first sighting of a gaily decorated hot-air balloon as a good omen. She steadfastly refused to take it any other way—she would need all the luck she could muster for her meeting with Archer Hanson.

The headquarters of the Hanson Development Corporation was far out in Albuquerque's North Valley, where orchards, small ranches, and expensive new subdivisions blossomed along the Rio Grande. Meredith always enjoyed this drive along the narrow, twisting road since it took her past one very special pasture that was fenced in with thick railroad ties. Inside this heavy-duty fence were living relics of the old West, a herd of buffalo. The sight of the beasts' barrel-chested bodies never failed to delight Meredith.

Today, however, she was too intent upon rehearsing the words that would convince Mr. Hanson to let her interview him to notice the shaggy creatures. She pulled up in front of the renovated adobe that served as the corporation's headquarters and entered through an enclosed courtyard.

"May I help you?" the receptionist, a brunette with a headful of doll-like curls, asked.

"Yes, I'm Meredith Tolliver. I have an appointment with Mr. Hanson."

The receptionist ran a polished nail down the appointment calendar in front of her. "I'm sorry." She looked up coolly. "But when you didn't arrive fifteen minutes ago at your appointment time, Mr. Hanson called in one of his foremen for a conference. He just arrived. Would you care to reschedule?"

"No." Meredith shook her head, annoyed at herself and her silly scarf for her tardiness. "I'll wait until he's free if that's all right."

"Suit yourself," the receptionist replied in what struck Meredith as a rather unprofessional tone.

Meredith found a seat, almost glad for the delay. It would give her a chance to review the file she'd collected on Archer Hanson. Or rather had attempted to collect. It was a pretty thin and sketchy affair, which was one reason she'd been so intrigued by the man. From the articles she'd culled from the financial section of the *Albuquerque Journal*, it was quite evident that Archer Hanson was a pivotal force in the state's economy, possibly *the* pivotal force. It was hard to tell, though, because all either she or the *Journal* had been able to come up with were reports on matters of public record, such as the filing of the building permit for the multimillion-dollar convention center complex that had become the hub of downtown Albuquerque, or the opening of his solar research firm a couple of years ago.

Though no one had ever put Archer Hanson's whole

story together, Meredith had traced back bits and pieces of it. She'd discovered that his father, Gunther Hanson, had made a fortune in the Texas oil fields in the sixties. The common assumption was that the old man had bankrolled his only son and that he was the one who had played puppet master to Archer's career.

Maybe that was another reason why this untold story appealed to Meredith so strongly. If anyone knew about the machinations of wealthy fathers, she did. The thought disturbed her, but she clung to it anyway. If her painfully gathered insights could help her capture this story, she couldn't afford to let them slip away just because they stirred up the old hurt.

She thumbed through her notes again. They were long on the hard one-dimensional facts that could be culled from Dun & Bradstreet financial reports about Archer Hanson, the entrepreneur, and terribly short on information about Archer Hanson, the man. In all her preliminary research she hadn't even come across one photograph of him. Based on the fact that Hanson senior was in his mid-seventies, Meredith had reckoned that Hanson Junior must be in his early to mid-fifties.

Without any conscious effort on her part, she'd evolved a mental image of the man. To have accomplished what he had over the past years, he would have to be something of a workaholic. Given that assumption, Meredith had imagined a stoop-shouldered, bald man of enormous mental capabilities who had gone a bit to seed physically.

She smoothed a nonexistent crease out of her skirt, glad that she had decided to wear what she now considered her "corporate camouflage." The Hanson headquarters presented the understated elegance of the very powerful. Meredith saw it all around her. She knew what property in the North Valley cost and how expensive old adobes had become. Hanging on a wall behind the receptionist was an original Fritz Scholder. She knew that museums could barely afford to acquire the Native American artist's work. Being in the heart of the corporate beast again caused her palms to slick over and her stomach to pull into a hard knot.

The phone purred.

"Yes, Miss Tolliver is here *now.*" The receptionist emphasized the last word almost as if she were scolding Meredith for her tardiness. Meredith quickly dug through her purse for a tissue to wipe her palms. She wanted a dry, confident hand to extend to Mr. Hanson.

The door to the office opened and a weather-beaten man holding a battered cowboy hat backed out.

"Okay," he said, "I'll get right on it. Be back with you in a day or two." The man jammed the hat onto his head and closed the door behind him. He leaned in close to the receptionist on his way out and confided to her in a low voice: "Boy, is he ever riled about the slowdown at the mine. Told me if I didn't get things cleared up pronto, he'd have my hide."

Meredith could just imagine how upset Mr. Hanson was at having his cash flow impeded. Knowing what she did about mine conditions in general, she figured the slowdown was some kind of labor protest that the foreman had been ordered to stamp out. A thread of guilt pulled tight within her at the memory of her own involvement in a world where the bottom line always came before human concerns.

"You'd better get on it, then, Mr. Nelson," the receptionist replied coolly to the distraught foreman's whispered confidence. She looked away as he departed and quirked an eyebrow in Meredith's direction. "You can go in now." Her tone implied that any fool would have already figured that out for herself.

Meredith gathered up her file, notebook, and purse. A mild flutter pushed her pulse up. Sternly she reminded herself that this was hardly the first time she'd stepped into the lion's den of corporate power. She'd once occupied one herself. Or something fairly close. She'd advised shipping tycoons, oil billionaires, and industrial magnates without giving it a second thought. Of course, she had never cared as much as she cared now, and that, Meredith supposed, made the difference.

She turned the knob and stepped into a whirlwind. As impeccably furnished and immaculately cared for as the reception area had been, Hanson's office was just as slapdash and chaotic. Papers were stacked everywhere. Empty foam cups were stacked in precarious pyramids. It was impossible to tell much about the furniture because every piece of it was buried beneath annual reports, yellowing copies of *The Wall Street Journal*, and casually discarded pieces of clothing.

It took a moment for Meredith to turn her attention from the turmoil to the object of her visit. She searched behind the mountain of papers on the desk and found a jeans-clad man, his booted feet propped up on the desktop, talking on the phone. His rangy body was stretched back in his swivel chair so far that he was close to lying down. He was glowering at the ceiling, completely unaware of Meredith's presence.

Surely, Meredith thought, Archer Hanson had stepped out for a moment and this was his son. A quick glance at his profile registered that this man couldn't be older than mid-thirties. Given her approximation of Archer Hanson's age, this man must be his son. He looked the part of the idle rich kid too, she decided, with his wind- and sun-reddened face and the kind of leanly muscled body that was most at home ranging over a tennis court or a polo pony. She'd grown up with spoiled, entitled boys just like him. She hoped he wouldn't stay around once his father returned.

"Right," he barked into the phone. "I heard all that

already. But I don't want excuses and rationalizations. I want action."

His angry words blistered the air around Meredith. She pitied whoever was on the other end of the line. Probably a car mechanic, she hypothesized, who couldn't get this rich kid's Jaguar back to him quickly enough. He was so caught up in his temper tantrum that Meredith was able to observe him at her leisure. A thatch of hair, as blond as hers, yet just as wildly unruly as hers was neatly straight, swept back from a high forehead dominated by dark brows and lashes. This contrast between blond and sable lent his face a striking air of drama.

Abruptly he turned to her. Meredith was startled by the eyes she found turned upon her. The irises were the kind of blue that made her think of the deep end of the pool on a hot summer day. Now, lit as they were by the flame of rage, they took on that unearthly aura that sometimes radiates from light, light blue eyes. For a moment Hanson's son looked like a crazed malamute. The effect was heightened by the dark lashes that framed the rage-paled eyes. With his ear and mind still turned to the person on the other end of the phone, he stabbed his forefinger in the air a few times, pointing toward a chair. Meredith unscrambled his message and took a seat.

"Fine. I told Nelson that I wanted a full report in the

next day or two. Why don't you see to it that he has some good news for me, or you'll both be looking for new jobs."

Disapproval curdled Meredith's expression as Hanson's son slammed down the phone. She *had* known too many men just like him. Born into privilege and luxury, they spent their pampered lives terrorizing and bullying everyone unfortunate enough to cross their paths as they acted out their grotesque parodies of the real power that their influential fathers wielded. It was a parody she had come horrifyingly close to perpetuating herself. She was determined that Hanson's son would not get the chance to exercise his petty tyranny over her.

Before he could speak, Meredith stated her mission in a prim voice, "I'm here to see your father, Archer Hanson."

The fury staining Hanson's cheeks gradually subsided. As it did, the color in his face seemed to seep into the crystal eyes, darkening them to a slightly more ordinary hue. As he collected himself, Hanson appeared to finally notice Meredith. He crossed his arms over his chest and, still leaning far back in the reclining chair, cocked his head and studied her. He put one finger to his lips in a mock pensive pose.

"You're here to see my 'father'? Archer Hanson?" he asked with a superciliousness that was not lost on Meredith.

She felt her dislike crystallize into an icy hostility that seamed her lips into a tight, prissy line. It was all so disgustingly familiar. The sassy rich kid toying with what he took to be his inferior. Never mind the underling's sense of dignity; that was all too easily sacrificed for a moment of amusement.

"That's correct," she replied with all the curtness she could inject into the answer.

A smile crept across Hanson's face. Meredith knew that her bristling, spinsterish appearance and answer were the source of his amusement. It had amused others before. Combined with her fair hair and porcelain skin, the aloof professional demeanor she had cultivated when she started to work for her father had earned her the nickname Ice Princess. Hanson probably thought that his smile would be enough to melt even the heart of an Ice Princess. She suspected that he probably had ample evidence with which to back up that theory.

"First of all," he said through a barricade of orthodontically perfect teeth, "my father's name is Gunther Hanson. And second, I'm Archer Hanson."

Meredith was on the verge of disputing that claim when the rakish smile disappeared and the casual posture was dropped. It became all too apparent in that one moment that this man had no need to parody power, for he generated an abundant supply of his own. Meredith had survived for years in her former profession by developing catlike emotional reflexes. She summoned them up now and refused to let embarrassment disconcert her.

She stood and stiffly stretched out her hand. Archer Hanson leaned forward without standing and took it.

"I'm Meredith Tolliver. Perhaps you've read my column in the local paper."

"No, Miss Tolliver, I'm afraid I don't get much time to read popular periodicals."

"I doubt that it would interest you much anyway. It's a financial column geared for the average person. I also freelance for several business magazines. The editor of *Enterprise* wrote recently asking if I might be able to do a profile on you, Mr. Hanson."

"So old Charlie is at it again, eh?" Hanson smiled broadly as Meredith thought of Charles Wendler, editor of the country's most respected business publication, being referred to as "old Charlie."

"I hate to burst any bubbles, Miss, Miss . . ." Hanson whirled his hand in the air as if groping for the name that eluded him. It stung Meredith a bit to realize that she had made no more of an impression upon Archer Hanson than he had upon her.

"Tolliver," she supplied stiffly.

"Right. Tolliver," he burst out as if she'd correctly answered an especially difficult item on an oral quiz. "But you're the fourth reporter Charlie has tossed my way. You wouldn't have gotten past the receptionist except that she's new and I haven't had time to explain to her that I don't care to see any member of the press at any time."

"I certainly didn't intend to force myself on you," Meredith answered coolly. Inside she was shrieking with the desire to turn sharply on her heel and leave. Preferably with a satisfyingly resonant slam of the door behind her. Much as it galled her to even appear that she was pursuing this insufferably arrogant man, she had no choice. If she planned on establishing herself as a business writer, she absolutely couldn't go back to Charles Wendler empty-handed. "It's just that there's been so little written about you beyond the bare bones facts of your business dealings. I'd like to flesh out that picture a bit."

"Miss Tolliver, if it were up to me not even the barest of my bones would ever appear in print." Hanson did nothing to soften the brusque finality of his comment. "I haven't been terribly impressed by my few experiences with business reporters. They've been underinformed and overzealous and I'd prefer just to avoid the entire issue. So, if you will excuse me, I'm sure you have a busy day ahead of you."

Rather than stand up as Hanson clearly expected her to do, Meredith slumped farther into her chair. "You're wrong, Mr. Hanson. I don't have a busy day ahead of me. I have a very empty day. I've finished my column for the week and have no other assignments. I'm running out of my savings from my old job and what they pay at the paper for my column barely keeps my cat fed. I can understand your feelings"—Meredith was not going to let the depression that was threatening to crush her creep into her voice—"but I am neither underinformed *nor* overzealous. I brought along clippings of my column and some of the magazine articles I've freelanced."

For a long moment Hanson stared at the odd woman who seemed to have collapsed in front of him. He carefully slid his legs off of his desk and faced her head-on. When he spoke again it was with the voice of a completely different person. It was almost as if, at the same time that Meredith abandoned her Ice Princess armor, he laid aside his hard-boiled facade. "Come on, then," he prompted gently, "let's have a look."

He extended a large hand toward the portfolio that Meredith clenched on her lap. She stood awkwardly before him and passed over the collection of her work. He leafed through it, pausing to read sections with an absorption so total that Meredith felt he'd forgotten she was there. The sound of his voice startled her.

"Unlike most of your colleagues, Miss Tolliver, you *do* seem to have a passing acquaintance with your subject." He continued studying the clippings spread before him. Suddenly he glanced up. "Why don't you tell me about yourself?"

Meredith, brightening somewhat at his encouraging tone, delivered a truncated version of her professional résumé. "Master's from the Wharton Business School in Philadelphia. Then a year on the Street," she said, watching Hanson's reaction to be sure that he understood that she meant *the Street,* Wall Street. He did. "Then two years with an investment firm in Chicago." She didn't add that the firm was the largest of its kind in the country outside of New York. Or that it belonged to her father. "I've been in Albuquerque for nearly half a year now."

Hanson scribbled some figures on his desk blotter. "That makes you what? Twenty-six, twenty-seven?"

"Twenty-six," Meredith admitted reluctantly, afraid that her relative youth would be seen as a handicap. She was surprised that Hanson had guessed so accurately. Most people assumed that, with a master's degree and several years experience, she must be considerably older than she was.

"Why'd you give it up? You were obviously a whiz kid, a Wall Street *wunderkind* on the express route straight to the top. Why are you out here scrambling around for freelance assignments?"

Meredith was no stranger to fielding hard questions and thinking under pressure, but this man's directness unnerved her. She yearned again to escape. This time from his laserlike scrutiny. If Archer Hanson weren't the one subject in Albuquerque who could guarantee her a feature story in *Enterprise,* she would have. But too much was at stake to indulge her pride. Instead she'd have to swallow it and at the same time convince him to agree to an interview. Meredith decided to try the truth. Or a small portion of it at any rate.

"I came out here a year ago last fall on a business trip and fell in love with New Mexico. When I went back to Chicago"—she paused, sorting through that tortured time in her life, looking for an explanation that wouldn't be either a complete lie or too close to the truth—"my whole world suddenly seemed gray and empty." It was an innocuous enough description. Meredith wondered grimly how the intimidating Mr. Hanson would react if he knew the facts it hid.

Her world had begun to come apart at the seams long before that trip. As her memory swirled briefly over it, one image surfaced from those memories: Meredith saw herself, alone, long after even the most ambitious workaholic had gone home, still slaving away in the plushly appointed office her father had insisted she take when she had started to work for him. It was an office that far exceeded her position as the most junior associate in the firm. Still he had insisted upon it, and Meredith had acceded to that wish just as she had to all his others ever since her brother's death. She took the office, then proceeded to drive herself slowly crazy in her attempt to be worthy of it.

That was when the dieting had started. Convinced that she was a grotesque embarrassment to her father and his firm, she had whittled away at what seemed to be lumpy mounds of fat. She had dieted until there was no fat and nearly no flesh left. But instead of the walking skeleton that everyone else saw, when Meredith looked in the mirror she found a disgusting, undisciplined blob. That was when the whispers behind her back had begun, and the visits to doctors that her father insisted were just social calls. When the word *anorexia* had entered her vocabulary.

"Gray and empty?" Hanson prompted. The piercing eyes urged her on and suddenly the interview was forgotten. Meredith found herself aching to tell this man her whole story. About her illness, about Chad, about the ongoing dilemmas she lived with. Quickly she reminded herself that Archer Hanson was in the mold of privilege and insensitivity that she had struggled so desperately to free herself from. She would tell him the truth, but only a palatable, sanitized version.

"Yes, Chicago was gray, my job was gray, the weather was gray, and I was tired of it. I suppose most of all, I was tired of the gray men who had been populating my life and their dreary vision of life as a one-track scramble up the ladder of success with no stops for joy or laughter. They were devoid of passion, emotion, all the things that make life worth living. After my initial visit out here, I couldn't stand the life I'd been living in that twilit country. I spent all my time daydreaming about moving out here where the colors are so vibrant they make your eyes ache."

Archer Hanson fixed her with a stare that made

Meredith think of her first glimpse of the New Mexico sky. Somehow she felt he'd understood everything she'd said. She'd forged a link with Archer Hanson. Surely he wouldn't turn down her request now. Surely he could see that she wasn't one of the bungling, inept reporters that blighted the profession she'd chosen. Buoyed up by that certainty, Meredith elaborated on her answer.

"Sure, I'm only making a fraction of what I made before. But there are other rewards. For the first time ever I feel like my life is my own. I don't feel as if I'm living out someone else's dream of success. I'm proud of the work I do, especially my column. I think it's important to make finance understandable to ordinary people. To keep it from being a closed game played by anonymous men who hold all the cards of wealth and power."

"Men like myself?" Hanson asked, steepling his hands on the desk in front of him.

Meredith suddenly felt that she had been lured into a trap, tricked into exposing herself. Still, she'd struggled too hard to uncover that self to deny it now. "Does the shoe fit, Mr. Hanson?" she asked with a disarming piquancy.

"That's somewhat immaterial here, isn't it? The relevant point is that I'd be a damned fool to let myself be interviewed by a writer who'd already pretty much made up her mind that I was going to wear that shoe whatever the fit."

Meredith forced herself to answer in a neutral tone. "I haven't come to any conclusions yet about you, Mr. Hanson."

"Haven't you? I wonder." He spoke the words in a way that left no doubt that he had seen Meredith's prejudices for what they were. "No, Meredith, I'm not going to allow this interview. But not for any of the reasons I'm sure you'll come up with."

In that moment, Meredith wasn't sure whether the fact that Archer Hanson had blocked her way into *Enterprise* magazine or his demeaning use of her first name irritated her more. "Well, then, *Archer*"—she took pointed aim at *his* first name and then gleefully fired on it—"I won't waste any more of your time." She stood crisply, almost as if the icy armor of the Ice Princess were freezing around her again, and leaned forward to collect her portfolio from his desk. As she did, Archer Hanson clamped one strong hand around a wrist that appeared matchstick fragile by comparison.

"Since we're already on a first-name basis, Meredith"—again he threw her name up to her, taunting the image of cool professionalism she wanted to project—"why don't we have dinner together? You can tell me all about reshuffling the cards of wealth and power and I can . . . well, perhaps a woman like yourself would be more comfortable telling *me* exactly what she'd like from a man like myself."

Meredith jerked her wrist free. Anger flushed a

blaze of color into her cheeks. "Of all the arrogant, high-handed . . ." She let the words trail off in her mind. Sealing her mouth into a tight line, she wordlessly gathered up her other things and left.

What in God's name had driven him to act like that? The question scalded Archer Hanson's brain the instant the door closed with a barely muffled slam. He wished it were possible to rip the boorish words that he had spoken from the air around him. He winced as those words reverberated in his mind. Perhaps he'd spoken them as some kind of instinctual protest against the prejudices she had worn as surely as her executive-lady demeanor. For a second he wondered if those instincts might have been wrong.

No, he answered himself, Miss Meredith Tolliver had definitely come into his office with a strongly preconceived set of notions about the man she was going to be meeting. His tip-off had been the way she'd looked at him. It was a look that he'd become all too familiar with in his boyhood.

A brief remembrance of those days, of riding out with his father to the old man's oil fields, came to Archer Hanson totally unbidden and fully intact. He saw himself sitting up as tall as a gangly eight-year-old could in the front seat of his father's brand-new candy apple red Cadillac with white leather upholstery, watching the miles of beige landscape fly past his window.

His father, with his stockman's narrow-brimmed cowboy hat clamped down on his head and half-moons of sweat forming under the arms of the long-sleeved shirts he always wore buttoned all the way up, kept the big car aimed straight down the middle of the road. The dust rolled in the windows as his father pushed the gas pedal down flat and they flew over those endless unpaved miles. Archer remembered thinking that no other boy had a father who could drive so straight and true. He'd nestled, utterly content, into the cushioning leather seat where his mother used to sit before she got sick and went to the hospital and never came home again.

That had been the same day that Archer first became aware that his view of his father as a shining hero didn't jibe with the opinion the rest of the world held. He'd gone with Gunther to check on some drilling not too far from their home in Fort Worth. All the men had smiled and kowtowed to his father, to the big boss, when they were speaking to him directly. Archer, though, remembered walking away, then turning back briefly. That was when he saw it for the first time, the unconcealed contempt the workers held for the man who ruled their lives.

Much as Archer resisted at first, his childhood illusions began to dissolve that day. In time, he too saw the man those workers had seen. His father was bombastic, high-handed, spoiled, and a rank abuser of privilege. In short, he was everything that Archer himself had been with Meredith. Everything that she had expected him to be. For he'd caught the same look in her eyes today that he'd seen more than a quarter of a century ago in the eyes of those oil field workers.

"Damn her self-righteous assumptions," Hanson breathed as he thought of her again. His burning annoyance mysteriously cooled, however, as he remembered the way her hair, that straight, silken curtain, had shimmered along the curve of her jaw as she'd leaned forward over his desk, touching him with the smell of perfume and the unconscious grace of her motions. He remembered her leaning there and the way her lips had hung above him like some unspeakably delectable fruit, plump and ready for the picking.

Irritation and arousal collided within Archer Hanson, muddling into a soppy pool of frustrated self-recriminations. He wished he could back up for only half an hour and start again. He'd still deny Meredith Tolliver her interview. But he wanted very badly to redo his refusal in such a way that he still might have a chance of tasting those lips.

Dammit all, Archer Hanson thought again as he plowed into the work waiting for him in a day already soured by regret.

Chapter 2

Meredith was still fuming when she wrenched open the door to her small efficiency apartment. Inside was a paradoxical mixture of possessions. Like the silver heirloom coffee service surrounded by the mismatched ceramic mugs she'd picked up at a yard sale. Meredith had balked at taking the silver service, but her mother had forced it on her, saying that her own mother had intended for Meredith to have it.

Then there was the handwoven Italian tapestry bedspread thrown over the rickety roll-away bed that she slept on. The monogrammed, silver-backed brush and comb set she'd grown up with now sat beside a discount store lipstick and a cake of soap she'd bought with the help of a cents-off coupon.

Even her cat, a Persian with a pedigree longer than the querulous animal's dense coat of blue-gray fluff, was a walking monument to the schizophrenic nature of Meredith's new life as he nibbled disdainfully at the generic-brand cat food in his monogrammed porcelain bowl.

The sight of her pampered pet, Thoreau, named in honor of an undergraduate passion for the early American writer, caused the nimbus of anger whirling around Meredith to dissipate.

"Oh, Thor," she sighed, slumping into a chair beside her kitchen table, "we both have such a long way to go on this new road I've set us on. Don't we, old boy?"

Thor looked up from the dish of food he was picking at desultorily. Winding a sinuous path lazily toward Meredith, the plump Persian sprang into her lap.

"You big bully," she laughed as the overstuffed cat began kneading her stomach. It was inevitable; Thor never sought the slightest bit of human attention unless his mistress was wearing either a dark outfit, preferably one that had to be dry-cleaned, or something like the raw-silk skirt with little nubbies that the claws he didn't bother to retract could pull out and unravel.

"Go ahead, you little lardbelly, do your worst. I'm through with the corporate camouflage. Not only is it unutterably drab, it doesn't even work." She stroked between his ears, and the soft kneading against her belly stopped. Thor's jade green eyes closed into two slits of feline bliss.

"Are you listening to me?" Meredith asked. Thor

replied with a deep rumbling purr. Thor. When had she stopped calling him Thoreau? she wondered. Probably about the same time she'd put aside her literature studies at college and changed her major to business. About the time Rory had died. Rory, a golden name for the golden boy who had been her brother and the shining hope of the Tolliver family. Meredith noted that it almost didn't hurt anymore to think about him. Almost. And it had only taken six years.

"Thor." She breathed the cat's name, but he didn't respond. Now, instead of symbolizing her love of literature, everyone who heard her call her cat thought she had some strange fixation on Nordic gods. Against her will she found herself thinking of Archer Hanson and wondering whether his ancestry was Nordic. She could easily picture him as a rampaging Viking with his white-blond hair and ruddy, hard-planed face. Could imagine his thickly muscled shoulders swinging a broad axe as he pillaged coastal villages. And coastal virgins? she asked herself wryly.

In a way, she thought abstractedly, we each represent opposite ends of the blond spectrum. She visualized herself, with her cool, aloof, porcelain-doll fragility, at one end of that spectrum, and Archer Hanson, with his wild thicket of hair, unearthly eyes, and flaming, sun-burnished magnetism, at the other.

Just as she had been trained to, Meredith followed

that detached intellectual perception to its source. It led to the emotional core of her reaction to Archer Hanson. Magnetism. Beneath irritation, humiliation, scorn, and any thoughts for the career she was trying to build lay attraction. She had been undeniably and overwhelmingly attracted to the man.

"Up, up, up." She stood abruptly, sending Thor skittering down the front of her skirt, pulling out more threads of raw silk the whole way. "Now look what you've done," Meredith moaned, though the lament was intended far more for herself than Thor. "I'm going to need to sell this suit, you know, to keep us both fed."

Thor flipped his puffy tail straight up toward the ceiling and padded away, regally unconcerned with his human's plight.

Meredith tore off the suit, wishing she could strip away the realization she'd so recently arrived at along with it. It was certainly humiliating enough to have been turned down and rudely propositioned by a man with more money than manners, but to come home with a crush on the lout? That was indeed a low blow and one she would most assuredly not let Mr. Archer Hanson land.

Changing quickly into the periwinkle skirt and gaily woven blouse she'd wanted to wear that morning, Meredith grabbed up her notebook and purse and, after an apologizing pat on Thor's head, slammed out of the tiny apartment. She headed for the public library downtown.

Almost as if she believed that by staying in rapid motion she could prevent Archer Hanson's magnetism from reaching her, Meredith drove faster than she should have, then rushed into the library when she arrived.

She spent the afternoon studying *Writer's Market*, the freelancer's bible, and perusing back issues of magazines she thought might accept her articles. After her failure with Archer Hanson, Meredith had faced the fact that she had to branch out of purely financial writing unless she wanted to return to Chicago in defeat. By the end of the day she'd come up with a couple of ideas that she thought might prove saleable, but knew that she'd need a bundle more. She drove home with one eye on traffic lights and the other scanning the streets for potential article material.

Even if she sent out a slew of prizewinning ideas this very night, Meredith realized as she plodded wearily up the stairs, it would be months before she'd have the articles written and published, and even longer before they were paid for. As she was unlocking her second-floor apartment, her neighbor, Phil, an engineering undergraduate at the university, popped his head out his front door.

"I've been straining to hear the pitter-patter of little keyboard clicks all day," he announced. "Where have you been?" Though she enjoyed her neighbor and was glad of his friendship, at times, like the present, Phil's youthful enthusiasm tended to make Meredith feel old and weary.

"At the library. Come on in; I'll fix us some tea."

"Can't now. I have an organic chem quiz tomorrow afternoon. But, listen, I wanted to find out if you could be on our chase crew tomorrow morning."

"Chase crew?" Meredith echoed the words.

"You Yankees," Phil sighed, shaking his head in mock despair. "A chase crew for the Balloon Fiesta. Usually you have to go to a bunch of meetings and training sessions to get on one, but someone from our crew got sick, so we need another person. I told them I'd ask you."

"I still don't understand, Phil. What precisely does a chase crew do?"

"As you might suspect," he answered impishly, "they chase. Balloons, to be precise. Every balloon is assigned a crew of about half a dozen people. We stumble out real early, five-thirty, six, and help the pilot launch his balloon. Then, since the pilot has no way of guiding a balloon, we chase it around until he comes down. Then we help him pack it back up. The neat part about it for most people is that at least once during the fiesta, your pilot will take you up for a ride. What do you say?"

With her mind fixed so firmly on the track she'd set it on that afternoon, one thought immediately sprang up: Could be an article here.

"We really do need another pair of hands for a safe launch," Phil pleaded. "What do you say?"

"Aside from that five-thirty launch time, your offer sounds irresistible."

Phil's grin made him look even more like Howdy Doody than he normally did, stretching his wide mouth and freckles across his broad face. "All right!" he enthused. "The rap you hear at your door tomorrow at an ungodly hour will be mine. So be ready to roll, okay?"

"Okay," Meredith agreed as Phil's door swung closed. She was smiling as she entered her own apartment. An adventure was precisely what she needed to take her mind off of today's debacle. As Thor twined between her legs Meredith puzzled over which magazine to submit the balloon story to and what angle to take with it. After a dinner that was simple but, like all her meals had been since she'd left Chicago, scrupulously balanced nutritionally, Meredith outlined the query letter she would type up tomorrow and went to bed.

Meredith's dream that night was of soaring through the sky in a Viking warship with its full white sails billowing in a reckless wind. And of being clasped in a warrior's embrace that was both far too strong and far too compelling for her to break. Along with the image came all the old, familiar anxieties, both named and nameless.

At six the next morning Meredith was pacing her tiny apartment, much to Thor's annoyance, and wondering what had become of Phil's predawn departure. Just as she was about to go next door to investigate, a loud pounding signaled that Phil had arrived.

"Jeez, I'm sorry," he announced sheepishly, still dazed from sleep. "I was booking it until three this morning and just slept right through the alarm. We'd better hustle. Drat, I hope we don't miss the launch."

As they started out the door Phil stopped her and glanced down at her feet. She was wearing her hiking boots. "Good shoes," he commented. "We'll probably end up doing a lot of tromping across fields. If you have a pair of leather gloves, you'd better bring those too. You can get a nasty rope burn on those balloon lines."

Meredith fetched an old pair of ski gloves and they were off. Outside, the cold and dark of night still held sway and she slipped on her kelly green parka over the raspberry sweater she'd topped off her jeans with. The vivid color combination warmed her soul as much as the wool and goose down warmed her body. She and Phil piled into his Jeep Wrangler and set off for the Balloon Fiesta Field on the northern outskirt of Albuquerque. She and Phil were snuggled deep in the silence of early morning as they watched the earth wake up while they tried to do the same.

A thin line of pink stretched out in the dark sky above the Sandia Mountains to the east, limning their granite bulks in the pastel radiance that announces dawn. Meredith looked off to the west. There, above the jagged silhouette of the five extinct volcanic cones that crowned the West Mesa, reigned a gleaming silver dollar of a full moon. Meredith was transfixed by the loveliness of the dawn moon, staring at it for several long minutes as the Jeep rolled northward. The vehicle melded into the line of cars making their way to the launch site. They passed a special city bus, crammed with sleepy passengers headed for the Balloon Fiesta. The Jeep's headlights picked out a bumper sticker on the pickup truck ahead of them. It read, "Follow Me, I Chase Balloons."

Meredith glanced up from reading the sticker and was stunned by the sight that greeted her. There, hovering in the sky above them, floated a giant orb, glowing orange in the navy darkness. As suddenly as it appeared, the globe was gone.

Though Phil didn't actually look up to see the balloon himself, he heard a characteristic whooshing sound and caught the look of surprise that crossed Meredith's face and guessed its source. "It's a balloon," he explained, though she had been able to figure that much out for herself. "They light up and make that noise when the pilot hits the burners. That releases a stream of propane gas that ignites to keep the warm air inside the balloon heated up. The flame lights up the entire envelope."

Meredith nodded her comprehension, unable to drag her eyes away from the now-empty sky.

Then it appeared again. The balloon had bobbed through the western sky until it drew alongside its luminous twin, the dawn moon. The blaze from the burners had illuminated the balloon's design. It was a radiant unicorn rearing up on its hind legs and stabbing his single glorious horn at the vastness of the empty universe above him. Meredith was transfixed by the wholly unexpected beauty of the sight.

Phil, absorbed in negotiating the tangle of traffic that had suddenly developed, missed the display entirely. The Jeep bumped off the highway onto the frontage road that led to the back entrance of the field. A guard checked the pass on Phil's front windshield that verified he was a chase crew member and then flagged him on through the special entrance. They pulled into the parking area located on a bluff overlooking the launch area below where fiesta activities centered.

Meredith was surprised at the number of people who'd gotten out of warm beds so early on such a chilly morning. It looked like a carnival with endless rows of cars parked around the periphery of the field and thousands of people milling about at its center where balloonists were unloading their gear and concessionaires were selling steaming cups of coffee to frozen spectators.

"We'd better move it," Phil advised, sliding out of the Jeep. Before locking up he patted his pockets, then looked around inside the vehicle. "Dammit!" he cursed himself. "I forgot to bring the directions to our balloon. The field is divided into a grid and I can't remember what our coordinates are."

"You remember what the balloon looked like, don't you?" Meredith asked.

"Sure. It has a really unusual design. But look at how many balloons are down there. Six hundred are registered from more than nineteen countries. They're not all here today, but still . . ." His voice trailed off miserably as they both looked out on what now seemed an unending sea of people clustered around the slack heaps of uninflated balloons.

"We'll find it, Phil," Meredith offered with more optimism than she honestly felt. They headed down the hill toward the launch area. Once there, Meredith truly did feel as if she were in the midst of a carnival with all the people and activities around her serving as the midway. Nearly everyone was bundled up in parkas and ski hats. Balloon Fiesta officials in bright blue and yellow jackets buzzed about, attending to the thousand and one details that go into keeping an event that was expected to attract 700,000 spectators during its nine-day run functioning smoothly.

As they reached the first balloonist and his crew, Meredith's footsteps slowed. The uninflated balloon envelope lay on the ground like a sail drooping off the main mast in a becalmed sea. The size of it surprised her.

Meredith figured it must be sixty or seventy feet long. A dozen crew members and onlookers were spread along its length. At the pilot's signal they all grabbed onto the nylon skin and began lofting it toward the sky as if they were trying to resuscitate the flattened beast. Gradually a pocket of air formed in the envelope.

"Come on, Meredith." Phil coaxed her away from the watching crowd. "During the course of the coming week you'll see this whole operation so many times you'll be sick of it. But for right now we've got to find the Cloud Waltzer."

"The who?" Meredith asked as she pulled herself away from the intriguing operation.

"Cloud Waltzer. That's the name of the balloon we're assigned to."

"Cloud Waltzer." Meredith ran the syllables over her tongue, liking the feel of them.

Hurrying after Phil, she passed an assortment of balloon aficionados: A man in an Australian bush hat pinned up on one side surveying the action through a pair of field glasses. A chubby woman with a frizzy perm that matched the topknot of the poodle she had nestled beneath her sweater. A sleepy child wearing his father's jacket and dragging the sleeves in the dust as he toddled after his parents. The giggly members of a high school drill team all festooned in high white boots and spangles, shivering as they waited to perform. An entire fifth-grade class following after their teacher in the course of a special, early morning field trip. And cameras. Everywhere Meredith turned someone was pointing a lens toward the crews working to resurrect the balloons.

As they approached the concession stands, Meredith became acutely aware that she hadn't had her morning caffeine ration. "Phil," she called out after her gangly friend, "I'm stopping for a cup of tea. Can I get you one?"

Phil glanced uneasily from Meredith to the turmoil of balloonists beginning to inflate their crafts. His shoulders sagged slightly at the prospect of trying to locate the Cloud Waltzer. "Make it a hot chocolate. I'll search out the area and be right back."

Meredith nodded and got into line, amused by Phil's eagerness. Once she stopped moving the cold seemed to catch up with her and seep under her parka. She huddled in closer to herself. Even a chorus of whooshing hisses, like the one she'd heard earlier when the pilot of the unicorn balloon had turned on his burner, couldn't make Meredith turn around: She was intent upon jockeying her way through the crowd to a hot cup of tea.

The sun was peeking over the Sandia Mountains by the time she made her way to the head of the line. She paid for her tea and Phil's cocoa and turned to locate him. For the second time that day, serendipity overwhelmed her. Behind her the shriveled shells of dozens of balloons had been pumped full of life. They loomed there like an enchanted city, topped by domed minarets, that had magically materialized within the space of a few minutes. She walked forward, mesmerized by a display of colors and designs unlike any she'd ever witnessed before.

Her eyes were tugged from one brilliant globe to another. At first all the balloons seemed to be covered with vivid stripes—fire-engine red, sunny yellow, sapphire blue, hot pink. Stripes that ran straight up for sixty feet. Stripes that zigzagged crazily across newly swollen girths. Stripes that encircled the balloons, making them appear to be the most fanciful of giant tops. Then, from the pandemonium of color, Meredith began to pick out even more striking designs. To her right rose a balloon emblazoned with all twelve signs of the zodiac. Ahead of her was another that looked like a vastly overinflated world globe with all the continents and oceans marked out. Another sported the French fleur-de-lis. A carousel complete with prancing horses twirled around the circumference of another.

Laughter bubbled up within Meredith as she caught sight of other, more whimsical creations: a giant gum-ball machine, a dragon spitting fire, Pegasus winging across ruffling nylon. There were even a few floating puns, like an ace of hearts obviously meant to symbolize an ace high. The Rocky Mountain sunrise, complete with tall pine and snowcapped peaks, Meredith figured, must symbolize a Rocky Mountain high.

She walked amid the riot of color and design thinking that if there ever were an absolute antidote to the dull hollowness of her former life, this was it. As overcome as she was, though, she realized that her favorite balloon was still probably the one she'd seen drifting beside the moon, the one with the mythical unicorn rearing up to challenge the heavens.

"Meredith, you'd better hand that over before you dump it on someone." Phil relieved her of the foam cup of cocoa. "You're stumbling around like a sleepwalker."

"Phil, I've never seen anything so gorgeous in my life."

"Yeah?" Phil gave her his Howdy Doody smile, wishing that he were fifteen years older and ten times better-looking, but pleased all the same just to be able to make Meredith smile. "It is pretty neat."

"It's a lot more than 'neat,'" Meredith countered gently, almost whispering the words. "It's magical."

"Hey, I found Cloud Waltzer. She launched early with a bit of aid from some helpful strangers and floated around for a while, then they tethered her to the ground at the west end of the field. They're getting ready to cut her loose, so we'd better be ready to follow. The rest of the crew is waiting for us where she's tethered."

They wended their way through the crowd to the Jeep. After a few minutes of jostling it around the other chase vehicles that were streaming out of the parking area in pursuit of their assigned balloons, they hit open terrain. Meredith spotted their objective, a balloon straining at the end of a hundred-foot rope. A thrill shivered through Meredith—it was the unicorn balloon! At their approach the ground crew set the balloon free, and it floated away as elusive as the unicorn of myth.

"Let's pile in, folks," an older man with a grizzled beard ordered the other crew members as Phil came to a stop. Chilly gusts blew in as doors opened and the four crew members scrambled aboard. The bearded man sat up in front. A portable CB radio crackled in his hand. He held it up to his mouth.

"Yeah, Cloud Waltzer, you're coming in. We're on your trail. Out." He turned to Phil. "We'll attend to introductions later; let's hit the road first." Phil rocketed over prairie dog holes and mounds of tumbleweeds as he tore out after the rapidly receding blob. The passengers in the back laughed and grabbed for handholds. Once they were under way, the bearded man introduced himself and the others.

"Carl Wilmers," he said, sticking a weather-gnarled hand the size of a bear paw in front of Meredith. "And that's Marie." A rosy-cheeked young woman wearing a white tam over her brown braids nodded. "And Tomas." A middle-aged Latino gentleman flashed Meredith a warm smile. "And my wife, Betty."

"Pleased to meet you . . ." Betty paused, the question in her gray eyes magnified by her bifocals.

"Meredith. Meredith Tolliver." Meredith supplied the missing name.

"Well, I'm so pleased you could join us," Betty said, her southern accent softening the words.

"We should have been out here earlier to help you with the launch," Phil said by way of an apology. "It was my fault. I was up late trying to cram half a semester's work into one night."

"Don't kid us, Phil," Carl joked. "You were probably out on a hot date and she wouldn't let you go home until the wee hours."

Phil reddened in response to the good-natured ribbing about his nonexistent social life.

"Hey, is that pickup following us?" Carl asked, twisting around in his seat to peer out the back window. Meredith turned, catching sight of a pickup truck raising a trail of dust behind them. "Good, he's there." Carl eased back into his seat, satisfied that the chase crew was intact.

Meredith took advantage of the silence that opened up to ask, "How do you all know each other?" She had already sensed that the group had not come together by accident. They seemed welded together by a playful sense of fun.

"That guy's my boss, if you can believe it," Phil said, poking his thumb in Carl's direction. "We all work together. I'm a part-time draftsman. Carl is head of my division. Betty is the company's bookkeeper. And Marie and Tomas are engineers. The guy up in the balloon owns the company. Got all that?" Phil asked with a smile.

"Pretty much," Meredith answered. "Just promise me, though, that you're not going to be giving any pop quizzes."

"It's a deal," Marie answered from the back seat, "if you'll reveal what you do."

"You mean what I'm *trying* to do," Meredith corrected her. "I'm attempting to establish myself as a business writer. So far all I've come up with is a weekly column in the *Journal.*"

"Hey, so you're the Meredith Tolliver that writes the 'Common Cents' column?" Tomas asked. "I read your column. Thanks to you, I'm going to be saving a bundle on my taxes this year. After I read your piece on Individual Retirement Accounts, I opened one up. I'd heard about them before, but never understood exactly what they were. Before I read your column, I thought they were just for tycoons."

"Thank you," Meredith said simply, though she glowed with pleasure at the compliment. It always delighted her to hear that she was accomplishing exactly what she'd set out to do with her writing.

"Hey, thank *you,*" Tomas countered.

"Did the big boss take anyone up with him?" Phil asked as he turned onto the paved road leading away from the launch area.

"His new receptionist," Tomas answered. "Even though it was my turn, she pouted so much that I told her to go ahead. She was really—"

"Hey, he's veering off." Carl's warning cut through Tomas's assessment. Ahead of them Meredith watched as the unicorn balloon switched back to the south, changing its direction almost as if it were trying to elude its pursuers. "Take your next left," Carl advised Phil.

"The Box seems to be working," Marie observed, leaning forward to track Cloud Waltzer's reverse in direction.

"The Box?" Meredith echoed. "What is the Box?"

"The Box," Marie answered with an energetic preciseness that Meredith was beginning to suspect was typical of engineers, "is one of the main reasons why ballooning is so popular around here. Albuquerque has an almost perfect combination of just the right winds at just the right altitudes. Generally, upper-level winds are from the northwest and lower-level winds are from the south. So by changing the balloon's altitude, the pilot can travel back and forth within a vertical box. If everything's really going right, he can land where he took off."

"But that doesn't happen too often," Tomas chimed in. "And that's where we come in, tearing across the untracked terrain after a wayward balloon." Laughter brightened the interior of the Jeep.

"Speaking of untracked terrain," Phil interjected as

he swung off the highway onto a dirt road, "everyone hang on because we're headed for more of it."

The radio in Carl's outsized hand sputtered to life again, spewing out static and a few unintelligible syllables. Carl brought the instrument to his mouth. "Come again, Cloud Waltzer. I don't copy."

The static cleared briefly and the last few words of the transmission came through. ". . . putting her down over the next rise. Over and out." The radio went dead, but Meredith's mind was only beginning to buzz with a disturbing suspicion. No, it couldn't be, she told herself, dismissing the flight of fancy. How annoying to have thought for even a moment that the voice on the radio could have belonged to Archer Hanson. Meredith was annoyed with herself at this latest evidence of the impact the insufferable man had made on her.

"He's losing altitude," Marie observed, craning forward.

The Jeep lunged over the dusty mesa, rocking and swaying with the unevenness of the dirt road that had dwindled to little more than a footpath. Ahead of them, the balloon slanted in closer and closer to the ground until it was barely skimming the tops of the undulating brown hills.

"We'd better park it and chase him down," Carl advised. "The wind's picked up. It might be a tricky landing."

"Tricky for most pilots," Tomas added. "Not that guy.

He could put a balloon down in a hurricane without even scratching the varnish on the wicker basket."

"True," Carl agreed. "But whether he needs it or not, let's give him a hand here, okay?"

Phil accelerated until he was ahead of the low-flying balloon, then maneuvered the Jeep around to the other side of the rise that the pilot had said he was aiming for, and stopped. The doors flew open and everyone unloaded.

"Around this way," Phil called to Meredith, who felt lost in the scramble. "We want to stay in front of the balloon if we can, then grab on to it if they need help landing. Get ready, here she comes."

The top of the balloon peeked over the rise the Jeep had circumnavigated. To Meredith it looked like the bald head of a shy giant building up the slow courage to show himself. Then the horn of the unicorn appeared and, bit by bit, the rest of the magnificent beast was unveiled. For a moment the unicorn seemed perched on the rim of the bluff, pawing at the tawny earth and reaching for the azure sky above. The underbelly of the balloon rose up beneath the beast, lifting him skyward again.

"Come on." Phil tugged at Meredith's parka, breaking the second spell that the unicorn balloon had cast over her that day. "Get over to the side. He's traveling low enough now to knock your head off." Meredith hurried off in the direction Phil indicated. Her back was to the balloon as it passed them by. Then they were scampering after it. Meredith was surprised at how fast the unicorn balloon galloped away from them after tracking what appeared to have been its slow, stately progress in the air. She was thankful for her thick-soled hiking boots as they trampled over thorn bushes and gullies.

At last they caught up with the balloon. The pilot was facing away from them, searching for the best place to put his craft down. The wicker basket the pilot and his passenger stood in now scraped a half foot above the ground. It touched down, then bounced up again and was dragged away as if the wind were reluctant to let this pretty new toy return to the earth.

"Grab ahold of the basket," Carl ordered the crew members who closed in around the balloon. Meredith hung on to the suede-covered rim of the basket and felt the mighty tug of the wind. She and the others were forced to hang on and run along behind it for several seconds before they got a firm grip. The pilot busily tugged at a line attached to the top of the balloon, hauling down on it to hold open the seam that allowed the hot air trapped inside to rush out. As the warmed air that had given it life blew away, the unicorn began to shrivel.

Since the pilot was still occupied with shutting off the propane burners and securing lines, Meredith saw him before he saw her. As he stretched up, struggling to release the balloon from the wind's dominance, his profile was gilded from behind by the early morning sun. His hair was a sparkling halo ruffled about his head. His expression was fierce as he battled to subdue the still-bucking unicorn. The muscles at his shoulders bunched into knotted cords that pitted their power against the wind, and won. He looked like the triumphant Viking warrior of her unsettling dream. At last the unicorn was tamed and it rested gently on the mesa.

Then there was time for Archer Hanson to notice the crew around him. The sunlight that played across his shoulders and hair seemed to funnel out through the gaze he settled on Meredith. He grinned as if he had expected to see her. The wicker basket was a shallow obstacle that he vaulted easily before coming toward her. Behind him the pickup, with a sign reading Hanson Development Corporation, pulled to a stop, and the driver joined the crew members that had ridden in the Jeep to begin dismantling the balloon.

"You're more determined than I would have given you credit for, Meredith." The sound of her name on his tongue somehow insinuated itself into a private place within Meredith where she would never have consciously allowed Archer Hanson. "How did you find out that the Cloud Waltzer was mine? Pretty clever of you to hook up with the chase crew."

Meredith stared for a second into those eyes that

seemed to see far more of herself than she cared to reveal. A sassy retort sprang to her lips, but she bit it back. Fate had given her a second chance. She could either turn it aside with a well-deserved prick to Archer Hanson's massive ego or she could capitalize on the opportunity. She listened to the steady pulse of logic that beat deep within her and chose the latter.

"I told you the other day, Mr. Hanson, that the interview with you meant a great deal to me." She said the words like an actress playing the role of a lifetime, mouthing lines that were alien to her natural instincts. "Besides . . ." Here she stumbled on a line that bridged the gulf between role-playing and out-and-out lying. She crossed the divide. "Besides, I adore ballooning. I go up whenever I get the chance. It's one of the main reasons I moved to Albuquerque." She glanced around, glad that Phil and the others couldn't overhear her deception.

He studied her without replying for the beat of three slow blinks, then spoke as if expressing an indisputable axiom. "Anyone who likes balloons can't be all bad."

Meredith congratulated herself for forcing even this admission from the redoubtable Archer Hanson. It was the tiniest of cracks in his facade, but one that just might be wedged further open. "I love balloons," she went on, hoping to cement whatever positive impression she might be making.

"What happened to the Wall Street whiz kid, the corporate superwoman I met yesterday?" he asked, eyeing her bright green parka, raspberry sweater, jeans, and boots.

"She stopped existing when I left Chicago," Meredith said, relieved to cross back into truthful territory. "I only drag her out when I think she's needed to help me get a story. Obviously she was out of place yesterday."

His laughter was rich and warm, the kind Meredith had always associated with a largeness of spirit. "Meredith, I like you. You wouldn't have dinner with me by any chance? Maybe I can talk you into coming for a ride in Cloud Waltzer with me?"

"And maybe you'll agree to be interviewed during the flight."

A momentary look of surprise was quickly chased from the ruddy face by the flash of his Viking grin. "Maybe I will," he boomed out. "Just maybe I will."

"Archer," a honeyed voice called out. It was the receptionist who had given Meredith such a chilly welcome yesterday. She'd been sitting in the pickup truck. "They need you to show them what to do. Oh, *hello,*" she said, catching sight of Meredith. "Didn't expect to see you here today."

Meredith smiled as graciously as she could, not wanting to spin any more fabrications for the moment. She had, or almost had, an interview with Archer Hanson!

It was only as Phil was driving her back to their apartment building after they both had declined Hanson's invitation to join the crew for breakfast that Meredith suddenly remembered—she was deathly afraid of heights.

Chapter 3

M*eredith was awake even earlier* than she needed to be, having spent a restless night bouncing back and forth between formulating possible interview questions and fighting down blind terror. She wondered how on earth—or in heaven, to be more accurate—she was going to keep up her charade as a ballooning enthusiast. Her fear of heights was so intense that she required heavy sedation to even set foot on an airplane. In her thirtieth-floor office in Chicago, she'd had to put her back to the window to avoid so much as glimpsing the expensive view.

And now, she asked herself gloomily, I'm supposed to go up a couple thousand feet supported only by a few scraps of nylon and a little hot air and pretend to like it?

With Thor weaving in and out between her legs, Meredith brewed herself a cup of herbal tea. She didn't need any caffeine this morning. She was fully awake and already nervous enough without coffee. Just as the warm, cinammon-scented beverage began unloosening the knot of apprehension in her stomach, Phil's knock sounded and the knot tightened back into a hard ball. Swallowing hard, Meredith grabbed her miniature digital recorder and leather gloves.

Carl, Betty, Marie, and Tomas called out greetings far too hearty for six-thirty in the morning as Phil and Meredith arrived at the launch site.

"So you're going aloft today, eh?" Carl asked through the steam of a cup of coffee he'd poured from a Thermos.

The question made Meredith realize that today would be the second day in a row that none of the regular crew members would be riding in the balloon. Her one-track focus on the Archer Hanson interview had blinded her to all other concerns, like common courtesy. The inquiry also represented a possible escape.

"It doesn't have to be today," she quickly volunteered, hoping she could both rectify her blunder and get out of the balloon ride. "I can go up any time this week. It doesn't even have to be this week. I'm in no hurry. You've been on one balloon ride, you've been on them all." She gave a brittle laugh. "I'm sure that you all are much more eager to go up than I am and you've certainly done more to earn a flight."

A smile cracked Carl's weathered face, then spread to the rest of the crew members. "I doubt that any of us is quite as eager as you might suspect," he said. "Balloon flights aren't much of a novelty for us anymore. You see, one of the major projects Archer has us working on now is the development of a solar-heated balloon. So we've all logged more than our fair share of time aloft in test flights. No, we mostly come out to help with the launches during Fiesta for the fun of it. To be with other balloon nuts from around the country and the world. Why, just the other day someone was telling me that there are pilots and balloons here from England, France, Australia, Japan, Germany . . ."

As Carl's international roll call droned on, Meredith's attention was captured by the plume of dust rising in the thin predawn light that announced Archer Hanson's arrival. He pulled up in the Hanson Development pickup. The wicker gondola stood upright in the bed of the truck.

"Morning," he called out as he swung out of the cab.

Meredith stood away from the others as they rushed forward to help unload the gondola and envelope bag. In the murky light Hanson wasn't quite the Nordic god he'd appeared to be yesterday. There was a softness about him that the harsh sunlight had obliterated before. Though with her conscious mind she denied that such a quality of sensitivity could exist in a man like Archer Hanson, in the regions deep within her, far beyond the control of her mind, something stirred.

That something was like a creature, kept too long

imprisoned, that sees the door to its cage open just a crack. The creature of her unconscious moved hesitantly, poking an exploratory paw outside the barely open door to test the feel of the earth after so many years of a concrete cage floor. The instant Meredith felt the creature escaping within her, she slammed the cage door shut once more. Flustered more than she cared to admit, she reached into her parka pocket and felt for her recorder, reassuring herself that it was still there and functioning properly. She was there to get a story. Period.

"Why don't you help at the mouth of the balloon?" Carl suggested as she approached the crew. They had already laid the envelope out on the ground. Meredith joined Phil at the point where it connected with the basket. Hanson was standing in front of the basket, which was tilted over on its side. He was busy directing a current of air generated by a gasoline-powered fan into the mouth of the balloon being held open by Phil.

"Glad you could make it," he said as Meredith grabbed on to the other side of the opening, helping Phil to keep it upright.

She smiled briefly in response to Hanson's greeting. The noise from the fan would have made any other reply difficult. They worked in silence, angling the loop as Hanson directed. Once a pocket of air had been trapped inside, he turned on the propane burner. It roared like a hoarse lion. Hanson aimed the flame toward the interior of the balloon. The hot air captured within, being lighter than the cold desert air without, was the spirit that gave the balloon life. Slowly, it rose. Cloud Waltzer's unicorn grew ever more eager to shed the bounds of gravity with each cubic yard of hot air it swallowed. Finally it tugged the basket into an upright position and the crew members held on to it to keep it from escaping.

"Are you coming, Miss Tolliver?" Hanson asked with a mock obsequiousness.

"Most assuredly, Mr. Hanson." Meredith could barely believe that the words of consent had tripped so lightly from her mouth. Fear made her arms and legs rigid as she attempted to haul herself into the gondola over the waist-high wicker sides. Then, before the fear had a chance to totally paralyze her, she was in and the hands of the crew members that had kept them anchored to the security of solid land were unclasping.

Meredith felt a scream rising up from the pit of her stomach as she watched the ground recede. Quickly she turned her back to the horrifying sight, knowing that she had made a terrible mistake. She closed her mouth on the scream, but her fear escaped through eyes widening into saucers of liquid terror. It also leaked through her face, washing it of all color except a faint fluorescent green.

Hanson was absorbed in the details of the takeoff. He made certain that enough flame was fed into the voracious maw above him to ensure an ascent swift enough so that they could safely clear the obstacles on the ground. Once he'd accomplished that, he had time to notice Meredith's frozen expression and sickly pallor.

Meredith easily interpreted the gaze he turned on her. Even if she'd felt physically able to continue her impersonation of an experienced and enthusiastic ballooning veteran, Hanson would never believe it now. Her ruse was over. She remembered the way he'd chewed out his mine foreman and knew that he would be just as ferocious when, after all the inconvenience of a launch, he had to land again. She braced herself to receive the scorn she deserved for her lie. Certainly she had extinguished any hope of an interview now. She waited for the scorching heat of his anger, but instead of the harsh abuse she was expecting when his full lips parted, he spoke to her gently.

"Is this your first flight?" he asked, the way a camp counselor might ask a tearful child if this was her first time away from home.

Meredith nodded, knowing that if she spoke her voice would be a quavery embarrassment.

"I know that it's probably hard to believe, but there's really nothing to be afraid of."

His tone was as soothing as the feel of the solid earth Meredith was intensely yearning for at that moment. She clung stiffly to an upright strut that connected to the cables at the mouth of the envelope. It was the one position in the tiny basket that kept the view of the ground below at her back. The higher they rose, the greater was the fear that welled up in her. Anxiety seemed to seep up from the empty air beneath them, stealing the strength from her legs and leaving them wobbly and unreliable. Now that same panic was invading her stomach with a growing nausea. She managed to let three words eke out between her tightly sealed lips.

"Let's go down."

The terrified plea in her voice spoke to the tender place within Archer Hanson that he sometimes feared had calcified from years of having to keep it barricaded behind the unyielding facade of business.

"Meredith." He spoke her name soothingly. "I'll bet if you'd just peek around behind you, you'd like what you saw."

Grimly, she shook her head "no." At the thought that this torture might continue, tears welled up in her eyes. "Please," she begged.

Acting purely on an impulse that went far deeper than the ones he'd honed over the past decade, Archer held his arms open. Meredith fled into their safety, burying her head against the solidness of his chest.

"It's all right," he soothed, stroking the silken fineness of her hair. He felt the tremors wracking her finely wrought body and knew then at what great cost she had managed to keep her fear under control. "It's all right.

We'll take her down. Don't worry, baby, it'll all be over in a few minutes." The endearment slipped out before he'd had time to censor it. His only thought was comfort.

As he stretched up with one arm to reach the line that would deflate the balloon, being careful to keep the other wrapped tightly around Meredith, his sheltering torso swung out away from her and she found herself doing precisely what she had most feared—looking over the edge down to the earth hundreds of feet below. For a moment she was bewildered. This wasn't the stomach-wrenching vision she had expected at all. It was as if someone had replaced an illustration from Dante's "Inferno" with something out of an airborne *Alice's Adventures in Wonderland.* The Fiesta grounds far below were dotted with dozens of gay splotches of color that were balloons inflating and just beginning to ascend. From Meredith's vantage point it looked as if an incredibly indulged young giant had overturned his Easter basket, spilling a rainbow of eggs across the brown earth.

Archer hadn't reached the rip panel cord yet, so Cloud Waltzer was still ascending. Or Meredith assumed that it was ascending. Surprisingly, though, it appeared that instead of the balloon rising, the earth was falling away. Whatever the cause, Meredith realized that she had absolutely no sensation of height. Without that key element, the fear that had been strangling her uncoiled and dissipated as swiftly as a wisp of dark smoke blown away by a spring breeze.

"Stop." She reached up to halt Archer's arm.

He looked down at her. She had the pure look of a delirious child just after a fever has broken.

"I think I'd like to stay up." Quickly she added, "Just a moment or two longer."

"I'm glad to hear it." His hand went from the rip panel cord back to the blast valve. He opened it up and a jet of flame howled out.

When the burner noise stopped, Meredith was struck by the incredible silence. There wasn't even the sound of wind rushing past her ears. Or the feel of it. "There's no wind up here," she marveled.

"There's wind all right," Archer said, checking his instrument panel. "A fairly stiff one as a matter of fact. It's just that we're moving at exactly the same speed as the wind. We're one with the wind, so it doesn't ruffle us."

Meredith felt that if she interviewed Archer Hanson for the next ten years, she might never uncover anything more basic about the man than what he had just said. Or, more precisely, how he had said it. An undercurrent of emotion had rippled through his words as strong, yet as nearly undetectable, as the one that carried them through the sky.

"Why don't you have a look around?"

Meredith started at the question and Archer's arm pulled her to him more tightly.

"I'll hang on to you," he joked, attempting to lighten Meredith's mood.

Closing her eyes, Meredith pivoted around within the comforting confines of Archer's one-armed embrace. She pulled in a deep breath and opened her eyes. The world lay at her feet. But not the world of ground-level folk. No, from her lofty perch the world was a tranquil, slow-moving place. It was a place where anxiety, all the myriad anxieties that had nibbled away for so very long at her, had no right to exist. The first one she jettisoned was her fear of height.

"Only birds and angels have any right to this view." She breathed the words, not wanting to disrupt the indescribable serenity.

Archer's chest rumbled at her back with an approving bass laugh. "I've logged hundreds of hours of flight time with dozens of different passengers, and that is the best explanation I think I've ever heard of why ballooning is so addictive."

They floated in a companionable silence over earth that was a patchwork of browns, beiges, and grays. So far below that they looked like plastic figurines, dogs barked and long-eared hares fled from the strange roaring noise that came from the sky when Archer fired up the burner.

"This is how I always imagined flying would be,"

Meredith said, unable now to tear her eyes from the panorama. "Just floating effortlessly like this."

"That's pretty much the way it took me my first time up," Archer replied, scanning the far horizon.

Meredith felt suspended in a fairy tale as they drifted toward the Rio Grande. Early morning sunlight glinted off the river, making it into a gilded serpent slithering through the lush greenness that kept it confined. To her left, curls of smoke unraveled like skeins of gray wool from chimneys throughout the city, signaling that Albuquerque was waking up. Overhead, so high that the whine of the engine was silenced, a jet hurtled through the air, slicing the sky with a ruler-straight trail. Meredith felt oddly sad for the passengers on board who might never learn what flying was really all about. She was equally pleased with her own introduction to the experience.

All these observations acted like the sluice that drained off the last bits of Meredith's fear. Once it had all been siphoned away, she became abruptly and acutely aware of the broad chest at her back and the strong arm wrapped protectively around her shoulders. Just a moment before they had been a comforting necessity. Now they were becoming far more. Meredith could feel his warmth enveloping her, swirling about her, carrying his smell. It wasn't the thought-out scent of an expensive men's cologne. Instead Archer Hanson smelled like clothes dried in sunshine and a fresh breeze combined with a more elusive scent. The combination of Archer's feel and smell was one that Meredith found increasingly arousing. It was a response that left her confused and threatened.

"I'll be all right now," she said evenly, shifting slightly to move out of Archer's grasp. She turned toward him in time to see the expression of contentment he'd worn replaced first by surprise, then embarrassment. Both were rapidly supplanted by a mask of neutrality that guarded against such displays of emotion.

"Your color's improved," he remarked, as if commenting on the weather.

"I imagine that if I looked as bad as I felt right after we took off that I must have been a fairly frightening sight." Her words strained for a lightness that she didn't feel. It almost seemed that when Archer had cloaked her in his embrace, he'd also wrapped a force field around her. Now she couldn't break free from it to chart her own course again. More brusquely than she'd intended to, she asked, "How about that interview you promised me?" She fished in her pocket for her small digital recorder.

"Promised you?" Archer took a deliberate step away. "As I recall there was a rather large 'maybe' hanging over this interview I allegedly promised you."

Meredith slumped and tucked her recorder back into her pocket. She was ready to concede defeat. She shrugged her shoulders and looked up at Archer. He was a disturbing man. Everything about him as he stood there before her—the thoughtful gaze that animated his eyes, giving them a depth of concerned warmth, the high forehead now gently creased with indecision, the sculpted lips curving with tenderness—was at odds with what she knew rationally about the man. She knew he was the privileged son of a rich man. She'd overheard yesterday how he'd squelched the trouble at his mine that she assumed was a worker protest. She knew that concerned, indecisive, tender men didn't survive and thrive in business the way Archer Hanson had. She knew all that, but it still wasn't enough to subdue the perplexing impact he kept having on her.

"I can understand your refusal," she answered with a mounting relief that her association with Archer Hanson would soon be at an end. "I haven't done much to win your confidence."

"Actually, you've come a lot closer than any other writer who's ever approached me."

"Close, but no cigar, eh?" She smiled. Her spirits, no longer inhibited by the burden of tying Archer down to an interview, rose by the second. After a few minutes of drifting soundlessly, like a lily pad carried along on a lazy river, Meredith was again recaptured by the delight of ballooning. Which was why, when Archer asked, "Tell me about your father," she didn't stiffen and evade the topic. The freedom of floating high above a care-ridden earth with a man she could no longer deny she found attractive, but one she would never see again, certainly one she no longer had to worry about treating professionally, acted on her like a truth serum. She felt liberated from the restrictions that usually constrained her.

"Old Andrew Tolliver senior?" she joked. "It's funny the way certain men ask me about my father. They're like young boys in Little League asking about Babe Ruth. But you're not a Little Leaguer, are you, Archer? And you too had your own Babe Ruth of a father to contend with, didn't you?"

Archer's response was lost in the growl of the burner as he opened the valve to release a blast of propane. The heat generated by the ignited gas poured down on Meredith like a heated rain. Several seconds later the balloon began a leisurely climb. Meredith knew that if she'd wanted to drop the subject Archer had brought up, he wouldn't object. But, for some reason, she wanted to tell him the whole story. To tell him more than she should allow herself to reveal. She compromised by giving him a sketchy outline of the rise of Andrew Tolliver.

"When my father entered the investment firm that had been in the family for a couple of generations, it was on a distinct downhill slide. My grandfather's other sons were bleeding the business dry. I suppose my father could have lived a country club existence like them, but instead he dived into the business and turned it around.

"There were a few lucky investments at just the right time. That's usually how the tale is told, just a few incredibly lucky investments. But behind the luck were twenty-hour days and weeks of research. One by one, he bought out my uncles until he had regained full control of the firm. My father was in his late thirties when my older brother, Rory, was born, and from day one he was the heir apparent. There was never any question that he would study finance. Although with what my father had taught him growing up, he knew more than most of his professors.

"I was sort of an afterthought, born a couple of years after my brother. My mother was never a strong person. I always considered her more as a sister, a frail, unworldly sister whom I had to shield from the harsh realities of life. Anyway, with my father so absorbed in Rory and the business, and my mother sort of off in her own world, I more or less raised myself. No one interfered when I announced that I planned to study literature and eventually teach. No one even much cared. Until Rory died."

Meredith realized that she hadn't meant to tell that part of it. Certainly she hadn't intended to let her voice catch and go ragged.

"And so you inherited the mantle." Archer summed up what had happened as if he'd been there. Meredith nodded affirmation.

"Yes, I charged in to fill the void that couldn't, would never, be filled. I switched my major to finance, then went to graduate school at Wharton. After a year of what my father called 'tempering' on the Street, I started to work at Tolliver Investments. And boy, did I work!" Meredith's laugh was dry. She attempted a smile, but it never reached her eyes. For her vision had turned inward, back to those nightmare days when she could never work enough hours, could never know all she had to know, could never fulfill her father's dream, could never, in short, be Rory. And then the dieting had started. But she couldn't tell him about that. Or about Chad. Or about how terrifyingly close she'd come to spending her life in a world she'd narrowly escaped.

"But you asked about my father, didn't you," she concluded.

"Actually," Archer interrupted, "you've answered my real question. Still want to do that interview?"

The question was so unexpected that it took Meredith a moment to comprehend it, then another to answer in the strongest of affirmatives. "What made you change your mind?" she stammered, still adjusting to this radical change.

"Let's just say that for reasons of my own, I decided you were the one person who could do a profile on me. There is another, less mysterious explanation; I want some publicity on a project I've been working on. A solar-heated balloon. You build your story around that and I'm yours. Of course, to do the story right you might have to come aloft for a few more flights." There was an impish quality to his grin that Meredith found as beguiling as the prospect of future balloon flights.

"You have yourself a deal, Mr. Hanson."

"Good." He nodded with satisfaction. "Very good." He twisted around. Far below a plume of dust marked the trail of Phil's Jeep and the pickup as they paralleled the course of the balloon. Archer picked up the CB radio. "Carl, you down there?" he asked conversationally, skipping the CB jargon.

"Come in, Cloud Waltzer, I read you."

"Carl, take your next right and cross the river. We'll be bringing her down in that field."

"Will do."

As the air in the envelope cooled, the balloon began to sink as slowly and smoothly as a western sun. They passed over the interstate and an eighteen-wheeler boomed out a greeting on its air horn. They floated on until they were hovering above a grade school. Out in the play yards children waved and ran shouting after the unicorn that galloped away from them. Meredith leaned over the basket rim, waving for all she was worth at the delighted children until they were but tiny stick figures in the distance. Soon they were skimming above the tops of the huge cottonwoods nourished by the Rio Grande. Then the river itself, flowing stolidly south, was beneath them.

"All right, a few landing procedures," Archer

announced, never taking his eyes from the empty field the balloon was drifting toward. "Face in the direction we're headed. Hang on to that strut you're holding now. And keep your knees bent. Got all that?"

Meredith nodded her head. The closer the balloon angled toward the earth, the more their speed seemed to increase. Meredith figured she probably wasn't Archer's first passenger to make that observation when he offered an explanation.

"It seems like we're going faster now than we have been. But that's only because you have things by which to gauge our speed."

As they angled in low over the field, it came alive with jackrabbits bolting away in all directions. And their apparent speed did seem to increase. Meredith clutched at the suede-covered metal, fearing for a few seconds that they would crash to the ground. From the corner of her eye she caught flashes of Carl, Phil, and the other crew members running across the dusty field toward the landing balloon.

"Hang on," Archer advised needlessly, blasting hot air into the balloon so that they leveled off. They drifted several hundred yards, scraping tumbleweeds with the bottom of the basket, until Archer shut off the valve and pulled the cord that opened a vent at the top of the balloon. The basket settled gently onto the ground. Carl was the first crew member to reach them. He, and then Phil and the others, grabbed onto the rim of the basket and held them down as the envelope continued to deflate.

"Ace chase!" Archer boomed out, congratulating the crew members for their vigilant pursuit of the elusive windblown bubble. With a feline grace, he swung out of the basket, turned, and offered a steadying hand to Meredith. The earth felt clumsy and ungainly beneath her feet after an hour of sliding over vaporous puffs.

With well-practiced coordination, Archer, assisted by the crew members, fell to securing equipment, detaching the envelope from the basket, milking the last bit of hot air from the nylon shell, and stuffing it back into its canvas bag to await the next flight.

"Okay, guys," Archer said, calling his crew together when all the gear had been stowed. "I'd like to make an announcement. That was Meredith's maiden voyage."

"A virgin balloonist?" Tomas asked with a gleam in his eye.

"That's right," Archer confirmed. "I suppose you know what that means."

"We most certainly do," Phil piped up, heading for the bed of the pickup, where he retrieved a box with a large canvas sheet stuffed on top. He stood behind Meredith and draped the material around her shoulders.

"What is this?" Meredith asked, not certain she liked the way everyone had closed around her in a semicircle with Archer at its head.

"This is the initiation ceremony for first-time balloonists," Archer answered. "Now, if you will all bow your heads." His tone was so solemn as he made the request and everyone else complied so quickly that Meredith did so too, lowering her head until she was staring at a bush bristling with goat's heads stickers beneath her boot.

"May the winds welcome you with softness." Archer intoned the words of the Balloonist's Prayer with a gravity befitting its lovely sentiments. "May the sun bless you with his warm hands. May you fly so high and so well that God joins you in laughter and sets you gently back into the loving arms of Mother Earth."

Meredith was so moved by the lilting simplicity of the prayer that she barely noticed the sound of a cork popping behind her. It was impossible, however, to ignore the chilly trickle of liquid down her back and the burst of a camera flash as Phil upended a champagne bottle over her head and Marie recorded the event.

"I christen thee, Balloon Novice," Phil laughed as Meredith whirled away from the escaping champagne.

"Don't waste the bubbly," Carl warned, taking the dark bottle from Phil and tipping it into his mouth. The crew members shared the champagne, all drinking from the bottle. Meredith was toweling her hair dry with the sheet when the bottle reached her. She took a sip. Archer popped open a second bottle.

"To solar ballooning," he said, raising the bottle in

a toast, then passing it to Meredith. Her second swig of champagne seemed to contain all the exhilaration of the last few hours. It bubbled up in her like the frothy liquid she was imbibing and escaped in a giggle she couldn't suppress.

"What's so funny?" Archer asked, moving to her side as the rest of the crew adjourned to the Jeep to search for the plastic cups Phil maintained were hidden within.

"Everything." The word rolled out on a merry note of bemusement. "I mean, don't you think this is a fairly comical scene? Here we all are, off in the middle of a dusty mesa, up to our knees in tumbleweeds, lizards, and jackrabbits, passing around bottles of French champagne and toasting solar ballooning. And here *I* am wrapped up in a sheet, with champagne drying in my hair. It's not even nine in the morning, and I'm bombed."

"May I say," Archer commented, leaning closer, "that you make an adorable drunk."

"You may say anything you like, particularly when I have my recorder turned on."

What a changeable woman, Archer thought, wondering if it was the alcohol that had rubbed away her cool professional facade and exposed the life-loving vulnerability he saw now in the face turned toward his. Or was this too a facade that would be gone with the intoxication of the moment? He remembered how she had felt in his arms. How content he'd been with her nestled there watching the world pass beneath them like pieces of half-forgotten dreams. He'd felt more peaceful, more right, than he had in longer than he cared to think about.

What was it about her that provoked such a response? he wondered. Her face gleamed in the sunlight. With her straight blond hair cut in blunt bangs across her broad forehead and her eyes creased shut in merriment, she looked like a blond Chinese child, if such a child were possible. He couldn't imagine her maneuvering her way around Wall Street or managing the portfolios of major corporations. Yet he knew she had and, more important, knew that she could. There seemed to be irreconcilable differences between what she was, what she had been, and what she appeared to be now. Even less easily understood was the way she affected him. He wanted nothing more at that moment than to kiss this enigmatic woman, and he was damned if he truly understood why.

"Archer," a slightly petulant female voice called out. He looked away from Meredith sharply.

"Yes, Courtney, what is it?"

Meredith glanced at the approaching woman and recognized Archer's receptionist. She had chosen to remain in the truck rather than join in the post-flight festivities.

"Nelson is on the truck phone. He's been waiting for you at the office for fifteen minutes. There's been more trouble at the mine."

"Tell him I'm on my way." He turned back to Meredith, but she spoke before he could.

"I enjoyed the flight more than I can tell you," she said, expressing her gratitude simply. "When can we start the interview? I imagine I'll need a few sessions to get everything I need."

Archer held up his hands to indicate how helplessly full they were. "The rest of the day is going to be insane. How about tomorrow? I'll call you when I get back to the office to let you know what's on the Fiesta agenda."

"Whatever's convenient for you," Meredith agreed, the champagne and balloon flight having left her far more tractable than usual. She hastily scribbled her phone number on a scrap of paper and handed it to Archer.

"Good," he said, hurrying off after his retreating receptionist. Then, pausing, he turned to face her. "Later on this week we'll be launching the solar balloon."

"What's her name?" Meredith had to raise her voice to travel the distance that had sprung up between her and Archer.

"The balloon?" he asked, putting his hand to his forehead to shade his eyes as he stopped for one last glimpse of this puzzling Meredith Tolliver. "We're calling her Cloud Waltzer II."

Chapter 4

"*Wear something long and slinky.*" That directive coming from any other man would have been intolerable, Meredith thought as she flipped through her closet in search of something that might meet those specifications. But Archer Hanson's order, delivered a few minutes before, delighted her as much as the prospect of going to the Balloon Ball with him did.

"Balloon Ball," she whispered, letting a champagne giggle leak out at the whimsical redundancy of it. She'd told Archer she'd have to check her wardrobe before giving him a definite answer. The answer in her heart, though, was a definite "yes."

Thor, curled up as usual on her bed, looked up peevishly at his mistress and her uncharacteristic outburst.

"Oh, go back to sleep, you grump. Something I don't understand and never want to end is happening in my life and I intend to enjoy it."

The cat kneaded a spot on the spread like a human sleeper fluffing up his pillow, then closed his perpetually bored eyes.

One by one, Meredith eliminated the few dressy outfits she had in her closet. They were all too stodgy, too drab, and far too conservative. They clashed discordantly with the sunny, rhapsodic mood glowing within her. Her mood dimmed momentarily as she remembered that her checking account hovered at an anemic two-figure sum and that she still hadn't paid her electric bill. She clearly couldn't afford to buy anything.

Euphoria bubbled up through her anew with her next thought. There was one thing she just *might* be able to wear that certainly wasn't either stodgy, drab, *or* conservative. But did she dare? She didn't allow herself time to ruminate on the question. Instead, she flung open a drawer and pulled out a rippling bit of floor-length finery. Technically, it was a nightgown, but Meredith had never worn the shimmering, peacock blue gown without thinking it fine enough for a debutante ball. Yes, she decided, she would do it. As if signaling her decision, the phone rang.

Meredith's heart stopped in the frolicking course it had been running since that moment when Archer had gathered her into his arms. Could he be calling so soon? She took several deep breaths and cleared her throat to rid it of the high-pitched giddiness that was tightening it.

"Hello." She was reasonably happy with the casual, warm tone she struck.

"Mer, that you? Sounds like you're coming down with a cold."

Chad. Meredith's heart sank. She should have known it would be him. He always waited until lunchtime to call her. Theirs had never been a late night phone call relationship. "No, Chad, I'm fine. How are you?"

"Can't complain, Mer, can't complain. Have you checked the *Journal* today? Echelon's going through the roof," he said, referring to the *Wall Street Journal* and to the mutual fund he managed for Meredith's father. "Remember those utilities you told me to stay away from? Well, we're getting an eighteen and a quarter return on them. What do you think about that?"

"That's terrific, Chad." Meredith could barely pretend interest in the financial banter that was the basis for all communication between her and Chad.

"Well, you don't sound like it's terrific. I thought you'd be pleased, Meredith. It's not easy, you know, doing my job *and* managing most of the portfolios that you left behind too."

Meredith felt the veins and muscles within her skull compress. They pulled tight and began to ache. "Chad, don't let my father overload you."

"Easier said than done. Some of us aren't free to just run off to New Mexico. Which brings me to the point of this, and every other call I've made for the last six months: When will you be returning?"

"And as I've told you every time you've called for the last six months, maybe never."

"Maybe never." Chad laughed as if she were joking. "By the way, your mother asked me to ask you how much you weigh now."

The dull headache abruptly broke into a thudding gallop. "My mother asked you to ask me?" she repeated disbelievingly.

"You know how your mother is."

Meredith did. All too well. Julianna Tolliver was a fragile china doll of a woman who somehow managed to manipulate those around her into doing her dirty work while she sat back playing the part of the saintly martyr. "Tell her that my weight is fine," Meredith answered, straining to keep the annoyance out of her voice.

"She says it's been a long time since you've sent a picture of yourself. She'd like to have one."

"You mean," Meredith corrected, "she'd like proof that I'm not lying. I'm afraid that both of you will just have to take my word for it that I don't look like something you could use to scare crows with."

"Come on, Mer," Chad whined. "You're not being fair. You know I believe you. All I'm doing is delivering your mother's messages."

"Tell her to use Western Union if she has messages

she wants delivered," Meredith snapped. She instantly regretted her retort as Chad's aggrieved sigh hissed through the receiver.

"I'm sorry. I know you're only interested in my welfare," she said, and in a way it was true. Chad *had* always been very solicitous of her, sticking with her right through the worst of her bout with anorexia. The problem with it all was that it was so foreordained, so programmed. When bright, handsome Chad Allbrook, graduate of Exeter and Yale, had come to work for Tolliver Investments, Meredith's father had moved him into the office next door to hers, displacing a senior member of the firm to do so. When she and Chad had started dating, Meredith had felt that, as usual, she was simply responding to the tug of the strings held by her father.

"Gotta run, Mer. Give your mother a call. She worries about you. We all do."

"Well, don't," Meredith started to say but Chad had already hung up. Wearily, all the effervescence of a few moments before now gone flat, she picked the rich blue gown up off the bed. What had she been thinking of? she wondered. She couldn't wear this in public. She trudged back to her closet and found a perfectly reasonable little black dress. She looked about as exciting as Mother Hubbard in it but, she reminded herself sternly, it *was* the only appropriate thing she had to wear. She couldn't go out in a nightgown, even one that didn't look like a nightgown. She simply couldn't. She'd have to either look like a frump or not go. And not going would probably mean not getting the story, which would ultimately mean surrendering and returning to Chicago.

She decided to go, but the happy anticipation that had glowed within her now cooled to a darkened lump. Meredith shooed a disgruntled Thor off her bed and slid beneath the covers. She escaped from the headache, disappointment, and tangled emotions caused by Chad's call by falling into sleep.

When the phone rang, Meredith was certain that only a few minutes had passed and that Chad was calling back. She groped for her phone and muttered a groggy greeting into it. The voice that responded jolted her into abrupt consciousness.

"Hello there, Balloon Novice Tolliver. Sounds as if you're exactly where I'd like to be at this moment. Starting the day off with a champagne breakfast is not the key to maximum energy or efficiency, is it?"

Meredith chuckled a nervous laugh as she struggled to collect herself. The sound of Archer's voice alone had unsettled her enough, then his casual comment about wishing he were in bed had thoroughly flustered her. Could he have meant with her? Whether he had or not didn't matter; with the first word he spoke his presence was as palpable to Meredith as if he were stretched out beside her. "Hardly," she answered. "I wanted to thank you again for initiating me into the wonders of ballooning. It was an incredible experience."

"It was for me too," Archer responded in a tone that told Meredith that ballooning had little to do with his enthusiasm. "Have I given you enough time to decide if you're coming tonight?"

"I'd planned on it." A touch of gloom dampened Meredith's ebullience as she caught sight of the black dress she would be wearing.

"Wonderful."

Could she be imagining things or did she actually hear a note of relief in Archer's response?

"It starts at eight. I'd suggest dinner except that I'll be tied up negotiating a labor contract with my mine workers. Tell me where you live and I'll pick you up as soon as I can tear myself away. I don't imagine it'll be much after eight."

Meredith glanced around at her tiny apartment and a stab of panic pierced her.

"Why don't I meet you somewhere," she quickly volunteered. "Where's the ball going to be held? I'd hate to have to make you drive out to pick me up and then backtrack in again."

A moment of silence followed. Meredith knew that Archer was trying to figure out how to respond to her odd suggestion. It didn't matter, though, how odd he thought she was, she couldn't allow him to see where she lived.

"I really don't mind, Meredith," he said in a deep, even voice that hinted at the kind of firmness that she knew to be a critical element in the makeup of an entrepreneur of his caliber.

"No, no, I wouldn't hear of it. Don't they usually hold these kinds of events in your convention center downtown?"

"I'd hardly call it *my* convention center, but yes, that's where it's going to be."

"Great, that's midway between your office and my apartment. I'll just meet you in the lobby outside the ballroom."

"Meredith, I don't like the idea of your walking through a downtown parking lot after dark. Please, I would love to come and pick you up even if you live in Santa Fe."

Meredith attempted a light laugh, but it sounded false and strained with desperation. "No, it's better this way. Less trouble," she added vaguely.

"All right, Mystery Woman, we'll do it your way, just so long as you're in that lobby tonight. You'll love the ball. It's always an extravaganza of color."

Meredith imagined herself in her plain black dress; she would be the little mudhen among the peacocks. "Archer, I don't think that . . ."

"Sorry, Meredith, I'm going to have to run. The delegation from the Antonito mine just came in. I don't want to keep them waiting. I'll see you at eight in the lobby. I'll be the guy with the rose between his teeth."

And for the second time that day, Meredith was cut off short. She didn't get the chance to tell Archer that she couldn't come that evening. She rolled away from the phone and toyed with excuses. She could call back and leave a message saying she'd come down with something highly contagious and frequently terminal. Something like . . . stage fright. With an exasperated snort, she identified the malady afflicting her and its cause—terminal timidity. She flung the covers away and jumped out of bed. She didn't flee Chicago to end up hiding out in Albuquerque, running in terror at the first hint of emotional involvement.

She picked the gossamer-light gown up off the floor. She was going to that ball, dammit, and it wouldn't be as the proper little Chicago mudhen. She was going as a peacock in peacock blue.

The evening was cool. Meredith pulled her parka more closely around her as she prowled the parking lot for a space as close as she could get to the entrance of the convention center. As she was locking the car, she realized how gauche her bulky parka looked over the brilliant blue gown. She shrugged off the down jacket and tossed it back in the car. Goose bumps would look better.

The convention center was an elaborate complex of

enormous meeting rooms, boutiques, restaurants, and the main ballroom. The lobby soared ten floors above Meredith's head as she entered. Her gaze instantly fixed on Archer. He was looking down at his watch. Meredith hesitated and moved into the shadows as he glanced up, searching the doorway. She watched him, astounded by the surge that quickened her pulse. How, she wondered bleakly, could she have ever mistaken him for a spoiled rich kid? An air of command and assurance that could never be simply inherited encircled him with its golden aura. He wore it with the same offhanded elegance he wore his custom-tailored tuxedo. She felt her nerve slipping away. She was way out of her league with a man like Archer Hanson and it frightened her. She wanted to run and would have except that he was already striding purposefully in her direction. If she didn't step forward, he would catch her trembling in the shadows. She moved back into the light.

"There you are," he exclaimed. "I was heading out to the parking lot to try and intercept you." He stopped speaking and simply stared for a moment that grew so long that Meredith felt her cheeks start to flame. His gaze was frozen by the mesmerizing blue of her gown. Slowly it traveled up along the classically simple lines to the draped neckline where the drooping folds of fabric curved over her breasts. "You look spectacular," he whispered, moving to her side so that only she could hear his words. "Of course, you could make a nightgown look like the height of elegance."

"You're looking pretty spiffy yourself," she joked, trying to divert him from pursuing his last comment any further.

With a warm laugh, Archer slipped a muscle-corded arm around her shoulders and guided her toward the ballroom.

Just as it dominated everything else during the ten days of the Balloon Fiesta, balloon-acy reigned inside the ballroom. A flock of scaled-down, helium-filled balloons hovered over the festivities. Beneath them, exactly as Archer had promised, was a dazzle of color as women swept by in their long dresses. Linen-covered tables scattered around the edge of the dance floor looked like giant silver dollars shining beneath the flicker of candlelight.

"Mr. Hanson, we're so glad you and your . . ." The maitre d' paused, scrutinizing Meredith. At last a smile of comprehension lit his face and he burst out, "Your sister could make it."

Meredith glanced up at Archer. His face glowed with a secret amusement that he shared by winking at her. With their matching blondness, it was easy to understand why the man had taken them for brother and sister. It appeared to be a misunderstanding that Archer was enjoying.

"Your table is right this way." They followed the maitre d' toward a section of tables that was roped off and designated "Fiesta Dignitaries."

"Excuse me," Archer said, halting the man's pleased progress toward the celebrity section. "My sister and I would prefer a more isolated table."

"Certainly, Mr. Archer, but the board will be disappointed."

"A more isolated table, if you please." Archer reiterated his request in a way that left no doubt that he was not accustomed to hearing his judgments questioned. They were swiftly led away from the spotlit section to the most remote table in the darkest corner of the ballroom. A boisterous, carnival atmosphere reigned that reminded Meredith of Mardi Gras in New Orleans. As they made their way back to their table, Archer was hailed from every side. Meredith was relieved when they finally melted into the shadowy corner.

Archer swept a damask-upholstered chair away from the table for Meredith. The moment they were both seated, Meredith felt as if they were marooned together on a tiny island of light. The ocean of people and merrymaking beyond ceased to exist.

"Hello there, Meredith Tolliver." He stared deeply at her as if it were a pleasure too long denied.

"Hello there, Archer Hanson." His name felt deliciously intimate on her tongue. It was almost as though she were completing a ritual that washed away their respective roles and reservations. She was no longer the dogged reporter and he the elusive prey. All that had gone before seemed now to be simply the route they had both taken to arrive at a cherished destination. All that was important was that they were here now, together; the mode of conveyance mattered not at all.

His unearthly eyes were dark now, colored by his vision of her and its effect upon him. Meredith wondered if the evidence of her arousal was as blatant. She was sure as she looked at the bold, unforgiving slash of his full mouth that it must be obvious that she was yearning to know its taste. To trace her fingertips along the hard thrust of his jaw, the high, Apache slant of his cheekbones. That she ached to feel the unruly spring of his hair beneath her palms.

"I trust your dance card isn't completely filled, m'lady," Archer teased as the lyrical strains of a waltz penetrated the silken cocoon they were spinning around themselves.

"I might be able to squeeze a humble petitioner like you in," Meredith answered with a mock aloofness.

"I should hope a sister could accommodate her brother." The little joke wrapped them in an intimacy that was far from brotherly. Archer's smile was a dazzle of whiteness against the sun-burnished planes of his face. At the edge of the dance floor, he paused and faced

Meredith, taking her eyes with his so that a mutual understanding flowed between them that what they were about to embark upon was far more than a waltz.

Meredith understood and acquiesced, the heat of that understanding flooding her with a drowning weakness. When Archer held his arms open to her and she stepped into them, she did so knowing that she had willingly taken the first step on a journey of passion that could have only one final destination.

She was trembling with the knowledge of what she had entered into as Archer took her in his arms. His sure hand on her back steadied her and prepared her for the assault of his nearness. They waited for the music to launch them as a ship awaits high tide. And then they were surging into the sea of swirling dancers. Archer was a masterful dancer who led with a gentle strength. They pirouetted around the cavernous hall with the thoughtless grace of a couple that has danced together for decades.

Meredith was surprised at how solid, how large he felt guiding her through the crowd. After a few seconds of reacquainting her feet with the box step, she abandoned herself to Archer's fluid guidance. The instant she did so, she was inundated by his feel, his smell. The hard bulwark of his chest brushing against the tips of her breasts was maddening. His warmth, scented with his clean male smell, embraced her. She fought the desire to turn her head to his neck and bury her face in the intoxicating aroma.

Almost as if responding to her suppressed desire, Archer pulled her closer, pressing his hard contours against her gratefully yielding softness. She felt the rigid fullness of his desire and her own answering hunger with no surprise.

Archer's voice was husky when he leaned down to whisper into the soft crown of her fragrant hair, "Shall we leave?"

She turned her face up to him. Her need for him was nakedly stamped in her expression. Without letting herself think, without allowing time for all the psychological demons that customarily haunted her to slither out of their hiding places, Meredith nodded assent.

They were making their way toward the exit when a rotund man wearing a plaid vest and cummerbund intercepted them. "Archer, thank God I found you. Tony at the door told me you'd arrived, but you weren't at your table. Listen, is your crew getting Cloud Waltzer ready for the tethered ascension? I hear there's already a sizable crowd gathered at the field and the television people are slated to show up and, of course, all they care about is whether the famous unicorn balloon is going to be there."

Archer smacked the heel of his hand against his forehead. "It completely slipped my mind, Andy."

The chubby man's face fell.

Archer looked at Meredith with frustrated longing. "Don't worry, Andy, I won't botch your P.R. ploy. I'll phone Phil and have him pick up the balloon and meet me out at the field. I'll take Cloud Waltzer up myself."

They hurried away. Outside the ballroom, Archer turned to Meredith. "I know this is inexcusable, but it looks as if the rest of my evening is going to be spent aloft. Would you be too offended if I asked you to come along on an earthbound flight?"

"I'd be offended if you didn't."

"Fantastic. Just let me rouse Phil." When Archer returned from the phone booth, they wound their way through the maze of shopping arcades that led to the private lot Archer had parked in. All the stores were open, keeping extended hours during the Fiesta. "How stupid of me," he exclaimed, stopping abruptly. "You'll freeze without some kind of wrap."

Meredith winced, not wanting to admit that all she had was her battered parka.

Archer looked around as if searching for inspiration. A shop window at the corner caught his eye, and grabbing Meredith's hand, they rushed toward it. "I'd like to see the cape in the window," Archer directed the saleswoman, who obligingly stripped a sumptuous emerald-green, velvet hooded cloak off of the mannequin in the window. She handed it to Archer, who draped it tenderly around Meredith. It was lined with taupe-colored velvet that immediately warmed and caressed Meredith, wrapping her even more securely in the luxurious fantasy of an evening unlike any other she had ever lived before or expected to duplicate again in her life.

"It's even better than I thought it would be," he declared. "It's so right on you, Meredith," he added in a voice intended only for her ears. "So right for this evening. I would be honored if you'd take it."

His courtly proposal contained a note of urgency reinforced by the pleading tilt of his eyebrows. Meredith was as powerless to refuse the extravagant gift as she was to break the enchanted spell woven by Archer Hanson's compelling masculinity. "Archer, it's gorgeous."

He beamed. "Then that settles it." Turning to the saleswoman, who had tactfully moved away during their exchange, he said, "We're in a bit of a hurry. Could you send the bill to Archer Hanson at Hanson Development?"

The name of the man who had built the labyrinthine center she worked in rang a bell of recognition with the saleswoman. She visibly perked up and chirped back her agreement.

Meredith hugged the voluminous cape to her as she slid into Archer's classic Porsche roadster. Archer captured her hand and drew it out from beneath the folds of the cape to rest on her knee, cradling his far larger hand. His long, powerful fingers with their clean, squared-off nails curled over her hand and lightly grazed the sensitive area inside her thigh. Tendrils of sensation spiraled out from his glancing touch and shot upward, bringing her secret core alive with a tingling awareness.

I'm a madwoman. The thought registered in a remote corner of Meredith's besotted mind. The barest touch from this man excited her more than all of Chad's most ardent maneuvers. She reflected on how different it was with Chad. Of their long, rational discussions about whether or not to, as Chad invariably put it, "have sex." Of the dry, clinical act itself. The comparison only heightened her uncontrollable response to Archer Hanson.

Meredith cleared her throat of its passion-betraying huskiness. "It's funny, right now, if this were a normal 'first date,' if such a thing even exists, I would be asking you questions about yourself, where you grew up, what you do, except I knew all that before I ever met you."

"And you filled me in with a pretty detailed outline of your life, complete with work samples." He squeezed her hand to signal the joking intent of his reference to their first meeting. "I suppose the most ponderous question weighing on my mind right now about you, Ms. Tolliver, is why, aside from the obvious fact that you are stunningly beautiful, am I so incredibly attracted to you?" As they drew up to a stoplight, Archer turned to face Meredith.

She was on the verge of giving voice to a flippant comeback, but the intensity blazing in Archer's face silenced her. He had meant every word he'd just spoken.

What little will she had left was utterly sapped by the naked wanting flaming in his eyes. In that instant, Meredith was lost. She leaned toward him the barest fraction of an inch.

Archer's strong, weather-roughened hands captured her gently tilting face. He marveled at the silken feel of her cheeks, barely believing that human skin could be so soft. He could have been cradling a magnolia blossom except for the vibrant life that pulsed beneath this unspeakably fragile skin, beneath those endlessly puzzling sapphire eyes, those tremulous, irresistibly swollen cherry lips.

Meredith felt time crack in two as Archer's magnificent, leonine head descended toward her. They were lost together in a place beyond the rule of clocks and watches. A lifetime and no time at all passed as his lips moved to taste hers. As they met, time was resoldered and years of sensation hurtled through Meredith. All the breathless nights of adolescent discovery she had denied herself were caught in the first touch of Archer's lips on hers.

As Archer tasted the limitless depth of Meredith's response, the image of her as a magnolia-frail vision evaporated. She was, every inch of her, a woman in all the most exquisite, responsive meanings of the word. He gathered her to him, taking her lips more fully, pulling her to his chest.

Meredith's hands found the straining columns of his back as he leaned out of his seat to cover her with a kiss that unloosed a flood of passion. His hot, ragged breaths, fiery against the sensitive down of Meredith's cheek, were answered by her own staccato exhalations. She was drowning in a wave of sensation. The smell of the leather seat covers mingled with the scent of Archer's breath and his undisguised male smell. As he leaned forward, the dizzying crush of his chest against her breasts awoke vortexes of tingling anticipation. A sweet ache deep within her told of the ultimate flowering of her desire for Archer.

He seemed to sense even that, her most intimate response. His kiss deepened. He demanded more of her and Meredith yielded it, parting her lips to him. His hands were now wild, seeking things, running with a frenzied desperation through her hair, along the arch of her neck, her trembling sides. His hands blazed new trails of wanting. Everywhere they passed, Meredith ached for their return. She heard herself as if from a great distance making faint, pleading sounds deep in her throat. Her hands were on the corded expanses of his broad shoulders, hugging him to her tighter.

His hands moved across the shimmering front of her dress, barely grazing the swells of her thighs, the gentle valley of her pelvis, the budding tips of her breasts, igniting flash fires wherever it went. Her body was raging now with wanting him, awake and flaming for a man with a heat she had never known possible. It burned so brightly that all the mental hobgoblins that had haunted her every other experience with a man were frightened away by the blistering light. Then, even the awareness of discovery was obliterated as Archer's palm curved over the straining fullness of Meredith's breast.

She had to have air. Moving her kiss-swollen lips to his ear, she caught shaky breaths. Archer trembled and groaned, answering her in the language of desire they were both learning to speak so eloquently to one another.

The jarring blare of a horn was a rude intrusion, startling them both. It took a second for them to realize that the world really hadn't stopped after all. Other cars had streamed past them as the light had changed several times, leaving them uninterrupted until the impatient driver behind them had broken the spell.

"Meredith Tolliver," Archer said, grinning sheepishly as he rammed in the clutch, adroitly found first gear, and got the Porsche moving, "what you do to me is clearly dangerous and probably illegal."

The floodtides of desire still churned within Meredith, but she made herself give a feeble laugh. "I guess my professional objectivity has just been blown."

"Not to mention my characteristic wariness with you 'media' types."

"Who knows what might happen now that we've

dropped our poses and defenses," Meredith hazarded. She felt like a skater sticking a toe onto ice marked with a danger sign.

"Who does know, Meredith? Do you?"

Meredith tried to interpret his expression, his tone, but found few clues to his cryptic questions. They drove on in silence until she spotted a cluster of orbs blinking on and off like gigantic, round fireflies glowing in the night. The Porsche rocked off the highway as they cut down the road to the launch site. Phil, with the help of several TV cameramen and late night spectators, was already inflating the unicorn balloon.

The emerald cape swirled around Meredith like the tangible evidence of the cloud of enchantment she felt wrapped in as they made their way through the crowd.

"Fantastic work, Phil," Archer congratulated his employee. "You're in for time and a half and then some for this. I really do appreciate it."

Phil shrugged, pleased with the public recognition, but still not looking away from the high-powered fan he was using to direct a current of air into the expanding balloon. "These guys," he said, pointing to the TV people, "are on deadline. They need to get some footage for the late night news, so they pitched in to get the thing airborne. Are you and Meredith going up?"

"Yeah," a short cameraman in a newsboy cap interjected. "The cape and"—he made a vague gesture that took in Meredith's face and figure—"everything would make a great shot."

"Why don't you take over here, then," Phil suggested, moving the fan out of the way as he and Archer changed places. Archer took over, opening up the burner to begin warming the air trapped in the envelope.

"Hang on to the basket, boys," Archer directed as the balloon rose from the earth, righting the basket with Archer in it. "Meredith, care to step aboard?"

She gathered her cape around her and took the steadying hand Archer held out to her as she climbed into the basket.

"Phil, are the lines all tied down?" Archer asked.

"Aye, aye, captain, your anchors are weighed. You won't be going out on high tide."

"Good work—then you can turn us loose."

The television crews turned their lights on and called out for the ascending balloon passenger and pilot to wave and smile. Meredith and Archer complied as the Cloud Waltzer slowly lifted off. Above them the balloon shone like a Japanese lantern as Archer kept the burners on so that the cameramen could film the popular unicorn prancing in all his splendor across the radiant globe. Soon, however, they were beyond the reach of even the most powerful light. In darkness and ever deepening silence, they continued to rise. By the time they reached the end of the ground tethers, the crowd noises far below were a dim blur.

Meredith felt an instinctive tightening in her stomach as the earth fell away, but even that slight apprehension dissolved as she surveyed the panorama below. The crowd immediately below her was lost altogether in darkness. She would have thought the field deserted except for the people clumped around the lighted concession booths ringing the field a mile away. Beyond them, Albuquerque was a splash of twinkling phosphorescence churned up against a sea of velvety blackness. The scene was unutterably peaceful. Meredith thought that in all the world, there was nowhere else she'd rather be than here, with Archer Hanson, rocking gently in a tethered balloon above a darkened world.

The blast of the burner ceased and his arms trapped Meredith from behind. They both looked out over the lights twinkling in the distance. "There is no way I could improve on this moment," Archer whispered, clasping his hands below her breasts and pulling her against him.

Meredith folded her arms on top of his, covering a part of his large, tanned hands with her much smaller, far paler ones. He rested his chin on her head, the silken down of her baby fine hair caressing the curve of his throat. He was astonished at how the brush of the undersides of her breasts against his hands excited him. No, he corrected himself, what he felt was beyond excitement. He was quite familiar with mere arousal and had known it in many different ways and to many different degrees with an equally diverse number of women. This was something else. It was closer to a delirium, a compulsion. It had an uncontrollability that was new to Archer Hanson, that tantalized him and, he noted with slight alarm, frightened him a little.

"You never did answer my question," he said. "What is it about you that attracts me so powerfully? And remember, we've already eliminated your beauty as a factor."

Meredith laughed nervously, feeling as if she'd somehow managed to fool Archer into believing she was pretty and, for the first time, regretted how desperately important it was that he never learn the truth about her, about the Meredith he couldn't see. The Meredith she must never let him see. "It must be that new mouthwash I used. Or maybe you're just trying to butter up the press."

"Butter? For the press? Margarine is too good for the swine."

"Swine?" Meredith echoed with a laugh.

"No, you're right, it must be the mouthwash. But I'd better run a quick test, just to be certain."

Still standing at Meredith's back, he bent down, his hands moving to cradle her chin and tilt it upward to receive his kiss. The moment their lips met, Archer's jest was at an end. They were lost again in the same urgent intensity of their first kiss. Every nerve ending along Meredith's back, from her ankles, up along her spine, to the nape of her neck, came alive as Archer edged closer to her. His hands stole in beneath the cloaking folds of the cape to span the length of her delicate rib cage. Then, as if taking possession of a great treasure, Archer cupped her breast in his warm hand. His thumb and forefinger found the hardened nub of her nipple thrusting up against the sheer fabric of her gown. Like a master locksmith, he rolled and fondled it until he'd found the combination that unlocked the response Meredith had kept so guarded from all others.

She felt her head fall against the firm support of his shoulder. The hungry urgency of his kiss fanned fresh flames through her. She swept back the cape to raise a hand to his face, delighting in the barely perceptible rasp of hours-old whiskers against her sensitized palm. As his mouth left hers, they heard one another's passion-hoarsened breathing. Each shallow inhalation testifying to the ferocity of their desire and building it to an even more unendurable peak. His lips found a nerve-rich strip of skin along her neck and left a trail of nibbling, inflaming kisses along it from the lobe of her ear to the scooped-out hollows of her collarbone.

A moan escaped from Meredith's lips and she felt her head pressing in helpless ecstasy against Archer's unyielding shoulder. Just as surely as Archer had led earlier on the dance floor, Meredith now set the tempo and Archer picked it up. Mindlessly, he responded to the quickening rhythm she had set, pressing her to him ever more tightly until the bold outline of his thrusting need was clearly engraved against the flesh of her lower back. The cyclone spinning through Meredith described an ever-narrowing circle as Archer's hand kneaded insistent messages along the tops of her quivering thighs and belly. The circle of delight constricted gradually until Archer found the center of her most intimate pleasure and began a narcotizing massage. Meredith had a fleeting image of herself melting, running like pudding down his shirtfront, but she was powerless to halt the voluptuous rapture.

"Meredith, Meredith." Her name was an insensate rumbling against her ear as Archer turned her to face him. With a drugged awareness, he realized that they were sinking, and he reached up and opened the burner. In the propane flame, Meredith saw the face of a thoroughly shaken man and knew that Archer was just as powerfully affected as she. After a brief roaring, the balloon bobbed back up to the end of the tether and they were isolated again in their floating crow's nest of dark and splendid privacy.

Facing her now, Archer parted the cloak and stepped inside until they were both wrapped in its enclosing warmth. Meredith clung to him as heated waves of longing buffeted her. She reached up and drew his head down, his lips covering her eager mouth. Locked together high above common concerns, trembling from the force of a mutual bewitchment, Meredith felt all her moorings slip loose. The choking ties that had bound her could no longer hold her captive up here, not with Archer's arms twined around her. For the first time in her life, she wanted a man with a desperate urgency she hadn't known she was capable of. That desire raked through her with a fierce ache that found the promise of relief in Archer's parched words.

"God help me, Meredith, I want you as I've never before wanted another person or thing on this earth. Stop me if you . . ."

But all Meredith had the power to stop were his words and the doubts they brought. Her answer was dictated by a relentlessly driving need. Haltingly, then with a growing courage, she reached out and began to unbuckle the turquoise-studded clasp on his belt. It was her sign to Archer that her need was every bit as strong as his, that it was a tempest that could not be denied.

The gesture snapped the straining bounds of Archer's control. With a low, primitive growl, his hands became unleashed creatures that roamed with a blind will. His fingers stroked a trail of fire against the bare skin of her thighs. The only barrier they encountered were a pair of thin panties easily stripped away.

The whisper of a zipper accompanied the uncharacteristically bold movements of Meredith's hands. The weight of the turquoise-laden belt pulled the suit pants down. They came back together with the sinuous fluidity of two people lost in a foggy dream, neither one knowing what to do or expect, yet each one moving in flawless synchronization with the other as though through a well-rehearsed routine. Beneath the cape draped over Archer's shoulders, the rock-steady crook of his arm came around Meredith to scoop her up. With artless precision, her legs parted to encircle his lean waist and the aching emptiness within her was filled. Archer, his large hands on her buttocks, guided her into a thrusting rhythm that was both her own and more than her own. It seemed it would go on forever, but she knew that life could not support such perfection, and driven by her crescendoing need, she was forced to dictate its culmination. The rhythm accelerated, hurtling them both to the act's completion.

Meredith's release rocketed her to a high plateau beyond any she had previously known. There, on those exquisite heights, everything was obliterated. She was scoured of past, problems, fears, even her self was gone. She was both reduced and elevated to a state of gasping ecstasy.

Archer's arms were quivering as he tenderly replaced her on the wicker floor of the balloon. Wordlessly, he bent down and retrieved the fallen underpants, holding them up for her to step into like the Prince with Cinderella's glass slipper. Meredith was unbearably touched by the simple, eloquent action. He stood.

"Archer." Her voice trembled. "I have so much to say to you, to ask you."

"I know. I do too. But before we begin, before words and reality and the rest of the world come crashing in on us again, hold me, Meredith Tolliver. Just hold me."

Meredith clasped Archer to her in a fierce embrace. They were still holding each other when the balloon, its cargo of air cooled by the night air, came gently back to earth.

Chapter 5

P*lease, come home with me,* Meredith. Stay with me. Let me love you properly." Archer's plea was delivered in the parking lot of the Convention Center. He'd pulled the roadster in next to Meredith's car to try one last time to keep Meredith from disappearing into the night.

Huddled beneath the cape, Meredith shivered with a chill that she couldn't seem to dispel. Once the balloon had touched earth, all the ghosts she had jettisoned during the shattering flight returned to haunt her. She was assailed by regret and apprehension. Fearful that she had made an irrevocable mistake, Meredith worried that the overriding impulses she had given in to might forever alter the course of her relationship with Archer. That their new intimacy might in fact doom it to a premature end. Her instincts now told her to run, to hide herself. She had exposed too much already.

"I really do need to be getting home," she said, hating the hard artificiality of the words she was forced to speak.

"At least let me see you home," Archer urged. "I'll have someone deliver your car to you first thing in the morning."

Meredith was touched by his sincerity and, for a moment, almost relented. But no, she couldn't afford to let Archer get that close. Not yet. Maybe not ever. "Oh, don't bother." She tossed off her reply in a tone that belittled the intensity of his emotion and mocked the awing power of what had passed between them.

Archer's shoulders slumped momentarily, then he stiffened them with a steely resolve. When he spoke, his voice was as defensively brittle as hers had been. "Have it your way, then, Ms. Tolliver. I imagine you would anyway, so I won't offer any more resistance."

Feeling something unutterably precious slipping away, Meredith scrambled to recapture it. "How about the interview? When do you want to get started?"

Archer turned his head and glowered.

Meredith could feel the weight of his annoyance and disappointment and wanted to pour out all the unnamed fears that held her in thrall, that prevented her from sinking into his arms, his bed. But she couldn't. Instead, she had to bear the burden of Archer's mistaken impression of who she was, of what she felt.

He sighed out his exasperation and resignation. Massaging the bridge of his nose, he said, "I'm booked solid tomorrow until eight or nine. Would you like to go out for a late dinner? You can bring your recorder and dive into the sordid life of Archer Hanson then, if you aren't afraid of what it will do to your digestion."

Delighted to hear the return of his humor, Meredith answered with a buoyant laugh, "I think I can handle the combination."

"Good. Tell me where you live and I'll come by for you when I'm done."

An icy stab of irrational panic lacerated Meredith. "No, no, don't bother. I'll meet you wherever you choose."

"Meredith, my girl, you do try a man, don't you? Come on, let's drop this cat-and-mouse game. Why am I not allowed near your home? I doubt that you'd have much trouble guessing the explanation I've already come up with."

The full force of his suspicion hit Meredith with a delayed impact. "That I'm married?"

"Or living with someone. Or otherwise engaged with someone you don't want me to see or be seen by."

"Oh, Archer, no." Meredith was stunned, though, of course, Archer's reasoning made perfect sense. Feeling her back to the wall, Meredith groped for an explanation. The truth, if she had the courage to reveal it, would seem far more unbelievable than any fiction she could fabricate. With the tenacity that only illogical fears can generate, Meredith clung to the conviction that the more of herself she exposed to Archer, the more he might learn how unlovable she felt. About how in Chicago she had turned her body into a brittle bundle of bones.

"Level with me, then, Meredith," Archer demanded. "There's not time enough in the world for me to spend any of mine with another man's woman."

"Another man's woman," Meredith echoed testily. "You make me sound like an assignable commodity. If you must know, I live with my aunt Adrianne." The lie slipped as easily off her tongue as if she had rehearsed it. "Actually, she's my great-aunt. My grandmother's sister."

"Why didn't you tell me that to start off?" Archer asked, obviously relieved.

"Living with an elderly maiden aunt doesn't exactly lend itself to an air of independence and glamour, does it?" Meredith asked. As soon as the words were out of her mouth, she realized that she'd overlooked a tremendous loophole: Phil. Not only was he her next-door neighbor, he also worked for Archer. "Not that Aunt Adrianne is at all interfering," she continued, trying to patch up the tale she'd concocted. "She's bedridden and prefers not to see strangers. Why, even Phil hasn't met her."

"I . . . I didn't realize," Archer started off haltingly. "I apologize for my accusations. They were unfounded and uncalled for."

Archer's gracious apology made Meredith wince under another spear of guilt.

"It must be a strain on you, caring for her," he continued.

"Not really." Meredith had no choice but to embroider on the lie. "Both my grandmothers died when I was quite young and Aunt Adrianne took their places. I could always go to her with any problem I had and she was endlessly understanding and always, unconditionally, on my side. It meant a lot to me when I was growing up and not terribly secure, to have someone who absolutely accepted me for what I was." The hollowness inside Meredith at the place where the fictitious and all-accepting Aunt Adrianne might have been seemed even emptier than ever.

"My grandfather sort of filled the same role for me," Archer confided. "I suppose parents are too close to their children to be able to love them for what they are. From day one, I was, first and foremost, an extension of the redoubtable Gunther Hanson. He was always taking me out of school so I could drive out with him to his oil fields or construction sites. As far as education went, it was better than any business degree in the world, but it made it hard as hell just to be a little boy."

Meredith understood more than she could ever say. She felt the depth of emotion in Archer's simple admission flow around her with the force of an ocean current.

"Well, maybe someday I can meet the reclusive Aunt Adrianne," he said with a hastily manufactured peppiness. "Until then, I bow to your judgment in making whatever arrangements you like for us to be together. Just be sure," he said, bringing her hand to his lips, "that we *do* get together." Looking into her eyes, Archer turned her hand in his and inscribed a message of longing on her palm with the tip of his tongue.

Meredith's starchiness melted into a warm, running torrent that coursed through her anew. She ached to succumb to the maddening invitation. To spend the night wrapped in Archer's arms. To wake to his kiss. Those desires battered against the wall of defenses imprisoning her. The wall held fast. "My aunt will worry if I don't get back soon." So shaken was she that her hand quivered as she withdrew it.

"My secretary accidentally threw away the scrap of paper with your phone number scribbled on it, so . . . ?"

"Oh, sure, I'll just send it to you," she said, punching his number into her phone and attaching her contact information.

Archer's phone chimed and he read over the message. "M. J. Tolliver? How formal. What's the *J* stand for?"

"Julianna. It's my mother's name."

"Pretty name."

"I never cared for it much."

"You're right," Archer laughed, "it's hideous. But

you're beautiful, M.J., and I can't seem to keep my hands off you." His grin flashed with a Viking radiance that mesmerized Meredith as his hands smoothed over her shivering shoulders. She felt the titanic pull of his attraction urging her to lean forward, to taste his lips again, to abandon herself to the oblivion she had found in his arms. Abruptly realizing how dangerously close she was to succumbing, Meredith jerked away, fumbling for the door handle.

Reaching across her, the iron bar of his arm pressed against Meredith's belly, Archer easily found the handle and flicked it open. But his arm remained where it was, branding a searing stripe of heat across the sloping valley of her pelvis. In that instant, Meredith knew the full measure of his power over her. She would be a willing captive if he chose to keep her. She could struggle no more. Her surrender was clear. As clear as Archer's recognition of it. With his gaze locking on hers, Archer slowly removed his arm. When she came fully to him, it would be of her own volition or not at all. Meredith was condemned to freedom.

Feeling like an addled bird, she hopped from the car. "Hasta lumbago," she joked weakly, cringing at the sound of the trite syllables issuing from her mouth. Unable to bear hearing Archer's response, she jumped into her battered Volkswagen.

Archer listened to the car sputter crankily to life as conflicting emotions churned against one another inside him. On one hand, he wanted to follow Meredith home. To watch over her and make sure that her wreck of a car didn't die on some darkened street. On the other hand, he was tempted to drive fast and far in the opposite direction. He wanted to flee the overload of feeling that had ambushed him. The instincts that served him so well in business now reasserted themselves, warning him that Meredith Tolliver was even more complex than she appeared.

When he looked up, the taillights of her VW had become tiny pinpricks of red in the inky black night. He engaged the clutch, then paused. With a decisive swiftness, he put the Porsche into reverse. He'd turn around and follow her, follow the mystery to its source. He'd confront her with his doubts and eradicate them before they had a chance to flourish beneath her infuriating reticence. Then, angrily discarding that adolescent notion, Archer rammed the gearshift into first and began the long drive home.

Sleep was impossible. Meredith lay in bed watching the lighted numerals on her bedside clock slither into a new shape as each minute passed. Alternating currents of joy and despair wracked her. One second she was hugging herself with sheer happiness. The next, she was mourning the inevitable passing of a relationship she would never be able to sustain.

Finally, around seven, she abandoned the charade of sleep and succumbed to Thor's yowling demands to be fed. She lingered over a mug of tea and the morning paper. As usual, the copy desk had peppered her column with typos that made her look as if she'd used a Serbo-Croatian dictionary to check her spelling. Forcing herself to focus on preparing for her interview with Archer, she sat down with a stack of back issues of *Enterprise* magazine. She analyzed all the profiles she could find, tearing them apart to study how they were put together so that she might use them as models for her piece on Archer.

Archer Hanson.

Time and again the name derailed her industrious train of thought, leaving her tangled in the sweet tentacles of fantasy. She would shake them loose long enough to jot down a question for the coming interview, then images from the night before would overwhelm her. If it were not for the extraordinary aliveness she felt deep within her, Meredith might have believed that the whole evening had been a fevered dream. Surely no woman had ever been loved as she had *except* in her wildest dreams.

She was so lost in fiery remembrance that at first she didn't hear the rapping at her door. When she did, hope and fear collided within her. Could it be Archer? Here? As powerfully as she yearned for him, she feared seeing him here. She saw the apartment she had found such contentment in with Archer's eyes and it appeared to her as it would to him, as a beggar's miserable hole and, worse still, as the repository of her secret self.

"Who is it?" The question quavered through the closed door.

"Delivery from Duke City Floral."

Meredith slumped against the door with relief, then pulled it open. A bored-looking teenager stood outside holding a spray of calla lilies.

"Sign here," he said, thrusting a clipboard at Meredith.

Barely able to tear her eyes from the magnificent blooms, she scribbled her name on the form. The delivery boy handed over the flowers and left before Meredith had time enough to collect herself and give him a tip. She twirled back inside the door, leaning against it as she shut it with her back. A card. The thought clanged her back to reality. She searched through the foliage for a card.

"Good morning, M.J.," it started off. A thrill of discovery welled up in Meredith at seeing his handwriting for the first time. The words were bold and dark and verged on being illegible. They had obviously been dashed off by a sure and quick hand, one unused to corrections or equivocations. "I trust you slept better than I did last night. I wanted to call first thing this morning, but thought better of it and am sending these instead. Don't ask 'Why lilies?' I just knew that roses were too trite and violets too delicate and everything else in the store was too forgettable. As you are none of the above, I settled on these. I'll call as soon as I can take a break. —A."

Meredith reread the note four times before laying the pale, white flowers down and finding a vase. The best she could come up with was a tall earthenware teapot. She cut down the stems and arranged the flowers, setting them on the bar that separated the tiny kitchen from the living room. She was lost in contemplation of their elegant beauty when more pounding on her door startled her. This time she didn't have to ask for identification. A gruff voice announced, "Deacon Movers. Delivery for Miss Meredith Tolliver."

Slightly bewildered, Meredith opened the door and came face-to-face with her grandmother's huge, elegant vanity swaddled in gray mover's blankets. Now thoroughly bewildered, she asked, "Where did it come from?"

The brown-uniformed moving man glanced down at the shipping invoice. "Chicago, Illinois," he read. "From Mrs. Julianna Tolliver." He looked up at Meredith's puzzled expression. "Didn't she tell you it was coming?"

Meredith shook her head bewilderedly.

"Well, it's most definitely here now. Where do you want us to put it?"

Meredith glanced behind her as if expecting to suddenly find another hundred square feet in her cramped apartment. By moving her chest of drawers into the bathroom, she created just enough space for the movers to squeeze the vanity into her bedroom. When they'd left, she slumped down on her bed. The vanity had been in her mother's room ever since her grandmother had died. She'd played dress-up, smearing lipstick on in front of the beveled glass mirror that opened into a triptych. The huge piece of furniture had fit in the mansion she'd grown up in with its twelve- and eighteen-foot ceilings, balconies, servants' quarters, and chandeliers. But here, in an efficiency apartment, it was like seeing the *Queen Mary* docked in a fishing pond.

Meredith didn't have much difficulty in analyzing the motives behind her mother sending such a behemoth piece of furniture knowing full well her daughter's limited budget, which implied a limited living space. The message was clear: If your present life can't support this bit of loveliness from your past life, it must not be much of an existence. The obvious conclusion (to her mother at least) was—come back to Chicago.

Julianna Tolliver's forte was wounded martyrdom. Meredith could even hear the echoes of her mother's hurt response if she were to protest the gift: "I always thought you liked your grandmother's vanity," she would say. "I only wanted to please you." Then Meredith's father would get on the phone, springing to his wife's defense as he always did and making Meredith feel like an insensitive clod, willfully hurting a frail, ethereal being unable to cope with a harsh world.

Meredith sighed and caught sight of herself in the oval mirror that stood taller than she did. The sight defeated her. Remembering Archer's note and his comment about violets being "too delicate" for her revived her spirit. Sitting up, she smiled at herself in her grandmother's elegant mirror and recalled an old saying: "When the world hands you a lemon, make lemonade." And the vanity, she told herself sternly, was most certainly no lemon. She reached a hand out to caress the burnished rosewood with its swirling grain pattern and to admire the exquisite craftmanship of the finely wrought piece.

She made up her mind. She wouldn't allow the size of the vanity or her mother's motives in sending it to her depress her. As her therapist in Chicago had pointed out to her, she was the person living her life, she had the right to make the decisions about it. And she *was* decided—she would neither retreat to Chicago and the life her parents envisioned for her, nor would she allow her mother to assume a role of hurt martyrdom by objecting to the gift.

Content with her small psychic victory, Meredith settled down and immersed herself in the *Enterprise* magazines. She savored each new question she concocted, gleefully anticipating Archer's answers to her pointed queries about unionism, trade deficits, Federal Reserve policy, and productivity. She had almost managed to take her mind off the phone when it finally rang.

"I'm sorry I couldn't call earlier."

Archer's breathless beginning caught Meredith with the force of a runaway locomotive. She had to scramble to keep pace with the landslide of emotion the sound of his voice unloosed.

"These guys from the mineworkers union seem determined to keep me from seeing the light of day for the next couple of weeks."

"I imagine that you're both fairly concerned about maintaining your own interests," Meredith commented drily. Glancing into her bedroom at the vanity, she was reminded of her mother's grandfather, a man who had made history for his skill at maintaining his interests. She'd been glad as a child that she didn't bear her notorious ancestor's name, especially during history class when she would hear Great-Granddad Moorington described as a "robber baron." He'd had his share of labor problems as well. A couple of them had led directly to some landmark court decisions that became the foundation for labor reform in the United States. Still, she had to admit that the old reprobate fascinated her. She wondered if that longstanding fascination could, at least partially, account for her attraction to the hard-driving Archer Hanson. She fled the disturbing thought.

"Archer, the flowers were . . ."

"Gaudy," he supplied quickly.

"No, of course not. They're gorgeous."

"I don't care if they are a bit overly dramatic, they fit

my mood this morning. Last night, Meredith, was so . . ." He paused. When he spoke again his voice was smoky with a husky intimacy that sent shivers capering along Meredith's spine. "My paltry vocabulary isn't up to describing last night."

"I know what you mean."

"Those lilies," he went on haltingly. "I bought them because they reminded me of your skin in the moonlight, all porcelain and cream and, oh, God, I wish you were here right now, Ms. Tolliver. I wish you hadn't left me last night."

"I . . . I had no choice," she finished lamely.

"Damn, Courtney's buzzing me. The delegation must be coming back. I'm going to have to run. Listen, is dinner still on tonight?"

"As far as I'm concerned, it is," Meredith answered spiritedly.

"Good. Great. A woman who knows her mind and speaks it. I hope it's all right with you if we eat at my place. I'm going to be wrung out by the time this day's over. Who am I kidding? I was wrung out when I stepped in the door today and you, Ms. Tolliver, are directly to blame. Anyway, I left word with my housekeeper to leave something heating in the oven. She's never let me down yet. What do you say?"

"As the interview-*er*, I'm completely at the disposal of my interview-*ee*. Whatever you say."

"Interviewer/interviewee, eh? I'll have to rearrange *that* dynamic, my pretty." He gave a melodrama villain's laugh. "I suppose that the embargo on my picking you up at your house is still in force."

"Yes, my aunt . . ." Meredith paused, horrified. She'd forgotten the name she'd invented for her imaginary aunt. "My aunt isn't feeling well," she finished abruptly. "I'll come out to your place."

"No, you won't. Not in that bomb you drive. I don't like thinking about the eager assistance you'd attract if that thing broke down on any of the lonely roads out here. I'll either send a car for you or come myself and wait outside. Take your pick."

Meredith chose the lesser of two evils, the car, and Archer rang off after she warned him to be prepared to answer some tough questions that evening.

As she placed the receiver in its cradle, Meredith was astonished to see that her hand was shaking. She was quivering again with nervous excitement. The feeling was both delicious and frightening. Ever since that day, almost three years ago, back in Chicago, when she'd first truly seen herself, finally looked at herself in the very mirror that now dominated her bedroom, and saw her emaciated body for what it really was, she'd been scared of losing control again. Now, with Archer Hanson, she felt as if she had about as much control over herself as she did over the weather. Compounding her mounting anxiety was the sudden realization that it was late afternoon and she hadn't eaten anything.

Was it starting again? she wondered. With icy hands, she forced herself to choke down some Greek yogurt and a pear. The all-too-familiar churning of conflicting emotions started up within her. Hoping to short-circuit the cycle of anxiety, she stared at the serenely lovely lilies. A dry snort of amusement tore from her nose as she remembered Archer saying that they had reminded him of her.

What would he send, she wondered bitterly, if he knew what she had been like? Weeds? Cockleburrs? Crazy daisies?

Stop it! The order was issued by a calmer, more rational part of her mind, the part that recognized and tried to shield Meredith from the destructive feelings of self-loathing that had led her to attempt to waste her body away to bare bones. Shaking, she wondered if the awful cycle were about to start up again, if the powerful attraction she felt for Archer would overwhelm her new sense of self. Sitting in the middle of the room, Meredith hugged her knees to her chest as if she were holding herself together while she thought about the past few years.

She'd never experienced these dramatic emotional upheavals at any time in her relationship with Chad. Everything was safe with him. He never pushed her, never probed too deeply. Never demanded that she share herself. And she had never wanted to. From the start, when her father had placed Chad in the office next to hers, she'd known what the setup was. Try as she might, she could never replace Rory. She wasn't a man. So her father arranged for the second best alternative, a son-in-law. Though he never would have put it into words, he'd chosen Chad. And because everyone had known from the start what was expected of them and what they would gain from the arrangement—Meredith, a suitable husband; Chad, a partnership in the family business; her father, an heir—she'd gone along with Chad's mechanical courtship. It had been safe. Something she could control and understand.

Archer Hanson was something else entirely. Meredith turned her mind like a team of fancy-driven stallions back to the task at hand. Dutifully, she returned to concocting questions to pose to Archer that evening.

But all the while, nibbling at the back of her mind was the fear of the questions he might ask her. Questions that she had no answers for.

Chapter 6

A***rcher was sitting on the*** portal, a porch that ran the entire length of the front of his rambling adobe house, when Meredith pulled up. She was embarrassed when the uniformed driver of the Hanson Development Corporation station wagon that had picked her up jumped theatrically out of the car to open the door for her before she had a chance to do it herself.

"Thanks a lot, Alex," Archer said, coming forward to shake hands with the driver. He was wearing a powder blue polo and jeans worn to a faded white at the knees and the back pocket, where he obviously stowed his wallet. They fit the lean contours and hard swells of his body with a comfortable familiarity.

"No problem, Archer. It was a kick. Hey, can I keep the uniform tonight? It's rented through tomorrow. Molly'll get a laugh out of it."

"Sure. Take the wagon too. No more pickups or deliveries tonight."

"Archer Hanson," Meredith fumed when the young man had left. "Why on earth did you go through that silly charade?"

"How else was I supposed to come up with a car and driver? You don't actually suppose that I keep a chauffeur on staff, do you? Besides, it's no sillier than your refusal to just let me pick you up. Come on, the libations are waiting." He led her to a chair on the porch and flopped down in one beside her. A frosty pitcher of margaritas was on the table next to him. He poured her a slushy glass, then leaned back with his own.

"I've just been sitting here trying to let the day ooze out of me," he said, looking off into the thick stand of cottonwoods that surrounded his rambling adobe house. The dark of a rapidly approaching night was beginning to meld the branches of the large trees into one solid, unbroken mass. Watching the feathery silhouettes disappear against a fading sky eased the buzz that had rasped through Meredith's head for the last few hours, and she began to really hear the peaceful country sounds of horses nickering in a distant pasture and wind whispering through the high treetops.

"It's lovely out here," she said, just starting to take the full measure of that discovery. Each breath seemed to cleanse her of the stale city air and fill her with air gentled by the exhalations of millions of trees and green things.

"Yes, sometimes I think I'd lose it completely if I couldn't make my retreat to this island of sanity every evening. How's the margarita?"

"Fantastic. Do you know, until I tasted this one, I thought I didn't like margaritas."

"Not like the national drink of the Southwest?" Archer echoed in mock alarm. "I'll let you in on my secret: I don't salt the glass rims."

"That's it," Meredith said, just noticing the missing ingredient. "That's why it doesn't taste like alcoholic Gatorade. Without the salt, margaritas are good."

"Without the salt, it's not a margarita," Archer corrected. "So let's rename it. How about the Meredita?" He held his glass aloft and they toasted the newly christened concoction.

The tight coils of tension that had been choking Meredith all afternoon and evening loosened. Once again, she chided herself, she had created turmoil where none existed.

"How was your day?" Archer asked, refilling her glass.

"It had its moments. The lilies first and foremost," she answered. Emboldened by the drink, she allowed her eyes to hold his and tell him more eloquently than her words could precisely what the flowers had meant. Then she went on to recount the delivery of the vanity.

"Whose bedroom did you put it in?" Archer asked, laughing with her at her surprise. Meredith had retold the tale, omitting her mother's dark motives. "Yours or your aunt's?"

Fresh regret stabbed Meredith. She wished she'd never told that lie. Even more, she wished she hadn't *had* to tell it. "Mine. It's getting a bit chilly out here," she said, anxious to change the subject. She pulled her shawl more tightly around her. It was handloomed in earth tones with a streak of indigo at the top that made Meredith think of the brown mountains south of Albuquerque and the intensely blue sky above them. Underneath it, she wore a simple gauze blouse trimmed with ecru lace and a swirling skirt in a bold geometric print that lent vibrancy to the entire outfit.

"Excuse me," Archer said, springing up from his chair. "I forget that not everyone has my metabolism. I think I was accidentally fitted out with one meant for a hummingbird. It's fairly high; consequently, I'm always about twenty degrees warmer than anyone else."

"We should compromise," Meredith laughed, helping him gather up the pitcher of salt-free margaritas. "I'm always about twenty degrees *cooler* than anyone else."

"I think something could be worked out." Archer blocked Meredith's retreat. Taking the pitcher from her hands and setting it back on the table, he enfolded her in his arms. "God, I've ached for this all day long."

Meredith snuggled closer to him, burrowing into his warmth. Shutting her eyes, she reveled in simply being held.

Archer pulled back and smiled down on her. "We'd better go inside and have dinner before I lose what little self-control I have left. Otherwise, I'm going to be tempted to try and make you forget your interview."

"Now, that *would* be disastrous," Meredith joked, following him into the house. It was as unaffected as his office. Tile floors, roundly curving adobe corners, exposed *viga* beams spanning the ceiling, defined the interior and lent it undeniable grace. But beyond those basics, it was clear that no professional decorator's eye had guided the contents of Archer's home. It was a comfortable jumble of sturdy, well-made mission-style furniture, pottery, and paintings that had nothing in common other than their owner's very idiosyncratic taste.

Meredith loved it. It was the kind of home she'd always wanted to grow up in. Her mother had redecorated every other year, slavishly following the directives of waspish decorators. The only items that her mother had refused to part with in the biannual purges were heirlooms from her parents and grandparents. In place of her own personal style, Julianna Tolliver, with her husband's unfailing indulgence, had substituted the trendy dictates of frosty professionals. But Archer's home was indelibly stamped as his.

"As you can see," Archer said, taking the pitcher and setting it down on a kitchen counter, "I'm not a serious contender for *Better Homes and Gardens.*"

"Which is exactly why I like it so much," Meredith replied without hesitation.

"Now, let's see. Theresa said she'd leave something edible for us in the stove." He pulled on an oven mitt and stuck his hand into the oven, where a cheesy casserole bubbled. "We're in luck," he exulted. "Theresa makes the world's best chicken enchiladas. Stand back." He hauled the steaming dish from the oven, then retrieved a crisp salad from the refrigerator. Like everything else about Archer Hanson, the meal was simple, unpretentious, and exactly what Meredith yearned for. They took their plates to the dining room table, which had been set with silverware that gleamed in candlelight. At the center of the table was a bunch of garden flowers—purple asters and chrysanthemums.

"On top of all her other talents, Theresa arranges flowers," Meredith joked.

"Actually, that was my little accomplishment," Archer confessed.

The vision of this nationally renowned entrepreneur, who had millions of dollars riding on his every decision, picking flowers for a centerpiece struck Meredith as unbearably poignant.

"I was going to claim the enchiladas too, but . . ."

Here his voice lowered and the teasing impishness vanished from his eyes. "I thought you would want to know me as I really am. Just as I want to know you."

Meredith shied away from Archer's intense stare. She felt as if he could look into her. It was clear he already suspected that she was hiding things about herself from him.

Her discomfort confirmed Archer's suspicions, suspicions he had wanted erased, not borne out. He quickly changed the subject. "Where are all these tough questions you promised me?" he asked, pretending that he hadn't noticed her uneasiness, that it hadn't upset him.

Meredith put aside her fork and fumbled in her bag for the miniature recorder she always took with her on assignments. The enchiladas, so appetizing a minute before, now held no appeal. She prayed that her appetite had been stolen by nervousness, that being with Archer hadn't triggered the feelings of inadequacy that had started it all before. Started the nightmare phase of her life she wanted to forget and for Archer to never know about.

"Let me check out the basics," Meredith said, controlling the quavery note that unsteadied her voice. She drew a notebook out of her purse. "Your name is Archer L. Hanson. Correct?"

"Correct, indeed. You *are* a penetrating interviewer."

"They'll get tougher, don't worry. What does the *L* stand for?"

"I was afraid you'd ask. Here's your first scoop. I can't think of another living soul I've ever revealed this to, but it stands for Little."

"Little?"

"Little," Archer confirmed with a nod. "As in Little Hanson, me, and Big Hanson, my father. Fortunately, it never caught on."

Meredith envied his ease in accepting his father's foibles, even one as quirky as intimating his own son was merely a miniature version of himself. She quickly ran over the rest of the background information she'd accumulated, making notes where Archer elaborated and correcting previous reporters' mistakes. Then she switched on her recorder and dived in.

"I imagine that your father helped you get your start," she said. "Is that what you attribute your early success to?"

Unexpectedly, Archer's eyes flared hot as the blue base of a gas flame. It reminded Meredith that behind the easygoing joviality she had been enjoying was a hard-driving man of unequaled intensity.

"You mean, did my father bankroll me and cushion all my mistakes? Did he pave the way for me with cash and connections?" Archer's anger was raw and he didn't bother to disguise it. "The answer to your question is no, though it would shock anyone who knows that my last name is Hanson. Yes, my father was rich. He was powerful. But he did it all himself. He was one of eleven children in a family of sharecroppers. My father grew up dirt poor and uneducated in a backwater town in Mississippi. The only things life ever handed people like him free, he used to tell me, were hookworms and rickets."

The crimson flush of color receded from Archer's high, wide cheeks. He paused a minute, then went on. "I'll tell you something, Meredith, but it's only for you. I don't ever want it repeated. Do you understand?"

Meredith nodded, feeling as if her recorder were an intruder that she no longer even wanted. She switched it off. Something far more important than any magazine interview was happening.

"I didn't always love my father. A lot of the time I didn't even like him. Sometimes I hated him." The words came out with a deceptive ease. "He made my life too hard in too many unnecessary ways. But I always respected him. He was afraid that if I were raised as a rich man's son, I'd never make anything of myself. So he created a kind of artificial poverty for me to grow up in. It seems almost funny now."

He smiled briefly, then added in a tight voice, "Almost. Because he only had one pair a year, I only had one pair of shoes a year. I collected empty bottles for spending money. My room was unheated in the winter and uncooled in the summer." A dry laugh escaped Archer's throat. "I think if he could have managed it, old

Gunther would have seen to it that I had to walk six miles to school every day, just like he did."

Meredith longed to put her arms around Archer, to hold him and soothe away all the ancient hurts. The hurts that never really go away no matter how old any of us gets. She felt honored in a way she barely understood that Archer was telling her this painful tale.

"Anyway," he continued with a forced briskness, "the point of all this is not to make my father out like some kind of 'Daddy Dearest,' but to correct this assumption that you and the rest of the world have made about my backing. No, Gunther never gave me a dime. But"—Archer smiled—"the banks *believed* he had and I used that belief to establish a line of credit far in excess of anything I deserved. That's how I managed to get my start. I invested every cent I could borrow in soybean futures at just the right time. They paid off and pretty soon I had something to back up the credit I'd finagled. Go ahead and switch your recorder back on."

Meredith complied with Archer's order. He leaned far back in his chair and looked at the ceiling as if a film of his life were being shown there. It was clear that he was not a man given to excessive rumination. He'd been so busy living his life and building his fortune that it took several moments for the details of how he'd accomplished so much in so few years to come back to him.

"Once I'd built up some capital, I looked around for

a little business to invest in. Of course, raised as I was, oil was the first thing to pop into my mind. I only had to remind myself of what a long shot wildcatting was, though, for that notion to pop back out. You need more money and more luck to make it as a wildcatter than I had to spare back then. But just as drilling for oil is unreliable, drilling equipment breakdowns are reliable. You never know when you'll hit, but you always know there'll be mechanical problems before you do. So I opened an equipment servicing company." Archer stopped and smiled at the memories of those lean years.

"We had to scramble. I mean every day of the week. I don't think there was any time there for about five years that I didn't have grease under my fingernails." Archer paused to glance down at his large, strong hands with their nails, squared-off and clean now. Meredith saw them for what they were, callused, not as she'd first suspected by the rigors of sailing and tennis, but by backbreaking labor.

Archer continued. "But we had business from the moment we opened. Invariably, some small-time operator would go belly-up before he could claim the equipment we'd repaired for him. Pretty soon, we had quite a backlog of unclaimed equipment. I added some new stuff and diversified into leasing. That was when I cleaned the grime off and went into management. We had contracts all over the country. Both service and leasing. Then the Saudis started inviting us over to help them out. It wasn't too long before I was spending most of my time in Europe and the Middle East consulting and negotiating one contract or another."

"You make it sound so simple," Meredith interjected.

"Do I?" Archer said, quirking an eyebrow. "I loved it, I'll admit that. It was challenging, hard, frustrating, heartbreaking at times, but I loved building something that was my own. For me it was a gigantic game. All money has ever been to me is just a way to keep score. I honestly believe that if kumquats were the agreed-upon medium of exchange, I'd be just as happy to have a huge pile of kumquats rotting in my backyard."

Meredith laughed.

"You don't believe me?"

"I do, that's what's so funny."

"How," Archer asked, "with me doing all the talking and you just sitting there listening, have I managed to finish my dinner and you haven't touched yours?"

"Just spellbound, I guess." Meredith dug into the enchiladas with what she hoped would appear to be an unrestrained heartiness. But her stomach had tightened into a hard ball that repelled food. Still, she made herself eat several bites. She didn't want to leave any clues, clues that might betray her to Archer.

"And now I have a question to ask you."

Meredith's heart stopped, but she smiled and answered, "Turnabout is fair play. Ask away."

Archer's hand closed the distance between them. A finger, roughened by work, but still long and graceful, stroked the back of her hand. "Where did you get skin like this? I thought it went out with parasols and whalebone corsets."

"I always hated it when I was growing up. Everyone else was outside tanning their skin to the color of shoe leather and I couldn't stick my nose outdoors without it blistering."

"You must have been an adorable little girl."

"Actually I was . . ." Meredith stopped. She'd been just about to tell him that she'd been chubby as a child, just like she was now. But she knew he'd only protest just like everyone else always did. Even she occasionally protested at the times when she looked in the mirror and saw the slender young woman she actually was. But deep in her heart, she couldn't root out that image of herself as a plump girl destined to be a fat woman. She even knew her self-image was irrational, but that didn't make it go away. ". . . pretty goofy-looking," Meredith finished.

"I don't believe that," Archer countered, his hand covering hers.

A flash of heat swept Meredith. She had been both dreading and dreaming of this moment. Two powerful instincts tugged at her. One was to open her hand, her self, to Archer. The other was to run, to hide herself from him.

"Meredith, I tried to tell you today on the phone what

last night meant to me. It was something unique in my experience. I've never felt for any woman what I felt for you. Never felt so out of control. Wanted someone as much as I did you."

The intensity of his searching look seared Meredith. She wanted to both escape his scrutiny and to surrender to it, let herself burn forever in its intensity. Archer's hand closed over hers in an anguished spasm as if so frustrated by the feebleness of his words that he had to reinforce them with his own strength.

"But it didn't stop after I had you. I didn't think it could be possible, but I wanted you even more. Do you understand me?"

Meredith nodded. She understood, oh, God, how she understood.

"I want all of you, Meredith. I want to know what's going on behind those sapphire eyes. Beneath that corn-silk hair." As if to emphasize his point, Archer's palm stroked the silken strands.

A storm of confusion, stirred by Archer's touch, whirled through Meredith. She feared she would splinter open, spilling all the unlovable mental debris she carried within her.

"I've told you some of my secrets, Meredith, tell me yours."

"Who says I have any secrets to tell?" Her voice wobbled over the evasion.

"Your eyes, Meredith. Your voice. The tremble in your hand. What is it?"

"Don't forget Pandora's box," Meredith cautioned him with a counterfeit lightness. She thought of Chad and how safe he was, never pressing her, never demanding to know what lay beneath the placid surface. Archer was altogether different. "Some things are better left in the dark."

"Not with us, Meredith. Not with what I want for us."

She thrilled at his protest and the future it implied for them. In the next instant, though, she was brutally downcast. There was no future for her with Archer Hanson, her past assured that. But there was now, the present, and if that was all there could be, she would have it. Her hand found his cheek. Her fingers trembled along the curve of his jaw, still smooth from the razor.

Archer trapped her hand with his, turned his head, and pressed her palm to his voracious mouth. His breath was warm and moist on the tender skin, his tongue expressive and questing.

The metallic taste of desire came to Meredith's mouth. Archer stood, pulling her from her chair.

"I want to love you, Meredith, love you the way you deserve to be loved."

His words, repeated from the night before, broke the dam and a molten river flowed through Meredith, drowning her fears and anxieties, suffocating everything except this moment. Her hands fluttered over the taut skin covering his biceps. "Yes, Archer," she whispered.

A low moan answered her as Archer pressed her to him. The seething power of his need was explosively evident. It pulsed from him like current from a hot wire. She was electrified by the contact of their mouths. His moved hungrily over hers, alternately filling her with the force of his need, then sapping her strength so utterly that she feared her legs would buckle beneath her.

When they actually did begin to give way and she swayed gently against Archer, he wordlessly took her hand and led her through the living room, with its vaulted ceiling and fireplace, and down the hall. Flickering lanterns lit the long corridor.

"This place is huge," she whispered, lowering her voice almost as if the house were a physical presence that might overhear her discussing it.

"Huge is a good description. It came with four more bedrooms than I plan on using for some time, but it also has more land around it than any other place in this area, so I put up with all the unnecessary space. This is the only bedroom I ever use. It has my favorite view."

Meredith stepped into the darkened room and was awash in luminous pools of moonlight that flooded in through the picture windows. The Sandias were framed in one window, their mighty peaks outlined in silver moonglow.

Archer flipped a switch and artificial light crackled through the room, revealing a thoroughly masculine lair. But Meredith didn't have time to study the decor for, with the light, panic streaked through her.

"No lights," she said swiftly, adding in a calmer voice, "Let's enjoy the moonlight."

Archer complied and the room was again cloaked in a velvety darkness gilded with silver moonlight. "However you want it, Meredith," he whispered hoarsely, moving toward her. "However you want it."

His arms twined around her, wrapping her again in the pulsing urgency of his desire. He tilted her mouth up and his own descended on hers for a kiss that was a serious beginning to what they both ached for.

Meredith felt hollowed out, emptied by the demanding savagery of his lips, his tongue. But that void was quickly filled by passion's inexorably rising tide. Her shawl slid off her shoulders and whispered to the thick rug as she reached up to Archer. His mouth nestled in the hollow of her neck, uttering primitive sounds in a language that her brain couldn't decode, but her body responded to flawlessly. His hands roamed with a wild willfulness over her shoulders, her back. They teased the upthrust tips of her breasts and stroked a path of fire along her belly and deep into her most intimate recesses.

He returned to her neck and began untying the ribbons that fastened her blouse.

"No," Meredith said, stilling his hand. Her protest echoed wildly through her mind. No, she couldn't allow him to undress her, to see her. She couldn't stand naked before him and let him see her inadequacies. She couldn't lose him. Not yet. "You first."

Archer's hands fell away from her blouse and hers found the buttons at his neck. Slowly, she undid them. Archer crossed his arms in front of his chest and pulled his shirt over his head. He was magnificent. Meredith remembered what he had said about her skin looking like lilies in the moonlight and thought the same of his. Except that beneath his were hard juts of solid muscle. The silvery light curved and bowed around his broad shoulders and over the corrugated firmness of his chest, his stomach.

Meredith, almost by way of paying homage to such perfection, kissed the small, stiffened nub of his nipple. A groan of pleasure rumbled in the chest beneath her lips. She ran her hands along the smooth, hard columns of his back. They were like warm marble chiseled by a master sculptor.

Quivering with excitement, Archer unloosed his buckle and the sculpture of his body was completely unveiled. A mat of tawny bourbon-colored curls covered his chest. It was mirrored by a darker thatch farther below. A dizzying spiral of delight whirred through Meredith as her gaze lighted on his stiffened manhood.

"Come here, darling," Archer coaxed huskily. As

he lifted his arms, Meredith watched, entranced by the bunching and rippling of muscles. He began again to unloose the ribbons at her neck. This time, she scampered away with a nervous laugh.

"Let's just lie down," she suggested, quickly burrowing beneath the covers on his king-sized bed.

For a second, Archer merely stared at her, tilting his head to one side and puzzling over her inexplicable behavior. Meredith trembled beneath the sheets as he came forward, then stood above her, his displeasure as plainly evident as his wilting ardor.

"Why are you hiding from me?" he demanded.

"I'm not hiding. I'm just . . ." She groped for a word that would explain but not expose. ". . . more comfortable here." Her voice withered away, ending on a small plaintive note.

Archer heard it and it melted his frosty anger. The bed rocked as he sat down beside her. "Meredith." His gentle voice made her think of how kind he'd been to her the day of her first balloon ride. "Doesn't the sight of my body give you any pleasure at all?" A stripe of moonlight illuminated his eyes. They were concerned, perplexed, and searching. Meredith again felt the titanic pull of her attraction to this man, an attraction that was both supremely physical and something far beyond it. It was that something beyond that drew the truth from her.

"Yes, of course it does. It gives me immense pleasure."

"Then why are you denying me the same satisfaction?"

Meredith was stung by his question. "If I had a body comparable to yours, I wouldn't hesitate to parade it about either."

"Meredith, don't be facetious. I already know the splendors of your body. I know them with my hands. Now I want to know them with my eyes."

The bed rocked beneath Meredith as Archer sat down beside her. "Your modesty is delightful but unnecessary." He began to tug lightly, playfully at the sheet that Meredith was gripping with a neurotic tightness just under her chin. The feel of the material slipping from her hands caused the panic seething within her to break into a full, rolling boil.

"No," she shouted. Archer instantly let the sheet fall. The rampaging emotions she had been struggling to keep under control for the last twenty-four hours now threatened to break loose. Meredith quaked with the effort of keeping them restrained. She turned her back to Archer, humiliated beyond words. She bit at her lip, trying to turn back the torrent of tears that threatened to fall.

Archer slid under the covers beside her and laid a gentling hand on her shoulder. "Forgive me, Meredith," he whispered in a voice that again reminded Meredith of his kindness to her on the day of her first balloon flight. It was his tenderness that began to unravel the bonds of her control. Archer felt the tremors start beneath his hand. He pulled Meredith to him, carefully keeping the sheet in place, and rocked her until the sobs started.

"That's it, sweetheart," he crooned, "let it out. I shouldn't have pushed you. It wasn't fair." He kissed the tears that streamed over her cheeks and held her even more closely against his chest.

Archer had held other women while they'd cried. Had dried the tears that he'd sometimes caused, but never before had he heard such quiet anguish and plummeting despair in their sobs. He bitterly regretted having triggered them, yet knew that, whatever lay behind them, he would, one day, have to uncover their cause.

Damning himself for the inadequacy of his will, for whatever spell this perplexing woman he held in his arms had cast over him, Archer felt the prickling in his groin that presaged the ineluctable return of desire. No, he shouted mentally at his traitorous body. But there was nothing he could do to stem the onrushing tide already swamping him. It only rose higher with each breath he took, each inhalation fragrant with her smell. With even her slightest movement, he became more agonizingly aware of her whisper-soft skin and the torturously curving body. Though he might never know its visual delights, his hands burned now to plunder the tactile bounty they held. This is impossible, he cursed himself. With a deep sigh of regret, Archer untangled himself and sat up.

"Where are you going?"

He heard the note of panic in Meredith's question and was even more confused than ever. "I assumed you wanted to be alone." There was an edge of hardness in his reply that he hadn't intended, but had to admit did reflect at least a portion of his reaction.

"No, Archer, don't leave me. Not yet."

Not yet? The words echoed in his mind, leaving behind a trail of questions. Questions that were obliterated by the touch of her hand settling on the back he had turned to her. It kneaded insistent patterns against the resisting muscles. Patterns that no force on earth could make him ignore. No matter how wrong or ill-timed or even dangerous his response might be, it was there. There as it had never been with any other woman. It was in his blood, the blood that even as he willed it back to its source, rushed with a blind will to his groin.

"Archer? Don't be angry with me."

"Angry? I may be mystified, confused, and frustrated, Meredith, but I'm not angry." Her hand slid around from his back to the flat slope of his stomach. It teased the springy curls that flared out beneath his navel. Then went lower. A sharp intake of breath met her touch. At the same time she said it with that bold gesture, Meredith whispered, "Love me, Archer." Archer groaned as the flimsy shreds of his self-control tore loose.

Though Archer had dreamed throughout the interminable day he'd just lived through of teasing each garment from the porcelain body next to him, he was denied the pleasure as Meredith herself hastily dispatched her clothing, shoving it out from beneath the covers onto the floor. His regret at the denied pleasure was quickly overpowered, however, as her naked length pressed against his in the materialization of something far more maddening than any dream.

Meredith met the frenzied heat of his desire with her own. The chaos of her emotions was refined into pure, undiluted passion. Neither one could delay their need a moment longer. "Please, Archer." The whimpering plea came from a throat no longer her own. Archer was as powerless to deny her as he was himself. They joined in a fiery union.

Meredith knew his primitive, thrusting rhythm as her own and answered it in kind. They moved together, seeking both release and elevation in union. Meredith felt the pitch of her need rise higher and higher until she was perched on a lonely peak far above any she had known before. And still she kept ascending. Higher and higher until Archer's labored breathing in her ear was a shrill, keening wind that finally blew her from her perch into a kaleidoscopic explosion of fulfillment. For several lost moments of precious oblivion, they lay tangled in one another's arms. Meredith felt the mad pumping of Archer's heart gradually settle back into a slower rhythm.

He slumped onto the bed and drew Meredith to him

so that they rested together like spoons in a drawer. He carefully adjusted the sheet around her shoulders.

For the moment, a moment she knew could never last, Meredith felt utterly safe and utterly loved. She pulled Archer's arms closer around her, shut her eyes, and luxuriated in the feeling. She pressed Archer's palm to her lips and covered it with kisses that spoke of the happiness he'd brought her.

They lay in a bliss-filled silence that went on so long, Meredith was sure Archer had fallen quietly asleep and she snuggled up closer to him. She herself was almost asleep when he spoke. His words revealed that his mind had been far from inactive.

"My beautiful, exasperating enigma," Archer sighed, kissing the dampened tendrils curling against the nape of her neck. "What could you possibly be hiding from me?" His hands slipped from her grasp and he ran a finger teasingly along the underslope of her breast. "Perhaps the tiny scar from a breast augmentation?"

Brimming with contentment, Meredith laughed at the outlandish suggestion.

"Of course not," he whispered, his hand sliding upward to capture the straining fullness of her breast. Meredith stilled the gasp of pleasure that threatened to break from her lips. "Nothing that feels this exquisite could be man-made."

Meredith could no longer answer with a laughing

lightness as his thumb and forefinger closed over her beaded nipple. Suddenly, it was as if the all-pervading satisfaction of only a moment before had never existed. With an excruciating sweetness, Archer continued his exploratory journey. His fingers now traced a tingling line along the base of her belly.

"Perhaps a botched appendectomy?" he playfully guessed, pretending to feel for a scar. "These fingertips have eyes, you know," he joked, tickling her with the ends of his fingers. The tickling slowed, then turned into caresses that lingered over Meredith's breasts, along the inward slope of her waist, over the fluffy triangle at the juncture between her legs. "And all they can see is unending loveliness. Unending loveliness."

The words trailed away, lost in the quickening tempo of Archer's breath. His grip on Meredith tightened, but his touch remained light as it tantalized the smoldering flesh along her thighs. He traced a path of tingling sensation up their inner sides. A paralyzing languor swept over Meredith as he expertly homed in on the magic center of all her desire. Her quickening response to his touch spurred Archer to a thundering renewal of desire. His mouth sought out the satiny feel of her skin, feathering her with kisses that tantalized her breasts, then slipped down lower. As his head disappeared beneath the covers, Meredith emerged from the drugged stupor she'd fallen into and realized what

Archer was intending. She stiffened and rolled away from his descending mouth.

An expression of pain was darkening his crystalline eyes when they reappeared. Before he could pry into the secrets she was frantically trying to keep hidden from him, she silenced his question with a kiss that arced a bow of fire between them. Then, before he could gather himself to began probing again, her own mouth was sliding over his sea-tasting skin on an inexorable journey downward. When it reached its destination, all questions, all conscious thoughts, were banished in a whirlwind of sweetly spiraling desire.

Archer groaned as her lips, her tongue, her mouth found him. Meredith marveled at the extent of her power over this twentieth-century Viking as he writhed from the impact of the waves of pleasure bludgeoning him into a state of senseless seeking. He groped for her beneath the covers, pulling her up to him. His taste on her lips was maddening. It was a lunacy that Meredith shared. She parted her legs and was filled by the surging length of his maleness.

Archer pulled her to him so that in the deepest reaches of her most private self, she knew again that they were one. They were still for several long moments, simply experiencing the wonder of their union. Then, swaying to rhythms older than memory, Meredith rocked slowly, experimenting with movements she had never before dared. Pulling the covers around her like a cloak, she sat up and new thrills shivered through her, emanating from the deepest source possible. With Archer's hands guiding her, they found a rhythm that was uniquely theirs. Meredith knew that neither she, nor Archer, nor any other two people who had ever loved one another before, had moved precisely as they moved together.

The movement and rhythm had a life of their own that captured her and took her sailing off to an exotic place of wild, careening fulfillment. As she floated gently down from the shattering ecstasy, Meredith had the same sense of wingless flight she'd had in Archer's balloon. It was a sensation that only birds and angels had any right to, and now she knew it too. That was her last thought before she drifted into a fathomless sleep.

Chapter 7

A*s broad stripes of daffodil-colored* sunlight crept across Archer's room, Meredith drifted lazily into the cozy limbo stage halfway between waking and dreaming. She was awake enough to be aware of a sense of handspringing joy percolating through her. She wasn't awake enough, though, to identify its source. For a few groggy moments she was back in the bedroom she'd grown up in in Chicago and it was the first day of summer. That was the last time she'd known such untrammeled exuberance. She lurched at the sound of Archer's phone ringing on the bedside table. It caused her to remember that Archer had slipped out of bed early to let her sleep in peace.

Archer returned and rushed to grab his phone. He was trying to keep his voice low so as not to wake her, but Meredith welcomed the sound of the deep, male tones. They satisfied some elemental longing within her that had been too long denied. She slowly opened her eyes. Archer's back was turned to her. She reveled in the sight. His years of hard labor and continuing physical upkeep showed in the densely mounded muscles of his broad shoulders that tapered away to his waist. Two indentations like giant thumbprints pressed in just above the rise of each hard buttock.

"Okay, Phil, I'll meet you out there. Have her ready to launch, okay? Appreciate it, buddy." Archer ended the phone conversation and leaned forward to replace the receiver. His back was transformed into an anatomy lesson as the bony ridge of his spine and the curving spokes of his rib cage jumped into relief. Meredith marveled at the splendid mechanisms that drove Archer's magnificent body. If only, she thought with a bitterness that was never far from her reflections, I had such bodily splendors to display.

"Sorry," he said, "I didn't expect any early morning callers."

"I should have been up hours ago," Meredith muttered, pulling the sheet more tightly around her as she searched the room for her clothes. A flutter of panic disturbed her tranquillity as Archer turned to her.

"Did you sleep well?" His marvelous voice caressed the simple words as he moved under the sheet, pulling her to him.

"Better than well," Meredith answered nervously.

There was too much light. She was too exposed. "Weller, wellest? I slept wellest."

"Wellest, indeed," Archer chuckled, his hands outlining the tightening muscles of Meredith's stomach. "You know what you look like when you're asleep?"

"You were watching me?"

"For quite a long time until I went into the other room. You look like a Botticelli angel."

Sliding away from his teasing fingers, Meredith asked, "And how does an oil field worker know about Botticelli?"

"I managed to cram a lot in during my off hours," he joked. "And don't change the subject. We were talking about you. And since we are, just where do you think you're going?"

With a growl of mock ferocity, Archer pounced on Meredith, playfully nuzzling her neck and capturing her in his arms. As always, his embrace sent the mental hobgoblins that plagued Meredith running for their hiding places. With her back to him, Archer drew her to him and they were joined in a way Meredith had never experienced before. Archer uncovered the bud of her most intimate self and, with infinite tenderness and skill, brought it to a shuddering flowering before he found his own quakingly powerful release.

"Meredith." Her name came in love-exhausted bursts. "There is something happening with us. You know that, don't you?"

His question was freighted with a cargo of deep implications. Meredith hesitated before she answered that she too felt it.

"I'm afraid to say anything more," Archer continued. "It's so new. So different from anything I've felt before. It seems so powerful, but also so fragile. I don't want the wrong words to shatter it. Do you know what I mean?"

Meredith pivoted in his arms to face him. "Yes, I know what you mean. I'm scared too. It's new for me as well. I'm afraid that . . ." She ached to let it all spill out. To tell him her fear that when he learned who she really was, it would all end. But it wasn't just a fear in Meredith's mind. It was a certainty.

She was not strong enough to bear the rejection she would surely see curdling his handsome face, muddying his vibrant eyes after she made her confession and he knew of her self-imposed illness, an illness that would reveal to him once and for all how confused she really was. For she still *was* that person. That was the last thing her therapist had told her. Anorexia never goes completely away. Just as the reformed alcoholic carries a propensity to abuse liquor with him to the grave, so too with her. She would always be an anorectic. She couldn't tell him. Not yet. She wanted too badly for what they had to go on, if only for a few more days, a few more hours. That would be enough. It would have to be enough.

"Afraid that what?" Archer prompted gently.

"Afraid that if we don't get moving, Phil is going to get very lonely at the launch site." Her joke was an evasion and Archer saw it as such.

"You may not believe this." All the softness had gone from Archer's voice and it was edged with a lancing menace. "But I am not usually an open person. Especially where my feelings are concerned. It took an effort for me to expose myself as I have to you. Don't you think it's about time you reciprocated?"

The question was a hairsbreadth away from an angry demand. It chilled Meredith. She cursed herself and her dilemma but could not speak. Her words were frozen along with the lump of fear that choked her. She listened to his breathing in the silence. It grew louder and louder until, with a snort of disgust, Archer threw aside the bedcovers and got up. He stalked over to a walk-in closet and whipped a pair of charcoal gray corduroy slacks off a hanger and stepped into them. Next he ripped a Prussian blue challis shirt off a hanger and put that on. The colors highlighted his brooding Nordic blondness.

Steadying himself and fighting back his fit of temper with a deep breath, Archer held up a bundle of clothes and suggested evenly, "Listen, I have no idea how close these'll come to fitting. I have a nephew who visits in the summer and he left these here. I think you're about the same size. If they fit and if you're so inclined, come on out to the airfield with me. We're going to be launching the solar balloon. Might be good material for your story."

Meredith bolted upright in bed. "The solar balloon? Really?" she babbled.

The brooding darkness left Archer's face at the sight of her childlike enthusiasm. "I thought that might perk up the eager cub reporter." He tossed the jeans, T-shirt, and tennis shoes onto the bed. "Suit up and I'll fix us some breakfast."

When Meredith didn't move from beneath the shelter of the bedcovers, Archer's happiness crumbled again. "I see, the visual embargo is still in force. Would you feel better if I left the room? The county? The state? What in God's name do you think you have to hide from me, woman?" he stormed. "We've already shared the most private act two humans can share. Doesn't that mean anything?" He stared at Meredith, desperate for an answer, an explanation. When none came, he withdrew from the bedroom, slamming the door behind him.

Meredith trembled. Tension drew in the nerves at the base of her neck and twisted them into a headache that sliced at the aching space behind her eyes. In a dull fog, she pulled back the covers. The morning was chilly, too cool for the light skirt and blouse she'd worn last night. She'd have to try the borrowed clothes. The jeans fit snugly over her hips that were as lean as those of the young boy who owned the pants. The brightly striped T-shirt was a gaudy mockery of the despair Meredith carried within her. She gathered up her own clothes and, like a soldier setting out on a suicide mission, headed for the kitchen. She cauterized the torrent of emotions churning within her with the thought that now all that remained was a professional relationship with Archer. It would have to be enough.

The sounds of sausage sputtering and coffee perking greeted her. Archer turned. His face was pale. Meredith melted at the sight of it.

"Archer, please forgive me." The words sprang from her as naturally as water bubbled from a spring. "Please, I'm trying, I really am."

"You are that, my darling," he said with bleak humor. "You are extremely trying. But I was pushing you again. I shouldn't have done that. I suppose I've been pushing all my life. It's a hard habit to break. Come on, have some breakfast so we can get out to the launch site before the sun goes down on our solar balloon."

His smile was a sun that Meredith had never expected to see again. She came forward to take the plate he handed her.

"Look at you," he exclaimed, his mood brightening by the second. "All you need now is a paper route, a baseball cap, and a few frogs in your pocket and you'd make the most gorgeous eleven-year-old boy on the block."

Relief caused Meredith to laugh a bit too heartily. She'd won a reprieve.

The scene at the launch site was a repeat of the one staged two nights ago. Meredith could barely believe that such a short amount of time had passed since the night of the Balloon Ball, the night in Cloud Waltzer. But it wasn't the prancing unicorn balloon that was being inflated this time; it was a second-generation model, Archer's pet project, a balloon that absorbed its heat, not from canisters of burning propane gas, but from the sun, the dazzling New Mexican sun.

Phil was already inflating Cloud Waltzer II. If all went according to the plans worked out at Solar Concepts, this would be the only time during the flight, except at landing, when a gas flame would be needed. The balloon rose. The top was covered with a thin black shell that would absorb the maximum number of rays. The bottom half was silver to reflect heat back into the envelope. It had an austere elegance, but Meredith missed the whimsical unicorn that she had come to identify so closely with Archer, almost as if he too were a creature of myth who could never exist for her in reality.

"Mr. Hanson." A television reporter trailing a cameraman approached Archer and stuck a microphone in his face. "Do you really believe this thing will fly?"

"Oh, we know it will fly," Archer answered. "We're

just not sure for how long. This isn't the first solar balloon, you know. It is the first built for long-distance flights, though. But we're still at the experimental stage with it."

"Why, then, are you going up? And why are you breaking your long-standing ban on personal publicity to do it?"

"I believe in solar energy, gentlemen and ladies," he said, nodding to the female reporters who'd joined the expanding crowd around Archer. Meredith too switched on her recorder. "If my stepping out of the shadows will in any way help move our country toward exploring this alternative more fully, then I'm happy to do so."

"Isn't that a rather contradictory stand for someone to take who made their fortune in oil?" a female reporter asked.

"It might be for some. It's not for me. Many fortunes, many industries, many businesses were built on oil, but the day of fossil fuels has passed. We, all of us, need to recognize that. I hope Cloud Waltzer II will help focus that recognition. Now, if you will excuse me, I have a flight to catch."

The gathering of newspeople chuckled appreciatively at Archer's quip. As he strode through the crowd, he stopped beside Meredith. "Why don't you ride with Phil," he suggested.

"Why don't I ride with you?" Meredith startled herself with her bold question. "I mean, if there's room."

"There's room, but are you sure you want to come? Like I said, she's still in an experimental stage."

"If you feel sure enough to go, so do I."

"I'd love for you to come." Turning to Phil, he asked, "Have you gone over the equipment checklist?"

Phil gave an absentminded nod as he hurried to keep pace with his boss as they made their way to the balloon. Carl, Betty, Marie, and Tomas, the whole crew from Solar Concepts, was hanging on to the basket that strained to escape their grasp. Meredith exchanged greetings.

"You going to solo like you planned?" Carl asked.

"No, Meredith's coming along."

"What a trouper," Tomas called. "I'm only kidding. Most of us have already been up during tethered flights. This is the first free flight, but it shouldn't be all that much different."

"All aboard." Archer, who'd already climbed into the basket, held a hand out to Meredith.

Funny, she thought, how far less frightened she was of going up several hundred feet in a relatively untested balloon than she was of letting Archer glimpse her unclothed. Even knowing that this was an experimental flight, in a balloon that had never flown free before, Meredith felt no fear. The crew members let the balloon go. Meredith gloried in the sensation of rising up to a warming sun with Archer at her side.

"Okay," he muttered, preoccupied with the altimeter

gauge that was charting their altitude. "If the design is viable, we should be able to cut off the burner now." Cautiously he turned down the valve regulating the flow of propane. The dancing blue flame withered, then died. Silence closed in around them.

"She seems to be holding steady," Archer observed after several tense moments had passed and the balloon hadn't lost any altitude. "Good old Sol appears to be doing his job keeping the air in the envelope heated."

As the minutes of serenely tranquil silence, minutes unbroken by the roar of the burner, lengthened, Meredith finally blurted out, "This is absolutely more bliss than any human has a right to."

"It would be hard to go back to propane after this," Archer agreed. "Hopefully we won't need to if we can maintain, or even increase, our altitude using solar power."

As if responding to his wish, the needle on the altimeter swung slightly to the right, registering a higher altitude.

"We're climbing!" Archer whooped. "She really works!" He grabbed Meredith in an exuberant bear hug.

She delighted in the powerful embrace that was augmented by the boyish enthusiasm animating Archer's features. He was such an intriguing blend of the hard-nosed pragmatist so adept at making tough business decisions and the whimsical dreamer who lived to chase airy fantasies. "The only thing missing is the unicorn," Meredith commented wistfully, "to make this whole flight seem like something out of a fairy tale."

"Are ye saying we should hoist our colors, matey?" Archer asked in a mock pirate voice that made *matey* sound like *mighty*.

"Colors?" Meredith echoed uncomprehendingly.

"Aye, the proud flag of this great ship o' the sky." With a grin that flashed its playful rakishness in the sun, Archer tugged at some lines and a banner the size of several bedsheets unrolled.

Meredith viewed it illuminated from behind before Archer could tie it down. "The unicorn!" she cried, for emblazoned there on the fluttering banner was the one-horned creature of myth capering as gaily as ever across the boundless sky.

"I thought you'd like seeing your old traveling buddy up there," Archer said, gathering Meredith into his arms again for a squeeze.

Meredith closed her eyes and was overtaken by the half-dreaming sensations of silent floating, warm sun, and the security of Archer's arms around her. She'd never felt so right. The far-off honking of a chorus of car horns brought her to a reluctant awareness. Archer craned to look out over the top of her head.

"Your subjects await you, m'lady," he jested, pivoting her in his arms so that she too could peer over the basket edge.

Far below, so small they looked like a child's toys, a line of cars was following them. Meredith recognized the logos of all three local TV stations on three different vans.

"Give the fans a wave," Archer coached.

"They'll never be able to see it from this height," she protested. Still, she hesitantly held up her hand, and feeling like a ridiculous parody of a high school homecoming queen, she leaned out and waved.

Her gesture was followed instantly by another round of raucous honks. Meredith responded with a far more energetic wave. Honks answered the second wave as well. For a second she was convinced that she'd set up a dialogue with the far-off cars when she glanced over her shoulder at Archer. He was busily working the lines that held the unicorn banner in place, making it rise and fall in the wind each time Meredith waved.

"You rat," she railed jokingly. "You had me believing they were honking at me."

Archer tied down the lines again and turned his attention back to Meredith. "They were. I was just giving them the right signals. The whole world should be honking and clapping and bowing at your feet, paying you homage." What had started out as lightly barbed teasing mellowed into something with an indisputable core of truth as Archer's gaze paid homage in *its* own way to the woman before him.

The honking became a distant, earthbound nuisance that they both easily ignored. The borders of their world had suddenly become very small. They extended no farther than the wicker basket they stood in, each wondering what the other was truly thinking.

"How do you do what you do to me?" Archer asked, his voice insinuatingly low. But he realized that he was the one who would have to provide an answer to the provocative question. His eyes seared her with a questing gaze. "I've never been so *consumed* by anyone before in my life. This is absolutely pagan, but I want you again, Meredith. Right here. Right now."

Like two wires split but still arcing electricity, Meredith felt the charge that never completely died away between them. "It's the same for me," she confessed, Archer's ragged honesty summoning forth her own. "But it's probably even more unique in my life. Before I met you, I'd even worried that I might basically be *a*sexual. I'd just never responded terribly strongly to any man before."

"You?" Archer questioned, remembering not only the heat of the response she stirred in him, but her own giving warmth as well. The memory flickered at his groin, waking him with a teasing excitement. "My darling, you are far from asexual. You can believe me on that score."

"I really haven't had too many worries since I met you," Meredith teased back enticingly, enjoying the sexual tension that crackled between them. She was safe up here. Safe from exposure, from Archer's scrutiny. She could revel without fear in a sensation she'd known precious little of in her life—that of desiring and being found desirable by a man.

"You're adorable in that outfit," Archer growled playfully. "You know that, don't you? Come here, I feel like doing nasty things with the paper boy."

Meredith laughed at his joke, at the notion that it was possible for him to do anything "nasty" with her. She laughed at the endless azure of the sky above. Her smile fading, she stepped forward. Suddenly, the entire morning, the balloon launch, even the months of research and development that had gone into the solar balloon, seemed nothing more than a prologue to this moment, to Archer's kiss.

A dizzying languor crept over Meredith as Archer's tongue found hers. She felt doubly adrift, floating several hundred feet above the waking city and floating as well in her own pool of rapidly warming desire. Just as the balloon responded to the invisible zephyrs that batted it about the sky, Meredith was a captive of her body's will.

His hand slid under the striped T-shirt to coax her nipples to tautened life.

"Archer," she reprimanded him, "someone might see us."

"Someone? Like who?"

Of course there was no one, and nothing except the

emotional phantoms that had populated Meredith's mind for so long. Oh, they whispered to her, you might have fooled him for now, but wait until he sees all of you, sees the not-quite-right body. Wait until he finds out why you really left Chicago. Wait until he hears the word *anorexia.*

The incessant buzzing rose to a terrifying pitch. Meredith knew only one way of silencing the destructive voices. She clung to Archer, her mouth drawing passion, strength, and reassurance from his.

The trembling fierceness of Meredith's kiss stirred Archer profoundly. He knew, he felt in his bones, that she was the woman he'd searched for all his life. Surely, the searing heat that flashed between them would be enough to melt the damnable walls she'd constructed around herself. It would have to be. Because, Archer swore to himself even as they shared one another's breath, he would spend his life alone before he shared it with a woman he could never fully have in all senses of the word.

A sixth sense stronger even than the surge of passion that was rolling over him alerted Archer that all was not well. His eyes flew to the altimeter. The balloon was falling.

Meredith, seeing the concern that furrowed Archer's brow, glanced down. The cars on the highway below were much larger than they'd been before.

"We're losing altitude." Archer's voice was calm and

steady as he checked out the craft for an explanation. "There's the culprit," he announced, craning his neck backward.

Meredith followed his gaze. The envelope puffing out far above their heads looked like a mosaic. The black coating was fissured by a multitude of cracks.

"The heat-absorptive covering obviously wasn't pliant enough," Archer observed caustically. Disappointment weighted down his every word. He was a man with a low tolerance for failure. "We'll have to use the auxiliary propane system." For Archer that was the final admission of defeat. He began rummaging through the small gear box.

Meredith felt a surge of tenderness watching his enthusiasm drain away. That emotion was replaced by mild alarm as Archer's search of the basket grew more frenzied.

"What is it, Archer?"

"The damned lighter, I can't find it." He patted all his pockets and scanned every inch of the basket a second and a third time. "Phil must have forgotten to pack it," he concluded. "You don't have a lighter? Matches?"

"I could rub two sticks together," Meredith volunteered in an outburst of nervous humor. When Archer managed only a tight smile, she asked soberly, "How serious is it?"

Archer checked their rate of descent on the

variometer. "We're picking up speed and, as the air in the balloon continues to cool, we'll pick up a lot more." Seeing Meredith's apprehension, he smiled his usual easy smile. "We'll make it. We'll just have to do it by the seat of our pants. We can't fire up the burners. That means no luxury landing. Just consider this your first parachute jump. Think you can handle it?"

"I'll try," Meredith promised.

"Good." His gaze lingered on her before turning to the stretch of earth below them. Meredith looked down and gasped. They were directly above the highway running north to Santa Fe. Vehicles from VW beetles to monstrous semis roared along its four lanes.

"Now, aside from the obvious," Archer said with deadly calm, "we've got two problems. The first is not landing in the middle of the interstate. The second is not running into those power lines," he said, pointing to the high-tension lines running along to the east of the interstate.

Meredith looked up at the maze of cables running from the crown of the balloon down to the metal frame and metal reinforced floor of the basket. The danger of contacting the power lines ahead was obvious. If they collided with the high-voltage lines, the balloon would turn into one big conductor, drawing electricity down the metal cables onto the metal-framed basket floor they stood on. There would be no chance of survival. Equally menancing was the four-lane interstate below.

"God, I wish I hadn't brought you along," Archer breathed fervently.

"Listen, Hanson," Meredith said in her best tough-cookie imitation, "if you can handle this, so can I. If you're going to wish for something, why don't you wish for the wind direction to change."

"Now, that *would* be helpful."

Meredith heard the tightness in Archer's voice. He was looking overboard. The balloon was stubbornly following the course of the highway. Worse, it was sloping in ever closer to the busy thoroughfare. She almost felt as if she could lean out and touch the high, flat tops of the trucks booming past beneath them. For reasons she barely understood, though, she wasn't afraid. Instead, an odd exhilaration beat through her. It was nearly a relief to face a real, tangible danger after all the psychic ones her mind had conjured up.

"What's your plan?" she asked levelly.

"Try to stay up until the wind shifts us clear of the highway and hope to hell it moves us to the west and not toward the power lines." Even as he spoke, they shifted, moving away from the highway. They moved east.

"We've got to dump her before we hit the lines," Archer shouted, staring straight ahead at the onrushing pylons. "Watch the highway," he ordered, grappling with a tangle of cables, "and tell me the instant we've cleared."

Meredith turned away from the treacherous power

lines. She could smell the diesel exhaust of the trucks blasting by and feel the balloon jerk as it was caught in the wake of their passing. At last the basket moved off the asphalt. The instant it was skimming above the shoulder of the highway, Meredith screamed, "Now!"

Archer hauled down on the rip cord, opening a huge panel at the top of the balloon. "Bend your knees and hang on!" he commanded, clamping an arm around Meredith and pulling her to him.

As the trapped air spilled out through the gaping hole, the basket dropped, landing with a bone-jarring impact. The last thing Meredith could remember was the feel of Archer's arms around her and the sight of the sere New Mexican earth rushing up to meet her. Then blackness closed in.

Chapter 8

A*s Meredith fought her way* into a groggy consciousness, the first thing she saw was her great-grandmother's vanity. For several disoriented seconds she thought she was back at the family estate in Chicago. That misapprehension depressed her far more than the dull throbbing in her head.

"Thank God, you're awake."

What was Archer Hanson doing sitting on her bed in Chicago? Meredith wondered as her jammed mental gears slowly began to engage again. What would her mother say when she found him here? Even in her befuddled state, Meredith knew the answer to that question: NOOFUD. It was her childhood shorthand for her mother's ultimate condemnation—Not One of Us, Dear. Only Chad Allbrook, of any of the boys she'd ever brought home, had escaped the condescending putdown. His family history was as monied and illustrious as her own, even though the Allbrook money was more a matter of history than Chad would have cared to admit.

Her eyes were as blank as a Kewpie doll's. Looking closer, though, Archer saw something in their fathomless blue depths. He saw fear. What, he wondered, haunted this vibrant woman he was coming to care for with such surprising intensity?

"Meredith, are you all right?"

Without waiting for an answer, Archer pulled her to him. "Come on, we're going back to the hospital. The doctor said you'd come around, but we're not taking any chances." Archer gently swung her blue-jeaned legs out from under the bedcovers and, kneeling beside her, tugged a pair of socks onto her feet.

NOOFUD, indeed, Meredith thought, the heartbreaking tenderness of Archer's gesture filling her with love. This man was worth a hundred Chad Allbrooks. Anger at her mother's snobbery and petty tyrannies finally broke Meredith free of the daze she'd been in.

"Archer," she said, her voice sounding rusty. "I'm fine. A bit stunned, but I'm coming around. What happened?" Slowly the gears in her brain were meshing.

Archer rose and stared into her eyes. The frightened vacancy was gone. Relieved, he sat beside her. "How much do you remember?"

She strained for the elusive fragments of memory. "I remember most of the flight." She bit on her lip in her effort to fish the lost bits out of a foggy pool. "I remember most everything until you pulled the rip panel cord."

"After that," Archer filled in for her, "we made what amounts to a crash landing because we had to get down before we ran into those power lines. I grabbed for you, but somehow when we hit ground, you banged your head. Thank God, the chase crew saw our dilemma and they'd already radioed for an ambulance. You were out all during the ride to the hospital. Do you remember coming to in the emergency room?"

Meredith shook her head. There was no recollection inside it of any emergency room.

Archer smiled. "Too bad. You were the very model of the assertive woman telling the doctor in no uncertain terms that neither were you going to remove your clothes, nor were you going to stay at the hospital. You were going immediately home, with all your clothes intact. He checked you out and said there was no indication of any damage. So he released you, provided that there would be someone with you who could bring you back in if you hadn't come around completely in the next couple of hours. I volunteered and Phil brought us back here." Wryly, he added, "Where all your clothes, except your shoes and socks, remained as intact as you'd ordered they be."

Archer gently lowered Meredith back onto her pillow. "But that's enough thinking for the time being. I want you to just lie back and rest. Don't go to sleep, though. The doctor warned against that. Just relax and I'll go try and rustle us up something to eat. You hungry?" he asked, tucking the sheet up around Meredith's shoulder.

She nodded, luxuriating in the rare sensation of being taken care of. She tried to remember another time when she'd felt so deliciously looked after. She couldn't. Even when she was a young girl, she'd been the one who'd done the looking after. She remembered struggling upstairs on the maid's day off with a tray she was barely big enough to lift and tiptoeing into her mother's darkened room. Julianna's face had been a tiny dot of white framed by her dark hair. Her eyes were covered with a moistened white cloth. That was how Meredith remembered her mother—always with a moist cloth over her eyes, forever shielding them from the light, the burdens of everyday life, from reality.

Just as Meredith was sinking into the infinitely cozy feeling of being taken care of for a change, and Archer was getting up, she was jolted back into full alertness by a delayed realization—Archer was here, in her apartment.

Archer felt her jerk against the sheets and saw the panic swim again into her eyes. He easily guessed its cause and sat back down. "It's all right," he soothed. "Whenever you feel up to it, you can tell me what happened to Aunt Adrianne." He stroked a few dampened wisps of hair back from her forehead, then trapped one of her slim, pale hands between his. It had turned to ice. "Don't worry about anything right now except clearing the cobwebs out of that beautiful head of yours." He leaned over to kiss her. The bed shifted beneath Meredith as he rose.

She stared at the ceiling. From her tiny kitchen came rattling noises as Archer hunted through her drawers and cabinets.

"Surely you have some coffee somewhere out here," he called to her.

"It's in the cabinet to the left above the sink," she answered, her voice a monotone. The decision she'd been trying to postpone had been forced on her. There was no way she could evade the inevitable any longer. Archer was too good a man for that.

"I've found your pot. Now give me a hint about where you hide your coffee filters."

"Underneath the counter. Second shelf from the bottom." There was a weary resignation in Meredith's voice as if she were at long last putting down a heavy burden. She listened to the cabinet door squeak open and heard Archer shuffle through its contents.

"All I'm finding here is a photo album."

"Look at it," Meredith instructed. Her whole body tensed up as she listened for the rustling of pages. The sound came. Then stopped. It was followed by silence.

"Who is this?" Archer asked.

Meredith couldn't force the words out of her constricted throat to answer.

"This isn't you, is . . . My God, it is! Meredith, what was wrong with you? Were you sick?"

She braced herself, looking down from the ceiling into Archer's questioning eyes. He stood at her doorway, the album open in his hands. Everything she had expected—the shock, the disgust it hid, the disbelief—they were all there.

"Yes," she answered, her throat dry, her tongue lifeless. "I was sick, but I didn't know it at the time."

"What was it?" Archer came into the room, filling it with his steady, masculine presence. "You were emaciated. How could you *not* know you were sick?"

"That *was* my sickness, Archer." Meredith paused, took a deep breath, and fighting back the powerful impulse to simply bury the truth, to lie and say she'd had some rare wasting disease, she spoke the awful words, "I had anorexia nervosa."

Archer had read about the disorder. He knew what it was. But he couldn't reconcile the bizarre symptoms, the pictures he held in his hand of a sad, skeletal girl, with the woman he was coming to love. None of them belonged together. "But you're over it, right? You've recovered?"

"I'm a fairly normal weight now, if that's what you mean," she answered, knowing that the worst part of her revelation still lay ahead of her.

"Does this have anything to do with why you didn't want me coming over? Why you forbid me to see you, to see all of you?"

Meredith nodded. Archer went to her side. She shrank from him. She'd won whatever feeling he had for her through deceit. Now it was time he knew who she really was. "Yes, I invented Aunt Adrianne as a way of keeping you from the truth. I didn't want you to know about me. About what I was . . ." She stumbled, but made herself finish. "What I am."

"And what's that?" Archer asked gently. "A person who's had a problem? Meredith, we all have. All of us, myself included, have our dark corners where we hide our secrets, our fears, our vulnerabilities. That's no reason to keep the world at arm's length forever."

Meredith shook her head with an increasing force. Archer had to know, she had to make him understand. He deserved that much at least. "You don't understand. I'm *still* the same person in those pictures. That's why I keep them: to remind myself that it could all start again. I still have to fight with it every day. Every time I run into a setback, a rejection, I start thinking that maybe it's because I'm overweight. That of course no one likes an undisciplined slob. With just a little shove, I could go right over the edge again."

"Meredith," Archer pleaded passionately, "it doesn't have to be that way. You don't have to let your past control your future. It's over. You can start living now. We . . ." Archer's words tumbled out with an increasing intensity. "We can start planning a future together."

She looked into his brilliant, searching eyes and was filled with a despair so profound that she couldn't speak. She saw such dreams, such life, such force there, and knew she could never be a part of any of them. She clasped her arms around her knees and rocked forward, burying her face. Try as she might to stifle the sobs welling up within her, she couldn't. She shuddered beneath Archer's encircling arms as the tears she couldn't keep dammed up within her burst loose.

Archer hugged her to him in silent comfort, letting her cry out her anguish.

Finally, in gulpy, choked words, Meredith told him the full truth as she saw it. "It can never be. Not with me."

"But why?" Archer demanded.

"Don't you understand?" she pleaded, looking up, her cheeks glazed with tears. She pointed to the open photo album. "That crazy woman is still inside of me. She'll always be there. That's why I never wanted you to come over here, to see me without clothes on."

"Why?" Archer probed, trying to fit the pieces together. A sense of urgency drove him. He knew that what he said, how he responded to Meredith's revelation, was crucial. That any hope they had of a future together depended on it. "Did you think I'd be shocked? Repulsed?"

"Well, aren't you?"

"Meredith, all you've told me about is your past. Let's not make it part of our present and future together. Please, angel. You deliberately left it behind you when you left Chicago; let's do the same thing now."

"You still don't understand," Meredith moaned forlornly. "I hid my home, my body, my past from you because, deep in my heart, I believe that none of them are good enough. That I'll never be good enough. I was in therapy for a year and even that didn't get rid of my feelings of inadequacy. And it does no good to have someone tell me that I'm crazy. That I have a good figure and am an all right person. That's the worst of it really, having someone tell me that it's all in my mind. I know that and hearing it just makes me feel even more inadequate. I feel even more undisciplined and self-indulgent and hate myself even more for not being able to even control my own thoughts. Can you possibly understand what I'm saying? What I am?" she pleaded with a heartbroken bereftness.

Archer grabbed her shoulders and made her face him fully. "Listen to me, Meredith. I understand what you're saying. I'd never tell you that what you believe is ridiculous. The strongest power on earth is the human mind. That's where we create the worlds each one of us lives in."

Archer's understanding was an unimaginable relief to Meredith. The final truth gushed out. "I don't think I'm good enough for you. I'm not pretty enough or strong enough or . . ." A fresh flow of tears washed away Meredith's words.

"I can't tell you that you're strong enough," Archer said, encompassing Meredith in his embrace. "I don't know that. But I can tell you in ways that no therapist ever could that you're more than pretty enough." He groaned out under the load of his mounting desperation. "If there's nothing else on earth I can prove to you, I can prove that." He captured her chin. Tilting it up to him, he channeled a gaze of burning intensity between himself and Meredith. He wanted there to be no doubt whatsoever that she was filling his sight, his mind, his heart.

Meredith met his gaze with a tentative wariness. Her lashes clumped around her storm-darkened eyes in teary spikes. Archer's grip of gentle iron and his unfaltering gaze told Meredith that there was nothing and no one else in the world on his mind. That realization forged an empathic link between them. In that moment nothing existed beyond the smoldering ice of Archer's eyes, the savage Viking planes of his heroic face, the boundless lure of his lips. She watched as they formed words.

"I lied. You're not pretty at all. You're exquisite." Meredith's swollen lips received his like a pillow cushioning a weary head. She tasted her own tears on his tongue as it entered her with a driving possession. He writhed in her mouth with a fury of abandonment. He wrote odes to her beauty and painted portraits of the longing it inspired across the hollows of her mouth. Her tongue flickered against his, answering his need with her own. She quivered at the depth and intensity of what they called forth in each other. It was somehow more powerful than anything they had experienced together before. She trembled, sensing that they stood together on the edge of a precipice. This time they would either join completely and unconditionally or she would lose him forever. Her heartbeat, already racing, quickened even more.

Archer felt the tremor of fear that rippled through her. He lay her back against the pillow and pulled the covers away, revealing the striped T-shirt and jeans. "Roll over onto your stomach."

Meredith sought out his eyes. There was a stern loving there that would broach no protest. She complied with his request.

"Now, take off your shirt."

The time of decision was at hand. She could cling to her secretive obsessions forever and doom herself to a loveless life of solitude. Or she could, with Archer's help, struggle to rid herself of her irrational fears. Facing the mattress, she shrugged off the striped T-shirt. Archer's hands found the fastener of her bra. A drowning voluptuousness surged over her as he freed her breasts and pushed the straps aside.

"You're tense," he commented as his large hands spanned the frail cage of her back and began a skillful massage. With unerring accuracy, his fingers found tightened bands of muscles and bunched nerves and unloosened them. Meredith purred with feline contentment as the strong, supple fingers wove patterns of relaxation into the fabric of her back.

"Now your legs and bottom," he instructed in a hoarse voice.

Meredith paused, her luxurious sense of ease stiffening as she considered Archer's order. But no, she couldn't turn back now. Couldn't sentence herself to a solitary life with only her mental hobgoblins for company.

Archer pulled the sheet up around her. She twisted over beneath its cover and shucked off her jeans and underwear, shoving them out onto the floor, then rolled back over onto her stomach. She tucked her arms underneath her, bracing herself against the inescapable exposure.

Archer lifted the sheet away. A gasp slipped from his throat. Trembling before him, against the background of the rosy mauve sheet, was a slender ivory band of inexpressibly lovely curves. Nothing he could say would be worthy of such alabaster splendor. He bent over and kissed her back precisely at the point where it began to rise into the womanly swell of her buttocks.

The honeyed touch of his lips sent delicious charges of electric warmth spiraling through her. They melted the icy nervousness that had tried to claim her. Feathering kisses up her tingling spine, Archer's hands began their narcotizing mission. He kneaded the springy muscles at the back of her thighs with a rhythmic insistence that sent sheets of flame pulsing through their throbbing juncture. With his thumbs working along the inside of her thighs, he gradually parted them.

Meredith felt her face burn at this newest unveiling. But her aching need for him was far too urgent to even consider retreating now from his plundering touch.

His fingers raked lightly along her thighs, propelling messages upward to her melting core. They teased her with fleeting passages, then withdrew, sending a spasm of need shuddering through her. His flickering touch tantalized the backs of her knees, the large muscles at the backs of her thighs, before it reentered the torrid zone it had left flaming.

The warm vapor of his breath fell over her spine. As his lips caressed each tingling vertebra, his hand slid along the cradle of her womanhood until, to Meredith's gasping relief, he found her moist innerness.

Feeling the magnitude of her womanly dampness, Archer rejoiced, happy in the knowledge that soon all restraints separating them would be removed. His voice was thick with wanting when he spoke. "Let me see you now."

The thought flashed through Meredith's mind: This will be the first time. Never before had she been brave enough to show herself to a man. Never, not even with Chad, who'd been only too happy to leave her in the prison of her compulsive modesty. If she were ever going to break through, now was the time. Holding her breath, she slowly rolled over. She thought her heart would surely burst in the following seconds. Seconds that passed like frozen, crystalline hours as Archer's eyes began to gaze at *all* of her.

Stupefied, Archer consumed and was consumed by her pale beauty, feasting on it like a heavenly banquet. He shook his head in rapt wonderment.

Meredith relaxed, seeing the obvious pleasure he was taking in the sight of her. A tiny hope flickered in her that maybe, just maybe, she wasn't as loathsome as she'd always believed.

Words had fled Archer's dazzled brain. In the only way he thought worthy, he paid homage to the vision stretched before him. Locking Meredith's gaze with his own, he parted the curling fluff between her legs and bent his head. His tongue found the flowering blossom of her womanhood.

Meredith watched the fair head lower and was electrified by twin bolts of thought and sensation. For the first time, the thought occurred to her that she might be beautiful all over, even in that place she'd always feared her ugliness centered. Then Archer was standing, holding his hand out to her.

"I want to feel you with all of me."

Wordlessly, trapped in an unthinking sensual haze, Meredith stood. Guided by a newly discovered expertise, her hands undid the buttons and zippers that held the wall of cloth separating her and Archer. The vibrant feel of his skin against hers, the intimate tickle of hair against her bare skin, was excruciating bliss.

"Come," he said, leading her to the vanity. He opened the mirror and pulled Meredith in front of it.

She shied away from her own reflection, shrinking from it like a superstitious native who had never confronted a mirror before. For not only had Meredith hidden herself from male eyes, she'd shielded her own as much as she could from a sight she was sure was too hideous to behold.

Archer held her firmly by the shoulders, turning her in his grasp until she faced herself. "Don't look away," he directed, gently forcing her head forward. "Look at yourself, darling. You were gifted with a magnificent body. Look at it. Really look at it."

In the tall, oval mirror, Meredith saw a man and a woman dazed with passion. She was surprised at how small she was next to Archer's leanly muscled bulk. Archer, standing behind her, took her hands in his and placed them on her breasts. Meredith felt the contracted tips beneath her palms.

"You should cherish what you've been given," he

murmured in her ear. "Even if you had been far, far less fortunate, you would still have a great deal to be grateful for." He molded her hands in his so that they could know the swollen contours of her own breasts. Guided by him, her hands slid downward, sloping with the hourglass configuration of her waist. Continuing to introduce Meredith to the glories of her physical being, Archer splayed her fingers out across the firm flatness of her stomach.

She looked into the beveled mirror. The reflection seemed steamed in an erotic haze. Archer watched over her shoulder as he spread two sets of fingers across her waist, then drew them downward. A thrill of daring shivered through Meredith as her palms passed over the tickling fluff crowning her thighs. Archer stopped them there and stroked her fingertips over the folds of her most intimate self.

"You're a beautiful, desirable woman," Archer whispered huskily, pressing down on her hand beneath his. The provocative pressure wrapped Meredith tighter in the bonds of pleasurable torment. She couldn't silence the primitive sound that escaped from between her parted lips. It was the signal that undermined Archer's teetering restraint. His hand freed hers and took its place. Meredith swayed against his solidness. Her head arched back until his mouth claimed hers. She turned toward his kiss like a flower following sunshine.

Archer's voracious mouth blazed a heated trail down

her neck. He paused to teeth the pointed crowns of her breasts until she was reeling with desire for fulfillment. He continued downward, nibbling at the corrugated swells of her rib cage, the juts of her pelvis, until he was kneeling before her. Meredith gasped as the silken tip of his tongue arrived at its destination.

She tried to jerk away from this ultimate intimacy, an act she had never known but secretly yearned for. Archer's hands held her fast about her slender hips and drew her back to the source of the dizzying nectar that pumped through her veins. His tongue spilled a fresh draught of the intoxicating potion over her as it skillfully probed. A velvet sliver of flame caressed her into a mindless surrender. Her entire will became bound up in the delirium that was lapping ever-widening waves of pleasure through her. She stopped straining against Archer's imprisoning hands and reversed the direction and intent of her motions until she was undulating to the insatiable rhythms dictated by Archer's conquering mouth.

Time, modesty, decency, past, and future all dissolved, erased by the crystal point of sensation gathering within her. Under Archer's masterful probing, the point focused to an acuteness that straddled the thin high line between agony and bliss. Meredith swayed in his arms, quailing before the magnitude of the sensual onslaught. And still Archer went on.

The crystal point of sensation sharpened to an

unbearable peak of intensity. Then, in a moment of rare and blinding ecstasy, she was vaulted beyond that summit into a shuddering fulfillment. The hard focus of sensation softened and broadened. It swelled through her body in billowing waves of release. She gasped out her pleasure and wilted into the unflagging support of Archer's steely grip.

He rose. His heartbeat thundered against Meredith's chest, pounding with a barbaric frenzy that could be denied no longer. His breath rasped against her neck in harsh staccato gasps. Hooking a foot under the vanity bench, Archer pulled the large stool toward them. Tangled together in a rhapsody of twining limbs, they sat down. Meredith was astride Archer. The sweetness of their joining filled her as nothing ever had. She gave herself joyously, gave back to Archer what he had reclaimed for them both.

Blinded by radiant pleasure, Archer shut his eyes. They trembled beneath their dark-lashed lids as he gripped Meredith to him, pulling her into another realm of satisfaction. She feathered wild, mindless kisses across those immeasurably dear lids. Archer thrust more deeply, as if his possession of her could never go far enough.

Meredith responded with a bold answering thrust. The erect peaks of her breasts stroked up and down across the wiry silkiness of Archer's furred chest as she rose and fell with the colossal surges of his passion.

Wanting that sensation to deepen even further, Archer captured a tantalizing nipple in his mouth, sending electric shudders raking through Meredith.

Wanting their impassioned duet to go on forever, they both strained against its inevitable end. But the force they generated was not to be denied. The tempo accelerated, hurtling them both to crescendoing fulfillment. In that culminating moment Archer locked Meredith against his heaving chest in an embrace of desperate rigidity, as if the birth pains of his final pleasure were ripping him asunder.

Meredith looked into his face even as she felt his spasms of completion echoing her own and was flooded by the surging tide of his release. She knew his pleasure as her own and was immutably moved by it.

In the mirror she glimpsed a man's head collapsed against a woman's full and comforting breast. She saw the woman's face aglow with the luminescent flush of absolute fulfillment.

She thought the woman beautiful.

Chapter 9

W*e're doing an apples/orange number* on ourselves with the Chinese."

Meredith snuggled closer to Archer and readjusted her recorder, balanced on his chest, as he went on.

"Their level of productivity is a function of their culture, just as ours is. Since this country's inception we've operated on a frontier mentality which had as its hero the independent freewheeler. His day is gone. The Chinese are communitarian people. Their culture is based on meshing. Individuals weaving in with the social fabric. America needs to start meshing more. Pulling together for national purposes. One good way for the government to start would be with more tax breaks for research and development . . ."

Meredith was thankful for the recorder, dutifully whirring away and capturing the insights and philosophy she was too exhausted to follow any longer. Night was darkening the windows. They had spent the day in a bliss-filled continuation of Meredith's initiation into the wonders and delights of her newly discovered body.

She curled against Archer's hair-matted chest. The bass rumbling of his voice resonated pleasantly through her. With no warning, he stopped. Meredith sat up and clicked off her recorder. "What is it?"

Archer leaned forward and nibbled playfully at her nipple. "I'm damned glad Aunt Adrianne's not here."

It was a sign of the astonishing progress she had made in one dramatic day, that Meredith could laugh easily at Archer's good-natured taunt. "Yep, had to put the old girl out to pasture," she joked. "She just wasn't needed around here anymore."

Carefully transferring the recorder to the nightstand, Archer enclosed Meredith within the protective circle of his arms. "And she won't be needed ever again," he swore gently into the downy cloud of her hair.

"Archer," Meredith began falteringly, toying with the dark curls on his chest, "I feel like my life just started over today." She looked up, her eyes large and searching. "Do you know what I mean?"

"I know, darling." The unshielded vulnerability in her eyes made him ache with a protective instinct that few in his life had ever elicited. He hugged her closer. "I've discovered places in myself with you that I never knew were there before."

"You have?" Meredith echoed him with astonishment. "With your help, *I've* uncovered lost continents, hidden galaxies within myself."

"You *were* a hidden galaxy, my celestial beauty. You were driving me crazy, forbidding me to feast my eyes on you." He playfully puffed up the sheet and poked his head underneath. With a playful growl of ferocity, he nuzzled her stomach. Scooping her up, he rolled onto his back, pulling her over to rest on his stomach. For a long moment they looked into each other's faces, memorizing the treasured contours.

"Oh, Meredith," Archer sighed. "There's so much I want to tell you, but it seems the only way I can do it is through jokes. That's a form of hiding too, isn't it? You were brave today, you truly were. Now, it's my turn to follow your example." Archer drew in a steadying breath. "My life changed from the day you strutted into my office in your little dress-for-success outfit with the puffy bow and all."

Meredith chuckled at the memory. "And I thought you were your own son."

"Right. Jeez, you made me feel like I *was* my own son. Even before I actually liked you, though, I was . . ." He paused, then with a wry grin went on. "I guess 'infatuated' might be a nice way to put it. 'Hot for your bod,' however, might be closer to the truth."

"Archer!" Meredith cried in joking reprimand.

"There I go, kidding again. The truth of it is, you feed a hunger in me that I didn't even know existed. It's never been this way for me with a woman before."

Meredith was profoundly touched by his admission. She had assumed that Archer was merely the accomplished master, leading her along a path he'd trod many times with many women. "Archer, I didn't even know enough to *dream* of what we shared today."

"I'm glad," Archer breathed. "I'm glad it was new for you. I almost felt like a virgin today." He plumbed her eyes for an answering comprehension.

"I did too," Meredith murmured.

"Oh, we're a pair," Archer whooped, exulting in the glorious novelty of a union that went so far beyond the physical. "Two experienced virgins."

Meredith was saturated with such bone-deep contentment that she couldn't prevent the beatific smile that wreathed her face in happiness.

"You know what the best part of it will be? What I'm looking forward to the most?" he asked.

"Tell me," Meredith prompted.

"Spending a whole night with you in my arms. Waking with you in my arms. I've wanted that so much."

Meredith was dumbfounded; Archer was speaking *her* heart, *her* dream.

When Meredith didn't respond, Archer quipped, "But you'd probably rather find out what I want from the

Federal Reserve Board, so switch on your recorder and let's get back to work."

"Suddenly," Meredith purred, "I don't give a damn about the Fed. And I've wanted you here, sleeping beside me in this bed, more than I can say. But before we find out how wonderful that will be, let's make sure we're both utterly exhausted."

She slipped a brazen hand downward and was stunned to discover a renewal of Archer's desire already building. When they made love, it was more a melding of their two spirits than the wild, all-consuming couplings that had gone before in that long day of discovery. To Meredith, it seemed as if she'd learned one more new facet of her body—that it could be an instrument for translating the subtlest emotional nuances. There was no need for words when they'd finished. They had already said it all in the elegant language they'd invented with their loving.

Just before she slid into sleep, Meredith, lying cherished and cradled in Archer's arms, thought, he was right, this *is* the best part.

Morning was a sunlit sonata that gilded Meredith's fresh, new world in a golden radiance. Not wanting to wake Archer, she made her breathing low and shallow. In sleep he looked like a Viking gently resting after his battles. The fierce glower that often furrowed his face as the day's demands were piled on him was gone. Meredith marveled, thinking of the sensitivity that lay behind such intimidatingly masculine handsomeness. She marveled again, remembering all that he had unlocked within her yesterday.

A silent prayer of thanksgiving formed itself in her mind. She *could* be strong enough for him, she concluded fervently. She *would* be.

As if roused by the force of her conviction, Archer stirred and lazily opened one eye. "Um-m-m-m," he muttered sleepily. "Just the person I was dreaming of."

Meredith slid into his arms, a chuckle gurgling in her throat.

"What's so funny?"

"Everything. Nothing. I'm just happy," Meredith admitted.

"Happy? Is that all?" Archer teased. "I'll have to see what I can do to make that ecstatic."

With a just-waking laziness, they made a kind of morning love that seemed to belong half to dreams. They were both slipping back into real dreams when Archer, suddenly remembering the existence of a larger world, jerked up.

"Dammit all," he cursed. "I forgot. I'm supposed to be down at the launch site right now being interviewed for *Wake Up, America.* Come with me?"

Meredith nodded.

After a hurried shower together, they dressed quickly.

Somehow, even in his slightly rumpled clothes, Archer looked magnificent. Meredith decided that with his bearing and manner, he could command respect wearing a plastic trash bag. She hastily slipped into a pair of jeans and a wine-colored angora sweater and smoothed her hair down until it was sleek and shiny as a wet seal's fur.

"How on earth do you do it?" Archer asked as he handed her into the Porsche roadster.

"Do what?"

"Manage to look more scrumptious every time I see you?"

"You're pretty scrumptious yourself," Meredith answered, passing off the compliment.

A large crowd was gathered at the launch site. A fair portion of it was clustered around the famous faces visiting from the national TV program.

"For a man who successfully avoided publicity for so many years," Meredith observed wryly as they approached the tumult, "you certainly dived into the media pool with a big splash."

"All the better for you. The more media hoopla I generate, the more play your profile in *Enterprise* will get."

Before Meredith could parry his accurate remark, a harried-looking man with a badge that identified him as media director for the fiesta approached them.

"Thank God, you're here, Archer. I've been stalling the *Wake Up* people, but all they really want is the solar balloon man. They saw footage of your crash yesterday and that's got them all wound up. Come on, Archer, let me feed you to the lions." He led them through a maze of spectators and technicians scurrying about with lights and sound equipment.

"Here's Archer Hanson," he announced to Matthew Lowry.

Meredith watched the face she'd seen on her TV screen every morning for years metamorphose into a live human being. She halted, ready to fade into the background as Archer stepped forward. But instead of letting go of her arm, he wrapped it even more securely in his own and pulled her into the limelight with him.

"You're not planning to abandon me now," he whispered. "Come with me. You'll class up my image."

Lowry was listening intently to his earphone. He nodded and looked up. "You're Hanson?" he asked Archer bluntly. Without waiting for a reply, his eyes flicked over Meredith. "Who's this? We just want the solar balloon guy, right?" He broadcast his question, glancing toward a production assistant. "Donna," he bawled at the assistant, "why do we have the girl up here?"

Meredith was disengaging her arm from Archer's, ready to leave, but Archer's hand clamped down on her.

"She's here," Archer said in a voice that brooked no argument, "because I want her here. She was on the flight yesterday."

Lowry was momentarily nonplused by having someone speak so forcefully to him. Meredith had quickly seen that he was not the jovial, easygoing man he pretended to be onscreen. He was an arrogant tyrant who ruled his program like a petty dictator.

"Leave the girl," Lowry barked. He turned to Archer. "Get ready for a live feed in about one minute. You'll be on national television."

Meredith barely had time to gulp away her shock. Archer, however, appeared unfazed as the production assistant positioned them in front of Cloud Waltzer II's dented basket. The envelope with its fissured coating was draped over the basket. Archer was oblivious to the tumult around him as he examined the cracked covering.

When the assistant shouted, "Places, everyone. Prepare for transmission," Archer reluctantly turned around. The makeup girl who had been blotting away shiny spots on Lowry's face scurried away.

In a lightning burst of delayed cognition, Meredith realized that millions of people would be watching her. That thought caused the air in her lungs to clot up. But before she could become any more panicked, the assistant was ticking off a countdown, then swinging a finger toward them. They were on the air.

"Hi, and welcome back to the Albuquerque International Balloon Fiesta," Lowry said, turning on his patented folksy charm. "We have with us Archer Hanson, the owner and pilot of Cloud Waltzer II, the solar balloon you saw earlier in the program when we ran the footage of its crash landing yesterday." He pivoted toward Archer. "Archer, that was some pretty spectacular maneuvering. How were you feeling yesterday about the time you saw those power lines coming at you?"

"Well, Matt," Archer answered as casually as if he were sitting on a bar stool next to the exalted personality, "I'll tell you, I was wishing fervently that we all had converted to solar energy years ago so that we wouldn't have all those lines strung across the countryside."

Meredith was astounded by Archer's joking easiness.

"But seriously," he continued, "our 'unplanned' landing hasn't diminished my enthusiasm for solar ballooning one bit. And just as soon as we get that absorptive covering right, I'll be back up there again." He paused and turned to Meredith, without glancing at Lowry, and said, "You might want to ask Ms. Meredith Tolliver, a noted business writer, who was my passenger yesterday, how she feels about the experience."

Meredith couldn't believe it—"noted business writer"—Archer had given her a plug on national television!

Lowry, who was trying to disguise his irritation at having lost control of his own program, asked, "Are you equally as enthusiastic about solar ballooning?"

"As Mr. Hanson?" Meredith asked, feeling suddenly shy about calling him Archer, as if the intimacy between them might be revealed if she spoke the name that was so dear to her. "I might be somewhat less of an advocate than he is, but let me put it this way: Ballooning is a rhapsody, and solar ballooning is a rhapsody in which the orchestra doesn't stop and tune up every few minutes. It's the ultimate uplifting experience."

Archer's laugh floated, rich and warm, on the desert air. "I guess it's easy to see why she's such a respected writer, isn't it, Matt?"

"Yes, it certainly is," Lowry babbled. He was by now clearly disconcerted at having a guest who wasn't intimidated either by his celebrity status or by the TV camera's cyclopic eye.

The assistant was flagging a hand signal to Lowry telling him to wrap it up. He mumbled a few inanities to Archer and Meredith about how pleased he was to have had them as guests on his program. He wished Archer good luck with the solar balloon, then the camera's red eye blinked off, and Matthew Lowry hustled off to the security of his mobile dressing room.

"'Ultimate uplifting experience.' 'Rhapsody,'" Archer crowed, quoting Meredith's words back to her. "You were fantastic!"

"I guess, for an on-the-spot improvisation, it wasn't bad," Meredith admitted. "I was inspired by your attitude.

You acted like you were talking to just any old Joe off the street."

"Who says I wasn't?" Archer asked.

They were laughing when Phil, out of breath, ran up to them to ask, "Archer, there you are, are you going up for the Key Grab?"

"Key Grab?" Meredith interjected. "What's that?"

"A dealership in town has donated a car," Phil replied, stumbling over his words in his haste to get the answer out. "The keys are taped to the top of a twenty-foot pole. Whoever can grab them gets the car. What do you say, Arch? It starts in half an hour."

"Would you like to go up with him, Meredith? Phil could pilot and you could grab."

Meredith was impressed by Archer's thoughtfulness. "Now what would I do with a new car when I have such a splendid vehicle already?" she admonished him teasingly. "No, you pilot, Archer, and, if I'm not mistaken, you could probably talk Phil into going along as your grabber."

"How about it, Phil?"

"I thought you'd never ask!" Phil whooped. "Let's hustle. Lift-off is at eight o'clock and we have to be two miles from the pole," he said, already charging off toward the pickup that had Cloud Waltzer loaded in the back.

"Wait for me?" Archer asked, squeezing Meredith's hand. Then he was loping after Phil, his loose, long-legged stride gobbling up the dusty distance.

Behind Meredith, the PA crackled to life. "Last call for entries in this year's Key Grab," a twangy, country-accented voice announced. "Pilots, please assemble at the field two miles directly northwest. This is your last call.

"For all you spectators, the competition will be starting in just twenty-five minutes. Should be a little tricky today because we've got some crosswinds kicking up. But that's just part of the challenge. It'll take a really top-notch pilot to maneuver a balloon within grabbin' distance of that pole . . ."

Meredith drifted away from the center of activity toward the concession booths housing a variety of Fiesta merchandise. One booth in particular caught her eye. It was filled with stained glass renditions of balloons. Early morning sunlight shot through the saucer-sized disks, bringing their gemstone colors to sparkling life. She was enchanted, wandering through the booth with the tiny balloons bobbing above her head like the glitteringly exotic fruit of a fairy-tale tree.

She couldn't resist the vibrant dots of color and purchased one in ruby and emerald. She'd hang it in her bedroom window as a symbol. The bright orb would stand for the new life she'd embarked upon, a life that would float free of the emotional weights that had kept her low for so long.

Outside the booth, Meredith took the piece out of the

flannel drawstring bag it was packed in and held it up to the full force of the sun. It vibrated with eye-piercing color. Its brilliance seemed to mirror Meredith's internal state. Fighting against the pessimism and dark expectations that had been her companions for so long, she prayed that the joyous colors would never fade.

"It's exactly eight o'clock, folks," the announcer twanged. "The first balloons ought to have started inflating by now. While we're waiting for them to reach us, let's go over the rules: Balloons can't inflate until eight o'clock. They have to take off at least two miles from the pole. There can only be two persons in the basket. Each balloon gets only one try at the keys. And most important, the person grabbing for the key must at all times have both feet on the floor of the basket."

Meredith fell in with the crowd that was flowing toward the pole with a set of brand-new car keys glittering at its summit. She thought of Phil's open, freckled face beaming expectantly and of his long waits in freezing rain and blistering sun at the bus stop and hoped that their late start wouldn't be an insurmountable handicap. Meredith's hopes nose-dived, however, when she saw the first balloon come into view. It was a great wobble of zigzagging color. A large pack of balloons hotly pursued it. Cloud Waltzer was not among them.

"Here they come now," the announcer said. "And they're all right on course."

The balloons swelled in apparent size as they drifted unerringly toward Meredith and ever closer to the pole planted in the middle of the field. Surely one of the pack would snatch away the prize before Phil and Archer even had a chance at it.

"Uh-oh." The announcer intoned the syllables of distress as the three leading balloons veered off to the west. "Looks like some of our leaders have been blown off course."

The three balloons all tried different strategies, firing up the burners to gain altitude or letting their crafts sink, all hoping to hit an air current moving in a different direction. None succeeded. The balloons trailing them were also adjusting their altitudes, trying to avoid the western current that was taking them all out of reach.

"That's a balloon called Plum Crazy," the announcer informed the crowd. "Up there high on your right."

Meredith followed his direction to a purple plum of a balloon.

"And that's Cherries Jubilee just behind it."

A balloon striped in hot pink and cherry red bobbed into view.

"Looks like we've got a danged fruit basket up there today. There's Orange Fizz and the Grape Escape coming at you now."

Meredith delighted in the image of a giant floating fruit basket scattered across the sky. But the whimsical names and luscious colors were no match for the capricious west wind that kept blowing all the contenders away from their goal. Then a blazing orb of fire red and flame orange appeared on the horizon far below the others. Like a plane flying low to avoid radar detection, the balloon was skimming the earth to stay beneath the sabotaging air current. Though it was still off in the distance, it was coming in straight and true.

As it entered the zone where the west wind had batted all the other pilots out of the running, the fiery balloon didn't waver. It was coming into the home stretch without any more complications ahead. Meredith sighed, thinking of Phil's disappointment.

"Looks like we've got a winner, folks. That's Hot Flash out of Houston. Funny thing, the pilot and his passenger are co-owners of a Cadillac dealership down Houston way."

Meredith groaned to herself. A Cadillac dealership. There was no justice in the world.

"That nasty west wind doesn't seem to be able to touch Hot Flash," the announcer continued. "She ducked under it and is heading right this way with no competition in sight. Whoops, appears I spoke too soon. I was so busy staring straight ahead that I didn't notice this aeronaut off to your right."

Meredith tilted her head in the direction the announcer had mentioned and there, appearing like the mythical creature it represented, was the cloud white unicorn galloping across an empty sky. Unlike all the other pilots, Archer was approaching from the east. The cobalt blue Sandias loomed behind him and the west wind that had foiled all the others was acting as his ally, blowing him right across the spectators' field of view, right toward the pole!

"That's Archer Hanson's Cloud Waltzer and it's coming in mighty fast. We could have a dead heat shaping up here!" the announcer shouted, expressing the taut emotion that had gripped the crowd at the unexpectedly dramatic finale.

Only when a jolt of pain shot through her did Meredith become aware that she was chewing her knuckle in a classically melodramatic display of nervousness. She managed to suppress that gesture, but when the majestic unicorn dipped low enough that she could make out Phil's gangly frame leaning out of the basket, she couldn't help screaming, "Come on, Cloud Waltzer!"

She feared that her cheering scream was futile. Hot Flash was coming up fast and sure on the pole. The passenger in the red and orange balloon stretched out as the balloon came within yards of the keys, then drew abreast of them. The passenger leaned even farther over the rim of the basket until his belly was hanging over the rim.

"Remember," the announcer cautioned, repeating the familiar rule, "all four feet in the basket must remain on the floor at all times."

Hearing the warning, the grabber slid back into the basket. But even if he'd remained illegally stretched out, he couldn't have reached the elusive keys. For even as the keys appeared within their grasp, the ineluctable west wind was finding the sails of their ship and blowing it ever farther away from the prize.

That same wind, ridden by a different captain, put the treasure within easy grasp. Meredith saw the disbelieving delight spread across Phil's broad face as Archer eased Cloud Waltzer in for a winning pass and Phil grabbed the glinting keys to his new car. The crowd broke the bonds of its hushed silence, bursting into wild applause.

"Now, *that* was one demonstration of exceptional piloting," the announcer congratulated Archer. "And that's the point of this event. It's a test of a pilot's ability to read and ride wind currents. Today's challenge was especially tough, but we had a pilot and crew who were equal to it—Archer Hanson and Phil Edwards."

The announcer's voice faded as Meredith joined the crowd surging toward the spot where Archer was putting down. She was as thrilled as she'd been the first time she'd seen him at the helm of his sky ship. His movements were so sure, so masterful. Just watching him, his authoritative maleness, Meredith felt her insides melt into a warm, slushy puddle at the pit of her stomach.

"Meredith, can you believe it!" Phil broke into her transporting reverie, dangling the silver keys in front of her face. He looked at the keys as if he expected them to vanish in a puff of smoke.

Meredith wrapped the exuberant sophomore in a congratulatory hug that caused him to redden in happy embarrassment.

Archer turned from shaking the hands held out to him and joined Meredith and Phil.

"Well, Archer, shall we go down to the lot and pick up our car?" Phil asked proudly.

"*Your* car," Archer corrected him.

"Mine?" Phil questioned. "What do you mean? Do you want me to buy out your half?"

"There's no half to buy. It's all yours, Phil. I only went along for the ride."

"You *were* the ride," Phil exploded. Turning to Meredith, he burbled on excitedly, "You should have seen him. I kept wanting to take off, to be in that first wave of balloons. But Archer just stayed put, studying them. He watched them and calculated the currents from their courses. Then, when we did take off, Archer went up way higher than anyone else until we caught an east wind that took us out toward the Sandias, off to the side of the field. Then he brought her down until we hit the west wind that was messing everybody else up and it just brought us in neat as anything." Phil shook his head and held the keys out to Archer. "No, you won that car. You deserve it."

Archer balled up his fist around Phil's, pressing the keys into the young man's hand, and declared sternly, "It's yours, Phil. I never would have even entered. You keep it. Besides, I don't need the hassle on my income tax return. How do you file a car you grabbed out of the sky?"

Meredith watched Archer's grin infect Phil as he took back the keys. She knew that many observers would have concluded that Archer's generosity was merely a function of his wealth. But she knew better. She'd seen too many wealthy men who were far stingier than any hard-pressed working person to believe that wealth equaled generosity. Chad came to mind, and the embarrassingly meager tips he always left when they went out and he picked up the tab. Tips she invariably supplemented.

"Can I treat the winner to breakfast?" Archer asked.

The agreement was unanimous.

After the balloon had been carefully stowed away and arrangements made for Phil to claim his prize, the three of them found a cozy restaurant that specialized in Mexican breakfasts.

"I am famished," Phil announced as they sat down in the sunny restaurant. "I think I'll just order the entire right side of the menu."

Meredith's laughter was cut short by the realization that she hadn't eaten in over twenty-four hours. Far more alarming than that, however, was the awareness that she wasn't even particularly hungry. Meredith had to force herself to make a selection when the waitress came by.

Her anxiety swelled as she watched Phil and Archer attack their meals with uninhibited relish. She looked down at her plate of *huevos rancheros* and could only appreciate on a visual level the artful blend of red and green chiles crowned with melting golden cheese. Her stomach had tightened into a hard knot that repelled food. It was frighteningly reminiscent of the awful days not long enough ago when the mere sight of food could induce panic in her. Back then, food had been inextricably linked in her mind with the illogical vision she'd cultivated of herself as an undisciplined blob.

She intercepted the concerned look that shadowed Archer's face as he watched her toying with her food. It was a look she'd seen before on her father's face. The familiarity of it sent icy chills digging into her belly.

"Anything wrong with your eggs?" Archer asked in a tone that was just a bit too determinedly casual.

"Too hot," Meredith answered hurriedly, forking up a biteful. She transferred it to her resisting mouth, chewed, and swallowed. "Good. They've cooled."

Mechanically, she shoveled in several more bites. It felt like those grim times after she'd finally gone for therapy and had to learn to eat again like a normal person. The whole time, she'd had to battle her terror that each bite would be the first in an unstoppable binge. Gradually that fear had subsided and, with excruciating effort, she'd reestablished normal eating patterns.

Were they crumbling now? she wondered darkly. Was the whole hideous nightmare starting again?

Chapter 10

After they dropped ***Phil off*** at the car dealership where a mob of reporters and his new car waited, Archer drove Meredith home.

"Can you believe that it's only been one week since we met?" he asked. "I wish we could spend the whole day celebrating our anniversary. Preferably in bed." He brought her hand to his lips.

"Sounds like a capital idea to me," Meredith joked only half-kiddingly. It *was* stunning to realize that she'd known the man beside her for only seven short, transforming days. For the first time in her life she could understand the stories she'd always considered outrageous before of people who met and married within the same week. Marriage? The idea flickered like a dangerous flame in the corner of her mind. It was a flame that could either rage out of control, destroying everything in its path, or it could light comfortable fires that warmed and illuminated the lives of the lucky ones. She chased the notion from her mind. She had never been one of the "lucky ones."

"Unfortunately," Archer continued, "I'll have to spend the next two days in Antonito doing an on-site inspection and hammering out some labor problems."

Meredith winced at his word choice. It evoked memories of her notorious great-grandfather, the robber baron. "Hammering? What kind of problems are you having at the mine? I suppose I should know for the article." It seemed odd bringing up the professional reason that had served as the catalyst for their coming together.

"I'd really rather the mine wasn't mentioned at all in any article."

Meredith was on the verge of laughing, sure that Archer was joking with her. But the grim set of his jaw killed her mirth. Meredith didn't answer. She'd honored other requests for selective silence from other subjects, provided that they hadn't interfered with her telling of a larger story.

"Believe me," Archer said, straining for a lightly self-deprecating tone, "the heart of the Archer Hanson story does not beat in Antonito, New Mexico."

"Archer, you must realize the position you're putting me in."

"Vis-a-vis your professional ethics, I presume," he asked drily.

"I *am* still bound by those obligations," she reminded him.

"Funny, I'd thought that you might be feeling the bonds of some new obligations. I guess I was wrong."

"Archer, you're not being fair about this."

He looked out the windshield, focusing on the Sandia Mountains to the east. A ruff of clouds ringed the peaks. He let his overhasty emotions drain away. He was unused to being at the mercy of his heart rather than controlling his every word and action with his head. "You're right," he admitted solemnly. "I was out of line. Let's forget I ever mentioned it. Work hard and I'll see you late tomorrow night. Deal?"

"Deal," Meredith answered, fighting down both the journalist's questions that were rising in her and her own sadness at even this brief separation.

"Gotta run," he announced, releasing her hand.

She turned to open the door, feeling oddly disturbed and bereft at his abrupt departure. Then a pair of strong hands recaptured her.

"Meredith."

Her name on his lips had the quality of an anguished question. He rotated her toward him. His kiss tasted of breakfast coffee. For the time-shattering seconds that their lips fused, the distressing buzz that was again gathering force within Meredith was silenced. As she stood on the street corner flagging a limp good-bye, though, it started anew.

She tried to shake the sense of foreboding loose by diving into work on the article. She reviewed the notes she had made so far. As she listened to the recordings she'd made only yesterday, the caressing magic of Archer's voice transported her back twenty-four hours in time. She relived yesterday, a day that had transformed her, from the moment she opened her eyes to see Archer Hanson here, in her tiny apartment, until he drove off. Notes lay forgotten as she was immersed in the wonderment of their long day of discovery. The memory chased away the dark clouds of doubt that had begun forming and subdued the ominous buzzing long enough for her to get down to work.

A couple of hours later she had her material roughly organized, enough so that she knew what research she still had to do. She arranged interviews with some of Archer's early business associates. Archer had happily supplied the names of both friends and competitors alike. His willingness to allow her access to those who might be detractors puzzled Meredith. Right from the start Archer had been completely open with her. He was fully aware that she was not writing a puff piece on him. That the profile came with no guarantee that she was going to present him in a favorable light. He knew that she wanted to take him apart and look at all the pieces, not just the ones that would glitter nicely in the public eye. So why was he so secretive about the mine?

Thor bounded up onto Meredith's desk. She stroked the cat absentmindedly as she went over what she knew about Archer's uranium operation. It was obvious from his financial reports that the mine was not a major consideration in the overall scope of his holdings. Maybe she *could* simply ignore it.

Thor began yowling and hopped off the desk. Meredith followed him into the kitchen to check his food and water bowls. As the dried chunks of food clinked into his bowl, she remembered that it had been four hours since breakfast. She also recalled how she'd merely toyed with the meal and that she'd eaten virtually nothing the day before. Worse, though, was the fact that she still had no appetite.

Methodically, she prepared herself a sandwich on whole wheat bread. It looked too formidable. She cut it into halves, then quarters, then eighths, hoping to reduce it to manageable segments. The act of slicing it up brought back an image of herself during the worst days of her illness, when she would allot herself one apple for a day's ration of food, then slice the fruit into dozens of paper-thin wafers. She tried to make them last the whole day by stingily doling them out to herself and then sucking on them until they'd disappeared in her mouth.

The memory was terribly unsettling. Meredith forced

the sandwich to her lips and made herself bite into it. She was choking down the third small section when she was saved by the clock. She had to be at her first interview in less than an hour.

Quickly she showered, then faced her closet. She'd scheduled two interviews, one with a bank president who'd gotten his start financing Hanson Development. The other was with Archer's first partner, a former oil-field roughneck. Meredith shuffled through her ward-robe, trying to come up with an outfit that would span the gap between the two men. She'd learned early in her career that it paid to look as much like her subject as possible so that they would perceive her as an ally rather than an inquisitive enemy.

She finally settled on a pair of well-cut navy trousers and a cream-colored, cotton blouse. She topped the outfit with a softly tailored blazer in heather tones that would look right at home in an executive suite. Then, when she met with the former oil field worker, she could slip off the blazer for a more casual look.

It was late by the time she finally returned home. Mer-edith was pleased; her interviewees had been extremely forthcoming. Perhaps because it was obvious from her remarks that Archer had already shared a great deal of himself with her. Whatever the reason, she'd collected some terrific anecdotes from the retired roughneck about Archer's flamboyant wheeling and dealing back in the early days. From the banker she'd gotten a sharper overview of Hanson Development and the major role it had played in much of New Mexico's growth.

Just as she was wishing that Archer would call, her phone started ringing. Swallowing back the excitement that tightened her vocal cords, she answered.

"Where have you been? Your father and I have been worried sick."

The voice was more familiar to her than any other on earth. "What are you talking about, Mother?" Meredith asked as calmly as she could.

"Meredith, we're so worried about you," she wailed. "We saw you on TV this morning on that program with Matthew Lowry. Why didn't you tell us your problem was starting again?"

"My 'problem'?" Meredith echoed archly, fighting to rein in the anger that had flared in her at her mother's accusation. "You can say *anorexia* to me, Mother. I won't wither at the sound of the word." Immediately Meredith was swept by remorse. How had it happened so quickly? How in an exchange of only a few seconds had they fallen so unerringly back into the old patterns of sniping followed by her guilt and her mother's hurt martyrdom.

"Well, excuse a mother's concern," Julianna Tolliver sniffed in the tone of noble hurt Meredith knew so well. "You just looked awfully thin. Terribly, painfully thin."

"I did?" Meredith asked. Her breathing had become

shallow and her pulse was skyrocketing. She felt her moorings slipping away. Her hand raced over her wrists, her pelvic bones. *Were* they jutting out too far? She steadied herself and tried to act like an adult rather than the bungling child her mother somehow always made her feel she was. "I can understand your concern, Mother," she answered in tones of calm rationality, "but I don't think I'm underweight."

"Meredith, darling, isn't that one of . . ." She stumbled. "One of anorexia's most devastating symptoms? Don't you remember? Even when you *were* so thin that there was a gap at the top of your thighs, you still thought that you were obese. Don't you remember how you resisted treatment?"

"But, Mother, I don't *think* I'm 'obese' now. I think I'm normal. Mealtimes *have* been somewhat erratic over the past week, but that will settle down."

"Promises, the endless promises you made to us that you could, you would deal with this . . . this anorexia. And you just got progressively worse. Meredith, dear, do you think it wise not to seek qualified help? You know the dreadful statistics as well as I do. People *die* from anorexia. Why, only last year there was that famous model. She thought she was doing fine too."

"Mother, do you need to bring this all up?" Meredith asked with a forced patience.

"Yes. Yes I do," Julianna Tolliver protested with a

feeble, yet somehow shrill stridency. "I just can't go through that ordeal again." Her voice collapsed. Sobbing, she choked out, "It almost killed me, going through all that the last time."

"Mother, calm down. Nothing—"

She was interrupted by her father's deep, authoritative voice. "Meredith, I don't care how you do it, but I want you back here," he ordered. "Your mother's right, you looked like hell. You're wasting away again and I won't stand by and let that happen again. We've already been in touch with your therapist and he says he can work you in. I'm sorry if I sound gruff . . ."

No, you aren't sorry, Meredith thought. She knew her father was never more comfortable than when he was intervening in people's lives and rearranging them in an order that suited him.

". . . but it's only because we're concerned. We don't want this anorexia thing to get out of hand again like it did last time. Your therapist says that if we can catch it now and nip it in the bud, treatment will be a lot easier."

"Dad, I don't need treatment," she protested, but her voice was neither strong nor sure.

"Okay, baby, you just get on back here and we'll talk it all over. You were a shrewd investor, Meredith, when you were working with the firm. You must still know that it's always a sound strategy to cut your losses when a gamble doesn't pay off. This Albuquerque move obviously isn't a high-yield proposition, so cut your losses and come on home."

"We love you and just want what's best for you," her mother chimed in reedily on an extension line. "You do know that, don't you, dear?"

Meredith bit back the bitter words that swarmed to her lips and instead spoke the truth. It was a truth that both bound the three of them together and tore them apart. "I know you do and I love both of you too."

Her hands were quaking by the time she hung up, her father's admonition to catch the earliest flight back to Chicago still ringing in her ears. Only in a remote corner of her mind did the vague questions form: Why didn't they ask about the crash landing? About how my writing is going? About anything other than my weight? Almost as if he sensed his mistress's distress, Thor sprang lightly into her lap and nudged gently against her hand until she started petting him.

The simple motion of comfort did little to calm Meredith's inner turmoil. A debate raged within her. She listened, stupefied, as one side of her argued for her to totally ignore her parents. Then another side came back with a stinging rebuttal, pointing out the validity in what they'd said. This side reminded her that she *had* wanted to ignore her parents when she was at her sickest. That she'd firmly believed the skeletal figure she saw in the mirror was an overweight blimp.

She dumped Thor off her lap and hurried into her bedroom, tearing off her clothes as she went. By the time she stood in front of the vanity mirror, she was as naked as she'd been the day before when Archer had forced her to see, to touch, to know herself. As she traced a finger over her belly, trying to judge if it was too sunken in, she wished desperately that Archer were at her side guiding her hand again. She'd felt so sure about herself yesterday, viewing her body through his eyes. Now she didn't know. *Were* her pelvic bones jutting out too far? *Were* the corrugations of her ribs too prominent?

Then her hand found the womanly swells of her hips and the buzzing voices chorused out: How could you have let Archer see them? How could *anyone* think you too thin? You're fat.

She reeled from the room, grabbing a thick flannel nightgown to hide under. It *was* starting again. It *was.* She'd lost touch once again with her own physical reality.

Meredith sat huddled in a chair waiting for the pounding of her heart to quiet enough that she could hear the voice of reason within herself. She wished with every fiber of her being that Archer were with her.

She jumped when the phone rang. She prayed it would be Archer. That he would know what to say, how to chase this nightmare away. Of course, it had to be Archer. Who else besides her parents would call at this time of night?

"Archer, I'm so glad you called," she blurted out in the same instant that she remembered there *was* one other person who would call.

"Sorry to disappoint you, Mer. It's just me, your alleged fiancé."

"Chad, I . . . I was expecting someone else."

"The balloon hero, I take it. Saw you two on the telly this morning. Nice way to find out that the engagement is off."

"Chad, the engagement was off before I ever left Chicago. I told you that I didn't plan on ever coming back."

"Yes, but nothing was ever formalized."

"Chad," Meredith said wearily, "there was never anything between us that *wasn't* formalized."

"And whose fault was that?" he dug in caustically.

"I'm not ascribing blame, Chad. I realize that a lot of what was wrong with our relationship was my fault. But it's over now, so let's try and remember the good times."

"Over?" Chad echoed belligerently. "After I stood by and nursed you through your crazy period? What other man would have put up with that? You think your balloon hero is going to be there waiting for you to make up your mind whether you want to starve yourself to death or not?"

"Chad—" Meredith tried to interrupt, but he was on a heated roll and not about to slow down for her.

"Because it's starting again, Mer. Your parents and I, we all saw it this morning. It's starting again."

"Archer doesn't think I'm too thin." Her protest sounded weak and shakily defensive. "He says I look fine," she ended lamely.

"Archer? Your father told me that Charlie Wendler mentioned to him that you were working on a piece for *Enterprise* on this Archer Hanson. What do you expect? That the subject of a profile is going to tell the writer that she looks like something out of a concentration camp?"

"Archer isn't the type of man who would play up to anyone, no matter what he stood to gain," Meredith boldly asserted. Still, Chad's words had stung, ripping as they did at her ever-shaky self-confidence. "He likes me for myself," she added weakly.

"Has he seen your 'self'?" Chad asked archly, making an oblique reference to Meredith's refusal to ever allow him to see her unclothed. A refusal he had not tried to override.

"Though it's none of your business, yes, he has." Meredith regretted that Chad had managed to worm the confession out of her. The long silence that followed betrayed his injured pride.

"Lucky Mr. Hanson," he sniped.

"Chad, I'm sorry. Sorry about the way things were between us and the way things worked out. I hope you meet someone else."

"Someone else?" Chad hooted. "Meredith, darling, don't think that you're the only one who's able to make new friends. You didn't really believe that you were my *sole* source of feminine solace, did you? That your frigid, repressed favors were enough to satisfy any man?" Chad's voice rose to progressively higher pitches.

"I think we've said enough, Chad. I'm going to hang up now."

"Oh, so the Ice Princess is withdrawing again," Chad mocked. "Well, you're not pulling the plug on me until you get the full picture here, sweetie. Your father set me up with you from the start. Told me all about your disease. He thought that a boyfriend might bring you around. Hinted about needing a son-in-law to take his dead son's place in the company. That's why I put up with all your crazy obsessions. Your frigidity."

"I'm hanging up, Chad. Don't call again. Ever."

As she was putting the receiver down Chad screamed out his parting shot. "No man could ever want you unless he had an ulterior motive."

Meredith hugged her knees to her chest, gripping her elbows until the convulsive trembling that shook her body had stopped. She felt lost on a midnight sea. She was adrift in an infinity of doubt with no compass, no star, to guide her back to shore.

Questions batted about in her mind like a swarm of mad moths searching for a light that had gone out: Was the anorexia starting again? If it was, should she go back to Chicago for treatment? Why wasn't she strong enough to simply ignore her parents and Chad and carry on, secure in the knowledge that there *was* nothing wrong with her?

And finally, most devastating of all: Why can't I just be normal? she wondered forlornly. That was what was worst of all. That all her pain seemed so self-indulgent. To the world it looked like something she inflicted on herself, something she could easily stop if she'd simply put her mind to it. If only, she wished desperately, it *were* that easy.

For long hours into the night, Meredith attacked those questions. She repeatedly attempted to dispel all her fears through the simple act of eating. But the sight, smell, and taste of food repelled her. Each time an attempt failed, she was plunged anew into a spinning vortex of doubt. Her hope that Archer would call flickered out as the clock ticked past the last two-digit number on the dial and started in on the wee hours.

With an heroic effort, Meredith calmed herself and brought her stampeding thoughts back from the edge of panic. She bullied herself into listening to reason: No, she was *not* anorexic. But, yes, it *was* within her to become that way again. Building on that foundation, she spent the next hours constructing a plan of action.

The sight of dawn streaking in her window startled

Meredith. The night had slipped away as she'd grappled with her internal tormentors. The sun redeeming a sleeping world from darkness illuminated the inevitable course she would have to follow.

She pulled on her parka, eager to be outside, away from the stale air she'd been breathing. The crisp newness of the unfolding day cleared her head. Everything was still except for the chattering of waking birds. The sun was reddening the sky above the Sandia Mountains. Meredith thought of how those defiant peaks had looked that morning just over a week ago when she'd first glimpsed Cloud Waltzer battling the sun and the moon for supremacy of the sky. That day seemed a lifetime ago. Or more accurately, like time completely removed from her life, a time untainted by it.

For the inescapable truth was, her life, her real life, was beginning again. The fairy-tale hiatus was coming to an end and with it her and Archer's time together. That was the conclusion she'd reached during the long hours of struggle. She'd finally decided after hours of fighting the realization that she couldn't use Archer as an emotional compass to keep her on course. She couldn't hope to build any kind of relationship if she would be forever relying on him for her own psychic orientation. It was fundamentally unfair.

Meredith lost track of how long she wandered, lost in

contemplation of what she had to do. When she glanced up again, a flock of balloons bobbed in the distance. Their tropically gaudy colors, once so enchanting, now failed to delight Meredith. Their vividness only served to highlight her somber mood. The bright promise they had once held now seemed a cruel mockery.

She was a fool to have ever believed that she could stay aloft in their high-flying company.

"I hope I didn't wake you." The call she'd prayed for last night and now dreaded came shortly after she returned to her apartment.

Meredith listened to Archer's voice, memorizing every cherished inflection. "No," she answered dully, "I've been up for quite a long time."

"Are you all right?"

"I'm better." She answered as truthfully as she could. "How about you? How are negotiations going?"

"Good. Getting a lot of problems ironed out. Listen, I'm going to have to get back to a meeting I ducked out of. I just couldn't go another minute without hearing your voice. I don't imagine that I'll be through here until late. It'll probably be close to midnight before I get in. I couldn't possibly presume upon you to see me then, could I?" There was a laughing charm in his tone. "I mean, that *would* be unspeakably rude, wouldn't it?"

The honey of Archer's voice coaxed a wistful smile to Meredith's lips. "No, Archer, it wouldn't. I'll be waiting for you."

Archer's heart was cartwheeling in his chest as he hung up. He looked out of the window of the Antonito mine headquarters. A wide open mesa rolled out farther than he could see. Planted smack in the middle of it was the conical thrust of Mount Taylor, a peak revered by the Indians of the area. He remembered all the questions that had boiled through him as a boy looking out at that sacred mountain. He felt now, for the first time, as if he understood the answers he'd found during that troubled time twenty years ago.

Those still-vivid memories collided with a remembrance of the fragile ivory body that had been unveiled to him and his blood warmed again. The fire she had ignited in his loins had mocked him almost continuously since that first day she'd walked into his office. How had he been able to sense the depths of tenderness and sensuality that had lurked beneath her professional primness? On a conscious level, he hadn't known, but the woman she truly was had affected him at a depth he might never truly understand. He still had so much to learn about her. So much he wanted her to learn about him. She alone among all the women he'd ever known would understand about his past. About the discoveries he had made staring out at Mount Taylor. He wondered if there really was only one truly right person in the world for everyone. He couldn't say, he was just thankful that he'd found Meredith.

Talking with Archer strengthened Meredith's resolve. It had reminded her of the well of goodness within him. He deserved a woman who wouldn't pump that reserve dry. Strong in the knowledge that she was doing the right thing, she was able to sit down and eat a meal for the first time in days. That most basic process also served to reinforce her decision.

Still, it was a decision that didn't seem entirely real to her. The prospect of carrying it out loomed ahead of her like some dark and brooding mirage. She crawled into bed and, exhausted by the emotional upheaval she'd survived, fell asleep under the shadows that were rapidly solidifying into her future.

She was jolted awake many hours later. Her lids flew open, but she saw nothing, so strong were the tentacles of the nightmare gripping her. Rory, her brother, was sick, too weak to walk. She'd been pushing him in his wheelchair. Suddenly the path had begun sloping precariously. Try as she might, she couldn't fight the precipitous slope. Her feet slid out from under her and the wheelchair was wrenched from her grasp. She ran—heart breaking, tears streaking her face—after the runaway wheelchair. It kept accelerating away from her, slowing down only in the instant before it toppled over the cliff at the end of the slope. In that moment, her brother, Rory, the smart one, the handsome one, the favorite one, had turned to her and smiled his golden smile.

A cavern of loss hollowed Meredith out, but she kept on running, still chasing after her brother, still trying to catch him in time. It was a familiar nightmare with a familiar end. With her dream legs windmilling wildly under her, she would always follow her brother to the end of the slope. Then, unable to stop, she would plummet over the cliff after him, jerking awake as she hurtled through empty, black space.

She awoke with a sense of impending doom that the dream had only heightened, not created. The loss she felt upon awaking was for Archer and for herself. Disoriented, she glanced at the clock. The digital numbers glowing in the dark read 9:53. She'd slept around the clock. It was late evening. Archer was coming.

Groggy as she was, she was still all too aware of the odious task that lay before her. For a few seconds she bridled at the unfairness of it all. Why couldn't she have been allowed just a few more days of happiness? She even considered postponing the inevitable. But in her present state of mind, what would that prove? No, it was better to cut it off now.

A shower revived her somewhat. She slipped into a violet, cotton robe that made her eyes look almost lilac. As she dried her hair, she thought of Archer stroking it for the last time tonight. As she applied a touch of plum-colored gloss to her lips, she imagined Archer's farewell kiss. Her sad reveries were interrupted by a forceful knock at her door.

"I managed to get away early," Archer explained, sweeping her into his arms as she opened the door.

His kiss was molten silver that poured into her veins, melting her resolve. She knew she should turn from the oblivion offered by his lips, but she was trapped. She couldn't bring herself to speak as his tongue made slow, dipping forays into her mouth, stealing the words that would separate them forever. She knew it was wrong, dishonorable, but she couldn't vanquish the need she had for him. She surrendered to the wooziness that was pulling a blanketing fog over her. It drugged her anxious thoughts, stilling them with an all-forgetting sleep.

His hands slipped inside her robe like stealthy night visitors come to rob the castle. They stole her determination as they glided over the bounty of her breasts, plundering their aroused crests.

"Could it only have been one night since we were together?" Archer's question was expelled on harsh, shortened gasps. "It feels like a month, a year, an eternity. All day I sat in meetings listening to my own voice, and the whole time I was imagining the feel of your breasts responding to my touch, growing firm and full beneath my hand, just the way they are now. It was agony. You're like a fever in my blood, Meredith Julianna Tolliver. I would be staring at some labor leader's face and all I could see was you."

He smoothed the robe down, off her shoulders, gently pulling it away from first one, then the other breast. His hands tantalized each one in the teasing unveiling.

"I kept thinking of your face the other day, that first time you let me see you, all of you." His voice was a rasp of arousal. He held her eyes, then satiated himself on the sight of her before unknotting her robe at the waist. His fingers trailed along the V of the robe's opening, parting it ever wider and sliding it down ever lower until his hands met just above the fiery core of her passion. He brushed an intoxicating hand over that most sensitive area.

A moan, half of desperation, half of delight, escaped Meredith. Aided by Archer, she quickly freed him of his encumbering clothes. He halted their rapacious frenzy while he removed the deep purple robe from Meredith with the adoring slowness of a sculptor undraping his life's masterwork.

"You're more beautiful than anything I imagined today or anything I'd ever dreamed of before I saw you." He continued the celebration of her body with a flurry of kisses that adored the delicate bones and hollows of her neck, the ivory column of her throat, the shell pink curves of her ear, the tips of her breasts. As he settled there his kisses intensified and he sucked at the roseate centers until the chasm deepening inside Meredith spasmed with the ache for fulfillment.

Swept now by the same maddening rhythm that was driving Meredith to grind her hips against Archer in an instinctive plea, he bent before her and trapped her writhing hips. A bolt of startled pleasure ripped through her as his hot mouth covered her and his finessing tongue sought out the folds within the delta of her womanhood.

Weakened by the power of the sensual assault, Meredith felt her knees buckling. Before she could collapse, Archer scooped her into his arms and she was wafted to her bed. She would not allow herself to think, to let the sadness that was building inside her like floodwaters behind a dam pour out. She switched off her mind and thought and spoke only with her hands. Hands that couldn't resist reaching down to cradle the rigid expression of Archer's straining desire.

He groaned at her touch, a primitive, abandoned sound that beat through Meredith, emboldening her and educating her emotions. She feathered kisses across his chest and down over the flat bands of muscle girding his stomach. Her lips skimmed along the arrow of crinkly hair, then stopped and parted to encompass Archer in the kiss that she had reserved for only him. He shuddered beneath her as her tongue darted along the root of his masculinity.

Meredith continued the bliss-filled torture until the

tickle of near satisfaction shivered up Archer's spine. He grasped Meredith by the shoulders, pulling her up to the sweat-dampened tendrils of his chest. They lay, pressed against one another in a fevered embrace, until the tickle subsided. Then he levered himself above her and she guided him toward the singing completion of all that had gone before.

As the storm of their passion subsided, Archer propped himself up on his elbows and looked into the face that haunted and transported him.

"I love you, Meredith."

The words were simple, but they tied up all that was in his heart. They could spend the rest of their lives unknotting the bundle and exploring its contents. "It's a relief to finally tell you. But you probably already knew." A bouncing ebullience enlivened Archer's tone. It *was* a relief to say the words that had been burning within him. He stared into Meredith's face. Her expression withered his happiness. It searched his, groping for words. "What is it?" he demanded.

Meredith's gaze flickered over the beloved contours of Archer's face. This last act of love had been a mistake. It had been wrong to delay. Even when Archer slid onto his side, she could barely suck air into her lungs. Still, she forced herself to speak.

"It can't be." She pronounced the sentence with a dead finality.

"What? What can't be?"

"Us."

"Oh, no, you don't." Archer reared up on his arm, looming above her like an enraged Nordic god. "No, Meredith, we've worked through all that." He shook his head, trying to turn back her words.

"No, Archer, we . . . I mean, *I* didn't. You don't, you won't understand."

"Give me a chance," he ordered. His command felt lifeless on his tongue.

And Meredith tried, but all the words tangled in her throat. She wanted to tell him about her parents' call, about Chad's call, about not eating, about her fears, but the task suddenly exhausted her. The only words she could force out from between her lips were, "It just won't work."

Archer sat up. He was trembling and felt as if he'd just taken a punch to the gut. Maybe the old rule he'd lived by before he met Meredith *was* best after all: Never leave yourself open. He'd let his guard down and now he was paying for it.

So sure of herself and what she was doing only a moment before, Meredith now felt shaken and unsure. She waited for Archer to make the next move, to say something. She almost wished that he would continue arguing. That he would refuse to give up what they had together. Scared by his silence, she touched his back. He flinched. "What are you thinking?" she asked.

He filtered air in and out through his teeth for several deep breaths before he answered. "Meredith, I'm not the hero in some cheap novel who can ignore words like the ones you've just spoken. Life, my life at any rate, can't be treated so lightly and I don't want people in it who expect it to be that way. If this is what you want, I respect your decision. Just don't call me, because I won't be calling you and coming around pleading with you to change your mind. Don't expect me to forget your words. I'm not a yo-yo and won't be played like one."

Something inside of Meredith crumbled at the chilling finality of Archer's words. She reached a hand to turn him toward her. "Archer, I . . ." She never finished her sentence, never knew if she was about to beg him to forget everything she had said.

He pulled away from her and stood, his back to the bed. He shook his shoulders as if throwing off a chill, then straightened them. His spine seemed to stiffen into a rod of iron. Without turning, he left the room.

Suddenly, everything that had been so crisply black and white when she had come to her decision was now muddied and gray. Meredith heard the sound of him dressing, the rasp of his zipper, the whisper of his shirt being hastily pulled on. Then the most desolate sound imaginable reached her ears—the scrape of a door being shut forever. She rolled away from the silence that followed and faced the window where she had hung the stained glass balloon. Without light to dance through the pane, it simply hung there, a dull, lifeless bit of colored glass.

Archer fled down the stairs. He was glad for the cover of night, glad because it hid what he hadn't allowed Meredith to see. What no human on earth would ever see or cause again. Before he stepped out into the cool darkness, he hastily wiped his sleeve across his face. The desert air quickly dried the tears smeared over his cheeks.

Chapter 11

Writing the profile on Archer made Meredith feel as if she were composing a eulogy to a lost love. Meredith sat slumped behind her laptop, desultorily pecking out a word at a time as she searched for a lead, for a way to start the story. She had less than a week before it was due at *Enterprise* magazine. That deadline loomed over her more threateningly and more impossibly with each second that ticked fruitlessly away.

Two weeks had passed since the night Archer had left, and still the pain was as raw as it had been when she'd heard the door closing behind him. In the first few days after he'd left, she'd hoped he might call. But the calls she received were from sources with more tales to tell of the wonderful Archer Hanson. The subject himself never phoned.

For another uncounted time, she wondered if Chad had been right. Had Archer been stringing her along? She thought of how he had lunged out of bed that last night without even turning to face her. Of how he hadn't tried once to get back in touch with her. It was hard not to think that he might have been just slightly relieved when she called it off.

And why shouldn't he have been, after he saw what an emotional cripple I am? she asked herself bitterly. She couldn't blame him for not wanting to haul her emotional load for the rest of his life. She was pulled from her thoughts by the impatient humming of her laptop; it was as if the machine were reminding her that there was work to be done, a great deal of it, if she was going to meet her deadline.

She reread what she'd typed so far: "Big-time ballooning and high stakes entrepreneurship—it's been a winning combination for New Mexico's Archer Hanson. Except that Hanson has added a secret ingredient: the sun." A spastic twitch kicked loose in her stomach.

She highlighted the paragraph and hit Delete—not for the first time today. The lead was trite and had a forced peppiness to it that gagged her on a second reading.

She wasn't putting everything she had into the profile. Some essential part of her was removed from the process, standing aside and wondering how Archer would react to the words she was typing. That, she realized, was *not* the way to write a good profile. She knew that a good journalist couldn't afford to let herself consider her subject's feelings. What she was doing, though, was far worse: She was dwelling obsessively on Archer. She couldn't stop thinking about him.

Something had to be done or she'd muff her first and, if she blew this assignment, only chance at becoming the business writer Archer had announced to the nation she already was. Somehow she had to regain her objectivity. The route was clear once she'd mapped out a destination: She'd visit his uranium mine at Antonito. It was what any good journalist would have done to begin with. She would turn over the rock he had asked her to ignore and see what crawly things scurried out. If she couldn't forget Archer, at least she might learn to remember him with disgust.

The drive out to Antonito was a straight shot west along Interstate 40, the famous strip of road once called Route 66. But Meredith barely noticed the scenery, so intent was she upon the images flickering across the screen of her mind. She replayed the events of their courtship again and again like a well-worn fairy tale she never tired of telling herself.

She started from the beginning, from the moment those icy blue eyes had turned on her like a splash of cold water from the North Sea. Then their second meeting, the glorious, incalculable chance of him owning Cloud Waltzer and of her becoming a part of his crew. She could still remember the metallic taste of fear in her mouth as she left the safety of earth on her first balloon flight. And how that bitter taste had turned to ambrosia.

It all *had* been a fairy tale, she kept reminding herself, the ball, the magic, festive air that pervaded the entire fiesta, the night of the tethered flight. She shook her head to rattle the images loose. None of it had been real, none of it could have been sustained in real life. Not *her* life. But the pounding of her blood as she remembered Archer lifting her off the floor of Cloud Waltzer's basket that night, of her naked thighs wrapped around his waist, was all too real. Just as the feel of his flesh, so solid and unyielding beneath hers, within hers, had been real.

She forced her attention back to the immediate present. As she looked out her car window a mirage seemed to have taken shape on the high, arid mesa that swept out far beyond her view. There, atop a sheer rock island several hundred feet higher than the surrounding plains, was what appeared to be the materialization of a village out of Don Quixote's Spain. The bleached adobe homes were clustered together, one defiant clumping of humanity amidst the unbounded vastness of Nature rolling on endlessly in either direction.

But it was no mirage, Meredith quickly corrected herself, remembering the guidebooks she'd devoured upon first coming to New Mexico. It was an ancient Indian pueblo called Acoma, "the Sky City," because it sat on those towering cliffs above the valley floor which itself was well over six thousand feet in elevation. She vaguely remembered that the pueblo had been occupied since sometime in the tenth century. More clear was the memory that the bloodiest battle in New Mexico's history had been fought there in 1599 between the Acomans and the invading Spaniards.

The Indians had defied Spanish orders by withholding supplies and killing some soldiers. High on their rock perch, the Pueblos had believed themselves invulnerable to attack. After two days of fierce fighting, the Spaniards with their steel armor and explosive weapons conquered the Indians.

She looked with new eyes on the land and the simple buildings that had weathered so much. Births, deaths, storms, wars, the coming of the white man, the passing of the old ways. And still they stood. The timelessness of the vista comforted her and placed her own sorrow in a different light. Certainly she ached for what could never be, for the love she could never share with Archer Hanson. But she too would endure. She hadn't cut her ties with the world that had spawned her to wither away out here. She would not only endure, she swore, she would grow strong.

Acoma Pueblo seemed to fade back into the high desert as Meredith sped toward Antonito, but she was still able to pick it out in her rearview mirror. She kept it in sight for as long as she could. When it disappeared altogether, she still clung to the determination it had forged within her. A new optimism percolated through her. She straightened her spine against the car seat and concentrated on the task that awaited her: the interviews at the mine.

Her upbeat attitude acted like a tonic on her sluggish brain, clearing out the cobwebs that had been gumming up its functioning for the past two weeks. Once again she started feeling and thinking like a journalist. A flock of questions, all the tough questions she needed to ask to uncover how the mine operated and what Archer's part in it was, came to roost in her newly uncluttered brain.

She pulled her digital recorder out from the tote sack on the seat beside her and switched it on. Methodically, she began reciting the points she wanted to cover into the microphone. She could transcribe them before she stopped at the mine. She figured that she would probably be confined to a few showplaces and prevented from seeing anything of significance. She made up her mind that she wanted to see it all. Her diligence might annoy Archer; it might ultimately even embarrass him when her findings appeared in print. But if she were ever to be a person in her own right, she would have to stop being an emotional rag doll. She had to have her own inner compass set and pointing to true north at all times. Right now, she felt secure and happy with the direction she was following.

She was surprised when a sign announcing the turnoff for Antonito appeared in front of her. The past sixty miles had passed without her even being aware of the distance. The road out to the mine was bordered on either side by high chain link fences that lent an ominous air to the approach. She was glad she'd phoned ahead to tell the mine foreman she was coming.

She'd debated whether or not to warn anyone of her arrival, knowing that they would alert Archer and that he might forbid her to set foot on his property. But that hadn't happened. The foreman had phoned back to confirm that he would be waiting for her the next morning. Looming in the distance was the cone of Mount Taylor, the peak that Archer had told her was sacred to the Indians. It seemed to hover directly above the mine.

She stopped just outside the gate at the entrance to Antonito Mine to replay her questions, solidifying them in her mind. At the gate, the guard stopped her.

"May I help you, ma'am?" He had the straight black hair and high cheekbones of the Navajo.

"I have an appointment with Hatch Nelson," Meredith answered.

The guard pressed a button on the intercom system set up in his little hut and spoke into it. Meredith wondered whether the elaborate security was to keep the uranium *in* or protesters *out.* Would the gate close, barring her from entering?

"Go right on in," the guard welcomed her after confirming her appointment. "Headquarters is straight ahead. Just head toward Mount Taylor; it'll look like you're driving straight into it."

The conical peak grew larger as she approached. It seemed the mountain was reeling her in, pulling her toward it by a mysterious force. She topped a rise on the desolate road and gasped as she looked down on the other side. All feeling of desolation vanished. Beneath her was a sprawling operation. Impossibly huge, prehistoric-looking machines and chunky buildings with steam pluming over their roofs covered acres of land at the base of the mountain. It was so unexpected and so vast that Meredith had a hard time comprehending that one man, Archer Hanson, had brought it all into being.

Headquarters for the Antonito mine was a small, functional, wood-frame structure dwarfed by the enormous metal buildings that surrounded it. The only thing noteworthy about the main office building was the cluster of Navajo men milling around in front of it. Suddenly, Meredith regretted having come. Though it was contrary to her every journalistic instinct, she really didn't want to uncover Archer's dirty secrets. The unhappy faces assured her that all was not well at Antonito. That the secrets *did* exist.

Inside, a secretary buzzed Hatch Nelson, the mine

foreman whom Meredith had seen the day she'd met Archer. He ambled out, his callused hand extended. From his grizzled gray hair to his scuffed boots, Nelson looked like a man who was always slightly dusty.

"Pleased to meet you, Miss Tolliver. I'm Hatch Nelson." His greeting was warm and open. It put Meredith on her guard. She wasn't going to be charmed into glossing over her inspection of the mine. She stiffened in resistance to the transparent display.

"Thank you for meeting with me, Mr. Nelson," she said with a cordial firmness. "I'm looking forward to seeing all of the mine." She stressed the word *all.*

"You bet," Nelson replied in a sprightly tone. "Archer said to give you free rein. Anything you want to investigate is yours for the asking."

Meredith tried to figure out what Archer's strategy was.

"I thought we'd start off with an underground tour," he said, heading off toward a structure that housed an oversized elevator.

The elevator ride seemed endless. It was like a balloon flight, only in reverse.

"How far down are we going?" Meredith asked. She could feel the denseness of the earth closing in around her as they hummed down farther and farther.

"I thought we'd have a look at the workstation at thirty-three hundred feet."

"Underground?" Meredith asked the obvious with her jaw dropped in disbelief.

"That's where they keep the uranium," Nelson laughed.

Meredith was finding it harder and harder to remain wary around the affable, easygoing man. She scribbled notes as he ran down some facts and figures.

"The uranium ore that we extract here is processed into a concentrate called yellowcake that has nothing to do with Betty Crocker." He laughed easily at the well-worn joke. "Most of that is shipped out of state to be refined into metal and then fabricated into fuel rods for power plants.

"We're located in what is called the San Juan Basin. The basin covers an area almost the size of New England."

The big elevator shuddered to a halt.

"Looks like we're here. All ashore that's going ashore."

They stepped into a vast excavation lit by a string of bare bulbs. It was cool and damp. Men in yellow slickers made bright spots of color in the gloom. Meredith was astounded by the level of activity. It was a beehive 3,300 feet beneath the surface of the earth.

Nelson pointed out various miners and explained what they were doing. Meredith nodded, but didn't jot down any notes. She wasn't looking for technical data about uranium mining. She was looking for more parts to the puzzle that was Archer Hanson.

The flash of a blowtorch illuminated the dark cavern. Sparks showered down on the asbestos-coated worker. Nelson explained what the man was doing, but Meredith paid scant attention. Unable to contain her real mission any longer, she blurted out, "What were those men doing at the main office? Protesting?"

Nelson was taken aback by the suddenness and the ferocity of her question. "Yep," he answered in his western drawl, "I suppose, in a way, you could say they was protesting. Protesting poverty and a dead-end future on the reservation. They're job applicants, Miss Tolliver, and they come back day after day looking for work here."

Meredith was unprepared for such an answer; in her surprise, she warned Nelson, "You know I'm going to be asking those men myself when we get back up."

The leathery face crinkled into an expression of suppressed rage and Nelson stomped off toward the elevator. Stunned, Meredith paused for a moment before running after him. She had no intention of being abandoned in the bowels of the earth.

The ride up was strained as Nelson visibly fought down his anger. Finally, in a voice tight with control, Nelson spoke. "Last person who ever called me a liar, Miss Tolliver, ended up in the hospital for a week. I wouldn't lie for myself and I sure wouldn't do it for Archer Hanson. Though I would do just about anything else on earth for that man. He ordered me not to tell you the big secret out here at Antonito, but you know what?"

The gleam in Nelson's eye made Meredith a little uncomfortable about being all alone with the man a couple thousand feet from daylight. "What?" she asked hesitantly.

"I'm going to ignore his order and tell you anyway. You came out here with a whole bunch of ideas already set in your mind and you need to have them knocked over. So here's the secret—Antonito has been operating in the red for just about five years now."

"Wha . . . ? But I've seen the annual reports," Meredith babbled.

"Doctored. Archer keeps the mine propped up with money from his development company. And do you want to know why?"

Meredith nodded her head silently, wilting under the heat of Nelson's obvious dislike for her.

"For men like those you thought were protesters. There's almost nothing else for them out here. Nothing except government handouts and some cheap wine to wash the humiliation down with. That's why Archer keeps the mine running. He'll go broke before he'll take these jobs away from the men here. Even if it means playing out a big charade with them."

The hydraulic whir of the elevator seemed to grow to a deafening roar when Nelson fell silent. When he spoke again, it almost sounded as if he were saying the words more to himself than for Meredith's benefit. "Archer and I had a big run-in a month or so ago. I told him that we're losing too much here. That he needs to shut down. I'd already gone ahead and ordered a slowdown to cut back on our losses, but Archer, he wouldn't hear of it. Got pretty riled up just at my suggesting it."

Meredith remembered the day she'd first met Archer, when she'd seen Nelson coming out of his office and had assumed that Archer had just ordered his foreman to stop the work slowdown that she had assumed was a labor protest.

The elevator ground to a stop and the doors creaked open. She followed behind Nelson, trying to keep up with his lanky strides and falling behind. Outside headquarters, a Navajo man, his hair pulled back and bound in the traditional style, broke away from the crowd.

"Hey, Mr. Nelson," he hailed the foreman. "You think any jobs'll be opening up soon?"

"I'm sorry, Luther, but like I told you yesterday, we won't be hiring again for a long time. When we do, I'll post notices at the reservation."

The man's shoulders slumped and he shuffled back to his companions, but none of them left.

That confirmed Nelson's story, leaving Meredith with

an entirely new and even more perplexing set of questions. She ran to catch up with the mining foreman.

"Mr. Nelson," she said breathlessly. "Why? Why does he do it?"

Nelson slowed his headlong retreat and turned to Meredith. He saw something in her face other than journalistic curiosity. Something other than a detached, professional interest. "Why do you want to know?"

The answer was on her lips before it had time to form in her mind. Like a wild horse kept too long corralled, the truth broke free. "Because I love him."

Nelson stopped then and faced her square on. "You do, don't you?" he asked, though the answer was already shining in her eyes. "All right, if that's how things is, I'll tell. But I guarantee you, young lady, if a word of this ever leaks out, a lawsuit'll be the last of your worries. *I* personally will be the first. You understand what I'm saying?"

"Yes, yes," Meredith muttered, unable to hide her eagerness.

"Well, let me see . . . it was about twenty-some odd years ago, I first laid eyes on Archer. He was a tall, gangly kid. No more'n thirteen. I was working as foreman for old man Hanson on a gas field outside of Grants. Old Gunther sent Archer out to the military school there in Grants and told me to keep an eye on him. Just like the boy was another assignment." Nelson paused and looked out on a landscape that was suddenly alive with memories nearly a quarter of a century old. He smiled to himself, then continued.

"Never saw a boy so quiet. Not shy, mind you. When Archer had something to say, he'd say it, and say it loud. He just seemed all tied up in himself. Considering what the old man was like, I can understand why he was that way."

"Why? What was his father like?"

"Hard." Nelson spit the word out. "Hardest man I ever knew and he was twice as hard on Archer. Gunther never wanted a son, he wanted a business partner. That's why he sent him out to that military school, to toughen him up." Nelson chuckled.

"But Archer, Archer wasn't having any of it. He ran away from that school as soon as he could. Just lit out for the desert. Ended up on the reservation. I think he'd have ended up dead if he hadn't. The Indians, I don't know how to explain it, there was just a kinship there right from the beginning. The school would call me and I'd go out and collect Archer. Then he'd turn right around and run away again.

"Maybe the Indians, since a lot of them had been shipped away to school, understood why a boy would run away. They never made a fuss over him. Just sort of treated him as one of their own. Let him be. That was the first time in his life that Archer had been around people who weren't playing up to him or scared of him because of who his father was. They couldn't have given two hoots who Gunther Hanson was. I guess that's why, around them, the boy was finally able to find out who *Archer* Hanson was.

"He never forgot them. From the time he first got started, he was looking for a way to pay it back to them. He found it with the uranium mine. For a while, she turned a tidy profit. But they just never worked out the problems with nuclear energy and demand has been slipping for a long time now. As soon as Archer realized what all the problems were and the long-range implications, he started up his solar energy outfit. He's trying to develop some kind of industry to replace the jobs here at the mine. But until he does that or goes broke trying, he's keeping the mine open."

Meredith nodded, too overwhelmed to reply. She mumbled a sketchy farewell and an embarrassed apology to Nelson, then left. Her head was still spinning from all that she had discovered by the time she stumbled into her apartment late that evening. She fought to keep the personal revelations separate from the ones she could use in her story, but they kept meshing together. Why had Archer wanted to keep her from seeing the mine?

She started to call, purely as a professional, to ask him that question. Before she could finish dialing the numbers, though, she replaced the receiver. Archer had told her not to call and she couldn't, not even for the sake of the article. Besides, she had to admit to herself, it wouldn't be for the article that she'd contact him. It would be for herself. All that was pertinent to what she was writing was that the mine at Antonito existed as it did. Why Archer might have wanted to keep its operation a secret was not relevant to anything other than her tortured feelings for him.

She had procrastinated long enough. Her deadline was now bearing down on her with an ineluctable immediacy. She had no time for any further research. She had to begin writing. When Meredith sat down with her laptop, it was with an undeviating will to work. She *would* get this profile done and it *would* be the best piece she'd ever done. She opened a new document and was confronted with the most terrifying sight a writer must face—a blank sheet of paper. Fortunately, on the long drive home, she'd blocked out a lead and decided on the tone and voice she would adopt for the profile. With her notes arranged by her side, she arched her fingers over the keyboard and began.

The maelstrom of emotion that she'd bottled up within herself burst loose, energizing her fingers as they tapped rapidly over the lettered keys. She took the heat and fury of her feelings for Archer and redirected them into cooler, depersonalized channels. She wasn't writing a valentine *or* a poison pen letter to Archer Hanson. She was filtering the rare personal glimpses she'd gotten of a remarkable man into a story that delivered what *Enterprise* readers would want to know about that man and the business acumen that had propelled him to the top.

Inevitably, as she worked a good quote or a particularly telling anecdote into the fiber of the story, the words she was recording would trigger a memory of a far different nature. Time and time again, Meredith caught herself staring off into space as she was snared by the compelling image of his proud golden head burning like a miniature sun beneath the furling banner of the prancing unicorn; rising over her shoulder as they both stared into the vanity mirror; and sinking ever lower, warming her with its radiant carnal energy until it came to rest between her thighs.

And time and time again Meredith would shepherd her wandering thoughts back to the course they had to take. She accepted these mental rebellions and didn't squelch them too ruthlessly. She had resigned herself to the fact that Archer Hanson would be in her thoughts for the rest of her life. She imagined she would think of him with her dying breath. The peace that had overtaken her on her drive out to Antonito as she passed the imperishable Acoma Pueblo had settled in, bringing with it a deep gratitude that she had been permitted to know the kind of love she and Archer had shared. Though it couldn't banish her grief at the end of that love, at her own inability to sustain such a transforming emotion, the peace she had found did neutralize some of her sadness.

She worked late into the night, making herself stop to feed Thor and to eat herself. She no longer had the time in her life to make such a fetish out of what should be a simple, straightforward process. When she was hungry, she ate, and that was that. She fell into bed exhausted and pleased with what she had produced so far.

The next morning she was back at the keyboard. Not even taking the time to change, she worked in the embroidered cotton Mexican dress that served as her nightgown. She was excited. As with all the pieces she'd ever worked on that had been successful, this one seemed to be writing itself. That was always a sign that she had chosen the right track.

She opened with the crash landing of the solar balloon, an incident that would grab readers from word one and also reveal to them a good bit about the man who had handled the dangerous situation so coolly. From that point, she'd segued into Archer's past, at least those parts of it that Nelson hadn't sworn her to secrecy about.

Untangling the threads that bound Archer's empire was where her expertise was tested. She unknotted the strands, detailing how he'd borrowed on one investment to finance another until he had a dozen different ventures whirling like plates on sticks. If he had ever stopped to rest at that point in his career, the banks would have put an abrupt halt to his balancing act and the whole thing would have come crashing down around his ears. As Meredith reconstructed his rise, she marveled not only at his energy but his instincts. He'd made a few wrong moves, a few bad investments, but not many. He'd gotten in on the ground floor of a number of energy and development trends, buying into ventures just before they became popular. She noted that this alone was a good sign for solar energy.

Then came the rough part, delving into Archer Hanson, the man. She had to weed her way through the barrage of impressions and anecdotes that bombarded her. She discarded the ones that were too intimate, the ones that would betray the depths of her relationship with Archer. Though shaping the story exhausted her, she was reasonably satisfied with the portrait of Archer that was emerging. She only hoped that she could bring him to life as vividly on paper as he was in the flesh.

Two days later she had a rough draft of nearly forty pages. What she had was basically good, but it was flabby. She remembered a famous bit of advice to writers that when they came upon anything they'd written that they found especially clever to cut it out, so she paid close attention to her own treasured bits. She smoothed over the transitions from Archer's present to his past, blending the two together into a seamless whole. She paraphrased several quotes, shortening them and integrating them more carefully into the piece. She questioned the portions that dealt with him as a man, worrying if they were too personal, too revealing. In the end, though, she relied on the journalistic instinct that told her they were good and shouldn't be altered.

It was nearly three in the morning when she checked the time. She staggered into bed, asleep before Thor had even settled himself on top of the covers. She was up a few hours later to make a few final tweaks. She was going to hand in a flawless manuscript to Charles Wendler. After trimming off the fat, she was left with twenty-five pages and six thousand words. Every single one of them had been polished until it gleamed. When she was completely satisfied, she attached the file to an email and hit Send.

It was done. After the initial euphoria wore off, Meredith felt oddly dejected. But before she could sink too far into her post-work depression, she hurried herself out of her apartment. A movie seemed like a good idea. She chose one at random. A love story. Not an especially good one. That didn't stop Meredith, though, from succumbing to an urge that hadn't overtaken her in a public place since her first day at summer camp twenty years earlier—she bawled her eyes out. She was shaken to her core by the grief she had suppressed in order to produce the profile on time. Now that she'd finished the assignment, she could afford the catharsis of tears, the luxury of abandoning herself to the turmoil of emotions still churning within her.

As she stepped into the darkness that had fallen on the city while she'd been lost in her cinematic release, she felt oddly cleansed, scoured of the debilitating sorrow and left with only the pure residue of her loss, the memory that she had, at least for a little while, been loved. Like Archer, who had suffered more than she could have ever guessed and finally found peace in helping the people who had offered him solace, she would cherish that immutable memory and use it to create a life worth living.

She filled the next few days with an assortment of projects, working out a few columns for the *Journal* and sending off several queries to other editors she'd worked with. In the middle of one such letter, Charles Wendler called. Suddenly, she felt like she was back in high school waiting to find out if her name would appear on the list of those chosen to be in the senior play. She hadn't been chosen then and for one moment she was afraid of feeling rejected again. In two words Wendler dispelled that fear.

"Great story," he announced.

"Wha . . . ? Oh, you liked it?" Meredith stammered.

"Liked it? I loved it. You did a superb job. Hanson practically leaps off the page, you made him so real, so vital. I have to confess to you, I didn't think you could do it. I tossed that assignment your way because three other reporters had failed to get the story."

"And because you wanted to do a favor for my father," Meredith added with no rancor. She just wanted Wendler to know that she hadn't been entirely ignorant of his motives.

"I won't deny that I'd prefer to be *in* your father's good graces rather than out, but I never would have let you touch the story if I hadn't seen your clips and thought they were good. Anyway, what's it matter? You delivered the goods. I love the solar ballooning angle. It'll make great art. The art director has already contacted a photographer there in Albuquerque to shoot some pictures of Hanson in his balloon. And we can use some of the TV footage of the crash to make stills. It will be a terrific spread. But that's not why I'm calling, or not the main reason anyway. I'd like to turn you loose on another subject we've been trying to nail down now for some time. Preston Denvers."

Meredith had heard the name bandied about in financial circles since she'd arrived in New Mexico. He was a behind-the-scenes man who had been making important things happen throughout the Southwest for the past half century. "Want to give him a shot?" Wendler asked.

Meredith readily agreed.

Her first thought after she'd hung up was, Archer isn't going to believe this. She couldn't wait to tell him, to run to him with the news of her assignment and Wendler's reaction to her story like a kid with gold stars on her finger painting. But no sooner had the thought crossed her mind than reality caught up with her and tripped her enthusiasm. Of course she couldn't tell Archer. But the headlong thoughts made her aware of how much of her drive had been generated by her subconscious desire to win Archer's approval.

She tried to submerge that impulse as much as she could in the next few weeks as she plunged into the new subject. Winning Preston Denver's approval required her full concentration as well as a weeklong campaign of persuasion and cajolery. When Denvers finally capitulated, Meredith could barely contain herself. Again her urge to call Archer and share the good news was so strong that she could barely contain it. But fortified by the memory of his final directive to her not to call, she fought off the impulse. The next few weeks were gobbled up with research as she immersed herself in the life and times of Preston Denvers.

She worried that this effort might not turn out as well as her first profile, mainly because she wasn't nearly as involved in the subject. But midway through her research she realized that her involvement with Archer had not helped her to write the profile, it had hindered her. She'd had to sort out her feelings every inch of the way with Archer; with Denvers there was no question that she was all business and that everything she collected on him or observed about him could be used in print.

Her straightforward approach soon won Denvers over and he allowed her access that had been denied to every other writer who'd attempted to tell his story. Among other things, he was a fancier of Arabian horses. One weekend he had Meredith flown up in his private jet to his horse farm outside Scottsdale, Arizona.

Meredith soaked up the atmosphere like a sponge. Though she'd grown up surrounded with wealth, the southwestern twists and touches all struck her with the freshness of things new and novel and she scrupulously recorded them, knowing that they were the essential spices that would ultimately give her piece its flavor.

Her every step seemed sure and direct as she switched from research to writing. With each paragraph, she gained confidence that her initial effort had not been a flash in the pan, that maybe, just maybe, she could carve out a career for herself in the field she'd chosen.

On a gray, gusty day at the end of November, Meredith finished the lengthy profile. As soon as she sent it off, she felt the familiar letdown of a project completed and the empty space it left behind. The deflation of her mood left her bogged down in a mire of regret.

She started home, but couldn't face the apartment that harbored so many memories of both the saddest and most exquisite moments of her life. She let the scything wind blow her where it willed. She drove aimlessly, not even realizing that she'd headed for the North Valley until she passed the pasture enclosed by a fence of railroad ties. The shaggy buffalo were huddled together, their backs to the chill wind.

She was on the road to Archer's house and had no will to resist the urge to continue. The barren limbs of the massive cottonwoods that lined the bank of the Rio Grande shivered in the cold. As evening approached, the little adobe ranches huddled in the shadow of the Sandias looked like charcoal drawings. Washed away by the thin, watery light of winter were the vivid colors that had lured Meredith from Chicago and given her the courage to start a new life. She yearned for their brightness, their warmth.

Archer's house appeared in the deepening dusk. The sight of it set far back from the road and silhouetted against an evening sky hit her with an impact she was unprepared for. So fierce was her yearning to see, to be with Archer just one more time, that she had to physically resist her desire to turn the wheel up the drive. But resist she did. She'd happily never see him again rather than drag herself to him in the condition she was in now, a tattered bit of humanity who could only function with him propping up her damaged psyche.

She gunned the idling motor and drove straight and fast. She'd take the long way home, looping around the valley to avoid passing Archer's house again. She didn't know if she'd have the strength to make the same decision a second time around.

Chapter 12

T***hanksgiving and Christmas blurred together*** that year, smudged at the edges by the work that poured in from Charlie Wendler. He was as impressed by Meredith's profile of Preston Denvers as he had been by her portrait of Archer. So impressed, in fact, that he called the morning of New Year's Eve with a bit of advice.

"Watch the newsstands," Wendler instructed her.

"I always do," Meredith countered. "Particularly around the time of the month *Enterprise* comes out. And even more particularly when my first article is due to appear."

"Well, be even more vigilant this month," the editor advised her enigmatically. "I think you'll be pleasantly surprised. I would have express mailed some advance copies to you, but I think it has more impact when a writer discovers her work on the newsstands along with the rest of the world. Listen, kid, I have to run. I've got the president of Chase Manhattan on the other line and I don't think it would be terribly clever to keep him waiting for very long."

"Very astute," Meredith kidded, pleased with the relationship that had developed between them. As she hung up she wondered what the surprise was that Charlie had mentioned. Maybe he had mentioned her story on the cover. Unable to fight off her curiosity, she headed for the drugstore across the street from the University of New Mexico campus. It had the best stock of magazines in town. There was a slim chance that they might have already received their copies of *Enterprise.*

In the car Meredith shrugged off her jacket. A warm spell had temporarily chased away winter. It looked as if Albuquerqueans would be welcoming the New Year wearing T-shirts. Meredith figured she'd probably see it in dressed in her old flannel nightgown. She'd been invited to a couple of parties around town. But since both parties would fête the business community, there was too great a danger that she would run into Archer. She was still not ready for that encounter.

Inside the drugstore, she headed straight for the business section in the separate room devoted exclusively to magazines. It appeared to be deserted. Her heart sank as she saw last month's issue of *Enterprise* sitting in the rack. Too bad; she could have used a pleasant surprise to help pass a lonely New Year's Eve. Maybe if Phil didn't already have plans, she'd invite him over for a late supper and fix something elegant and extravagant.

"You looking for the new issue?"

Meredith spun around. As she did a bald head fringed by wisps of graying hair poked up over the countertop. The clerk disappeared again, then materialized on the other side of the counter, dragging a box behind him.

"We just got the latest *Enterprise*s in this morning, but I didn't think anyone would be coming in for them until after New Year's so I didn't bother to unpack." He slid the box over to the aisle where Meredith stood, took a knife out of his jeans pockets, and sliced the thick strip of tape across the box's top. The box flaps fell open and there, splashed across the cover, was Archer's Viking grin. Once Meredith recovered from the shock of seeing him in full color, she was able to absorb the rest of the cover. It showed him waving from the basket of Cloud Waltzer. In bold black letters across the wicker ran the title, "Archer Hanson, New Mexico's BALLOON TYCOON."

"We'll sell a bunch of these," the clerk said, arranging a handful in the rack. He quickly cleared out several adjoining racks. The combined effect of staring at half a dozen Archers and the surprise of seeing her story featured on the cover practically unhinged Meredith. She grabbed several copies of the magazine and headed for the door.

"Hey, I'll take care of you up here," the clerk said,

moving back to the counter. Meredith blushed crimson. It looked as if she'd planned to make a hasty exit without paying for the magazines.

Back at her apartment she'd barely had time to begin glorying in her triumph when the phone rang. She answered, her mind still on the cover. Halfway to her ear, her hand froze. Whether it was intuition or the barely perceived sound of breathing, she didn't know. All Meredith *was* sure of was that Archer Hanson was on the other end of the line.

When she finally said, "Hello," her voice was wobbly and little-girl high when she answered.

"Meredith, that you?"

Archer's voice was the sound of memories and dreams come to life. It reverberated in Meredith's head, swirling a haze over her thoughts and tying her tongue.

"Yes," she finally choked out.

"You didn't sound like yourself for a moment. I have a copy of the magazine."

Meredith's heart, which had barely begun beating again, froze once more. She waited for Archer to continue, to deliver his assessment of her work. In that instant, she knew that she could win the Pulitzer for her article and it wouldn't matter as much as what Archer had to say about it.

"And?" she prompted him when the silence had grown longer than she could bear.

"And there are a number of inaccuracies and misrepresentations of fact that I'd like to talk with you about."

The bottom fell out of her stomach. At the worst, she'd been expecting some mildly qualified praise, but praise nonetheless. "Misrepresentations of fact," she echoed weakly, her mind whirling to discover what he could be referring to. "What do you mean?"

"I'd rather talk to you about it here, at my office, if you don't mind."

Archer's formal remoteness sent a chill scurrying along Meredith's spine. It was the guarded tone people adopt when they are acting under an attorney's directions. It silenced the questions crowding in on Meredith.

"No, I don't mind," she lied. "I'll be right over."

She blinked in the brilliant sunshine that was warming the city, but barely noticed the unseasonable radiance. Her mind was fully occupied with visions of what awaited her at Hanson Development Corporation. She imagined that Archer would have his team of lawyers already assembled and briefed and poised, ready and waiting to pounce on her. The word *libel* flashed on and off in her brain, rattling her even further. If Archer sued, no matter if he was totally wrong, her future at *Enterprise* would be over. No publisher in his right mind enjoyed working with writers who collected lawsuits. Far worse even than the specter of a libel suit was knowing that

Archer hadn't liked the piece. Hadn't even respected her craftsmanship.

Her palms were as damp as they'd been that first time she'd pulled up in front of Hanson Development. Only this time her stomach was also churning and her heart was fluttering as well. Seeing Archer again would have been sufficient in and of itself to elicit any of these symptoms, but seeing him with the threat of a lawsuit hanging over her caused her reactions to go into overdrive. Aside from a few company trucks the only car in the lot was Archer's Porsche. As she walked to the front door, she made herself take the steps slowly, breathe deeply, and think. Hard. By the time her hand was on the doorknob, she had worked out the semblance of a defense.

Archer opened the door. Hard as it was for Meredith to accept, he was even more handsome than he'd been before. He'd lost some weight and had acquired a few lines and shadows that gave his face an added interest. For one frozen fraction of a second, such a short time that both of them were able to pretend it didn't happen, they each stared into a face they had hungered for.

Pretending to clear his throat, Archer backed quickly away, swinging the door open. "Come on in. No one else is around."

"No one?" Meredith asked, peering around the office for men in three-piece suits carrying briefcases. She relaxed a tiny bit when she saw there were no lawyers waiting to ambush her.

"Just you and me," Archer said, lingering over the words in a way that freighted them with significance. "Well, shall we . . ." He paused and threw open his hands, holding them out to her, then abruptly slapped them together, his fingers twining over one another. Meredith wondered if the gesture suppressed the same nearly uncontrollable urge that was bursting within her—the urge to touch.

". . . step into my office," he finished.

Meredith gave herself a stern lecture. Just because there wasn't a battery of lawyers hovering about did not mean that she was out of danger. And just because Archer seemed slightly nervous did not mean that he had any deeper feelings for her. She had, once again, to do what she'd become so adept at over the past months—she had to compartmentalize herself, locking her feelings for Archer far away.

Archer slid his leanly muscled frame behind the desk and hunched over it, his shoulder muscles straining at the fabric of his shirt. Meredith took a chair on the other side of the desk. It might have been on the other side of the world, as distant as she felt from Archer. She couldn't help remembering another day—it seemed an eternity ago—when she'd first walked into this office and found him with his feet propped regally on the desk.

She waved the memory away as if it were a marauding crow. Such thoughts had no place in her current dealings with Archer.

"Archer," Meredith started off, hoping that the best defense *was* a good offense, "I honestly don't see how you could object to the article. I've searched my conscience and if I did err, and I don't think I did, it was in your favor." As she said the words, Meredith was fortified by their irrefutable veracity. Her voice gathered strength as she went on. "You couldn't have *paid* a P.R. firm to have gotten you any better coverage. To say nothing of having yourself and your solar balloon splashed all over the cover of the most respected popular business journal in America."

Archer's face hardened. Her impassioned words seemed to run off of it like rain off the chiseled heads on Mount Rushmore. "You lied," he said with a frightening blankness.

Meredith was stunned into silence for a moment by the accusation. "Lied? Where? I might have been subjective in a few parts, but I had to be. The piece was based on *my* subjective impressions. But aside from that, I can back up every assertion of fact in that article." Her voice and temper rose as she thought of all the extra time she'd spent corroborating all her data. "On anything that was the least bit questionable, I have no less than two sources and you, Mr. Hanson, are usually one of them." She bit off her words with a crisp finality, knowing that she stood on absolutely firm ground.

"Meredith, you lied." Archer repeated the charge. When Meredith opened her mouth to protest again, he silenced her with an upraised hand. "No," he ordered her. "Listen." He punched a button hidden beneath his desk and a whirring sound filled the office as though a swarm of locusts were descending on them.

"Archer, what is that?"

"Just listen," he repeated with the same icy control. The sound of another button being pressed clicked with an amplified volume over what Meredith guessed were hidden speakers. Then a recorded voice was speaking. With a jolt, she realized it was *her* voice.

"Yes," she heard herself say, "Chicago was gray, my job was gray, the weather was gray, and I was tired of it. I suppose most of all, I was tired of the gray men who had been populating my life and their dreary vision of life as a one-track scramble up the ladder of success with no stops for joy or laughter. They were devoid of passion, emotion, all the things that make life worth living . . ."

"You recorded me!" Meredith burst out as her voice faded in the background.

"I told you I'd had problems with overzealous reporters in the past," Archer explained. "I wanted to have my refusal on tape. Then, after I changed my mind, I didn't see any point in telling you that I'd recorded our first interview, just as I record all sensitive meetings."

"I still don't understand," Meredith muttered, becoming increasingly befuddled.

"That was merely Exhibit A. This is Exhibit B." Archer plucked his copy of *Enterprise* off his desk and stretched across it to hand it to Meredith. Her concluding remarks, the words she had labored so long and hard on, were highlighted in yellow.

"Read them," Archer ordered.

Meredith glanced away from the article into Archer's face. It was set in an expression of deadly seriousness. She began to read her closing words. "In a world of black and white and shades of gray, Archer Hanson is a polychromatic rainbow dancing on the horizon as vividly as one of his banner-draped, sun-heated balloons."

"Those two statements," Archer observed drily, "don't jibe with the last one you made to me. The one about our not being right for each other."

The scrappy brittleness was gone from Meredith's voice when she softly answered, "As I recall, you didn't disagree with me."

"No, I didn't. I've fought for everything I have. But there's one thing you can't ever take by force and that's love. It's either freely given or it's not worth having. I wasn't about to battle you for your love, Meredith. I've done that before, and it's a mistake. One I'll never repeat."

The last thing she'd ever expected to see on Archer Hanson's face was plainly evident—a look of hurt vulnerability. In that instant, Meredith realized how badly she'd misjudged him. Not once, when she'd taken him for an indulged rich kid, but twice. The second time she'd missed the mark was in her assumption that Archer was emotionally invulnerable. That he could have walked out on all they'd shared together and felt nothing but relief. She should have known better after what she'd learned about him at the uranium mine. The love he was talking about having battled for was his father's.

Meredith barely trusted her voice. It was quavery and small when she spoke again. "My love isn't something worth fighting for, Archer. That's why I told you it wouldn't work for us."

"Why didn't you just tell me that, tell me something, *anything*, in the first place?" Archer probed, but his tone had lost its granite edge.

"I would have if you hadn't bolted out of my apartment, my life. All that I could assume was that you were relieved I'd called it off."

"Relieved?" Archer leaned back in his chair and unloosed a dry, humorless laugh that bounced hollowly off the ceiling. "Were you 'relieved' when I left without making a fuss, Meredith?"

"Relieved?" Meredith said, echoing his incredulity. "Archer, I was devastated." That flat admission opened the floodgates behind which she had kept the swirling tides of her grief, loneliness, and love dammed up. She was swept away on a wave of emotion. She choked back the currents raging within her. "I'm not strong enough for your love, Archer. I was slipping back into . . ." She stumbled over the word just as her mother had, swallowed, and made herself spit it out. "Back into some anorexic patterns. Not eating, not wanting to eat. I was losing weight and, worst of all, losing my perspective. I was starting not to be able to tell if I was skinny or fat or safely in between. I couldn't risk having all that start again, Archer. Not for anything."

This time Archer's laugh was not the dry, hollow thing of a moment before; it was his own full-throated, robust sound of true amusement. "You silly little fool," he grinned. "I haven't eaten right since the day I met you. Did you ever stop to think that you might be in love?"

"Archer, if this is love, then it's a weak and destructive thing on my part and it's not worthy of you. I can't spend the rest of my life falling apart and then waiting for you to come home and put the pieces back together. To make me whole again. That's not love, Archer, that's emotional parasitism." She hesitated, waiting for his reaction. It was a very strange one.

"Why do you keep trying to destroy yourself, Meredith?"

"Destroy myself?"

"I've had a lot of time to think about this. It's practically all I *have* been able to think about for the past two months. You've even admitted that you denied yourself what you really wanted to do in life when your brother died and you went into finance. Then, when you couldn't perform the impossible by *becoming* your lost brother, you attempted a slow form of suicide that came perilously close to succeeding. Instead you made a courageous decision and chose life."

As Archer spoke the truths she herself had uncovered with her mind, she finally began to believe them with her heart as well. Like the perfectly executed illustration that accompanies the most insightful of texts, Meredith's recurring nightmare came to her. She saw herself through the dark mists of the frightening dream running after Rory, trying to catch his escaping wheelchair. She saw herself running still, even after he'd disappeared over the cliff. It was painfully obvious in that moment, with Archer's eyes boring into her as if he too were watching the drama being played out on the screen of her mind, exactly what she'd been doing. She *had* been trying to destroy herself.

Meredith felt her heart pound. She didn't want to hear his question. Didn't want to answer it. But his eyes, those dark, crystalline chips, wouldn't relent. They gouged into her, digging a reply from the deepest part of her soul, a part she had buried beneath years of pain and subtle rejection.

She tried to deflect the question with a brittle attempt at humor. "You certainly don't make a very good Freudian analyst. Shouldn't you have a little goatee and a notebook and shouldn't I be lying on a couch?"

"Don't do that, Meredith," Archer commanded, his gaze unwavering.

She didn't have to ask what he meant; she knew she was trying to hide behind a shield of humor.

"First you tried to eradicate you, who you were, by abandoning what you really wanted to do with your life and trying to take your brother's place in your father's firm. But that wasn't enough, was it?" Archer asked the question gently, in a way that only a person who had done the same thing could ask it.

She wondered how much of his childhood Archer had spent trying to turn himself into the person his father had wanted him to be. The undeniable fact that he understood what she'd done and why, and didn't condemn her for it, kept Meredith from closing her ears to the painful truths he was holding up for her inspection. She nodded in answer.

"No, nothing was ever enough," she whispered, barely noticing the tear that slid over her cheek, a dagger-shaped streak that pierced Archer's heart. "I remember once, I was about eleven. I'd never brought home a report card of all A's before. There were always one or two B's.

And they were what my mother commented on. Never the A's. But this one time I'd worked really hard. Studying after school. Never going out to play. And I had all A's. I brought the report card to my parents, waiting for, dying for a word, just one word of praise. My father looked at it. Then, without speaking, he passed it to my mother. She put on her little half-moon reading glasses and looked down at it. I was bursting, barely able to contain myself."

Meredith sucked in a deep, shuddering sigh as if it had all happened only moments before. "Then my mother just put my report aside as if it were a thing of no importance. 'But, Mother,' I said, 'I made all A's.' She looked at me over the tops of her glasses and said, 'Well, I should hope you did, my dear. A little girl without any friends had *better* make good grades.' "

Archer ached to fold her in his arms to soothe the hurt that had been burned into her so many years ago. But he knew that if there was any hope of them building a future together, he had to let her go on. To tell it all.

"I was never bright enough, diligent enough, popular enough, amusing enough, or even thin enough."

"But you almost killed yourself trying to be." Archer leaned forward as if pleading for her to understand. To understand what he was saying and, more important, to understand who she was. "And you're still doing it, Meredith. You're doing it right now by denying yourself the happiness that we could have together. For whatever reasons and rationalizations you care to come up with, that's what it all boils down to."

Archer's voice mesmerized Meredith. She barely breathed, so riveted was she by what he was saying and by the passion with which he delivered his message.

"If you can look at me right now, Meredith," Archer said, the heat in his gaze soldering a connection between them that she was powerless to break, "and tell me that you don't love me, I'll disappear from your life forever. It will be like you never knew me."

The desolation Meredith had known for the past two months became like a few minutes of discomfort when matched with the possibility that Archer's entire existence would be forever eradicated from her life.

"No!" As she began to wake from the spell cast by Archer's mesmeric revelations, she bolted from her chair. "No, Archer, please, no!" The strangled cry was wrenched from her.

Compelled by a call that went beyond words, Archer was drawn to her. His arms encircled her with a sheltering tenderness. But Meredith could not surrender to them. Not yet, not before she unburdened her heart.

"God, yes, I love you, Archer. I love you more than anything else on this earth."

"Why, then, have we been torturing each other this way? Why haven't we been together?"

She heard the question only as a deep rumbling against the ear she rested on Archer's chest. She drank in his feel, his smell like parched earth absorbing a long-delayed summer rain. For the first time in weeks, she felt whole, not a fractured mosaic ready to crumble at any moment.

"Archer, I've ached for you. You don't know how many times I almost called. I even drove by your house one night and it was all I could do to keep myself from stopping."

"You should have. You should have come to me."

"I couldn't. Not after you had forbidden me to call. Not when I still felt like a jigsaw puzzle with half the pieces missing."

"How do you feel now?" he murmured, his voice a velvet enticement.

"I feel as if I was born to be held in your arms," she whispered.

"You were, darling, you were," he answered with a rising ardor. "I can't begin to tell you how I missed you. I tried to seal off the hurt, to harden myself. But I couldn't. You opened doors inside of me that I never knew existed and I couldn't shut them. When I read your article, I realized that I could stop trying. It was a great piece of writing. I read it and thought that no one could have written about another person with such depth and understanding without loving him." Archer smoothed back the fine wisps of hair around Meredith's face, gently massaging her temples as he tilted her face upward.

"I clung to that thought like a drowning man hanging on to a piece of driftwood, I wanted to believe it so badly. But there were corners of doubt and fear in my mind. I even had another excuse ready when I called. I was going to say I was just ringing up to tell you that I'm going to be launching Cloud Waltzer III tomorrow. Even with that extra excuse in reserve, my hand was trembling when I dialed your number."

"My whole body was trembling when I walked in here," Meredith confessed. She opened her mouth to say more, but realized that a far more eloquent vehicle of expression was hers. Sliding her hands up over the broad expanse of Archer's shoulders, she brought the tips of her fingers to his sturdy jaw. With infinite care and a torturing slowness, she tilted his mouth down. At the same time, she raised herself up on the tips of her toes, skimming the awakening points of her breasts along the bulwark of Archer's chest as she reached up to deliver the symbol of all that pounded in her heart.

His lips met hers, and for a second they were both stilled by the awing significance of this moment. Then all thoughts were blown away by the cyclone of desire that touched down as their lips reunited. It howled through Meredith, a whirling funnel of need that sucked up remorse, sadness, and regret. It churned through her, leaving only a devastating path of passion.

"Archer, I've wanted you so terribly," she babbled, her voice a barely recognizable whimper of loving.

"Not half as much as I've wanted you." Hot breaths of need carried Archer's words to batter damply against Meredith's ear. The tickling tendrils that shivered out from that spot burst into great blooms of electric sensation when Archer's mouth closed over the arching column of her neck.

Archer felt the purring of her want vibrate against his lips. In that instant, all the frustrated desire, confusion, and despair of the past two months were converted into mindless, rapacious need. He had to exercise an almost superhuman strength to keep himself from ripping the annoying encumbrance of clothes from Meredith's quivering body, a body that had tormented him in fantasy for so many weeks. But he'd been too long denied not to savor the incalculable treasure that was now, unbelievably, his.

Meredith felt the tremor that shook Archer's hand as he lifted her top over her head. She saw that same tremor in her own hands as she slid them up under his shirt to push it away from the magnificence of his chest. Archer ensnared Meredith with the lethal power of his Nordic gaze. She was lost in it even as her hands reacquainted themselves with the sculpted swells of his chest, the corded strength of his shoulders, the rippling of his rib cage.

Archer's hands too were avidly renewing a passionate friendship. They devoured the silken smooth feel of her skin and the intoxicating delicacy of the fine bones beneath it. He unhooked the front fastening of her bra and was dazzled by the beauty that even his fantasy had proved inadequate at faithfully reproducing.

As he leaned slowly forward Meredith took the flimsy garment from his hands and parted it with her own fingers until it dropped from her shoulders into a puddle of fluff at her feet. Archer's mouth on the shell-pink crest of her breast was a molten potion that coursed through her, narcotizing her into a rubber-legged languor. As he sucked at the straining centers, it felt as if the ambrosial nectar that was melting within her was being drawn up from the very core of her femininity. She swayed against him, weakened by the many powerful emotions colliding within her in such a short period of time.

"Meredith"—her name blossomed in a warm vapor that caressed her ear—"be my wife."

The simple words jolted Meredith, rocking her more profoundly than any of the upheavals she had so far experienced in a day filled with them. Why did it jolt her so? Wasn't his request the very crystallization of all she dreamed of? Could she even imagine a future in which she and Archer *weren't* together?

"Why are you trembling?" Archer asked, his passionate caresses turning to ones of comfort.

"I . . . I . . ." Meredith started off before she finally stammered out her reply. "Yes, oh, yes, of course, I want to be your wife. I want you to be my husband. I want us to have children together. To grow old together. But I can't. Not yet. I've come so far in the last few weeks, found so much strength within myself. I can't stop now. I don't want to come to you, Archer, as anything less than an equal partner."

Archer opened his mouth to protest, then stopped himself. "I wouldn't want anything less," he said, his voice dull. "If it means I have to wait a bit longer, so be it. I've already waited my whole life for you, Meredith."

Emboldened by a love neither of them could deny, Meredith's fingers found the turquoise-encrusted buckle of his belt as his went to the zipper of her pants. She paused, though, stepping away from him. She felt suddenly shy, as though the past weeks, and now his proposal, had made Archer something of a stranger again instead of the man who had introduced her to her own body.

"The lights," she muttered.

A hiss of exasperation escaped Archer's lips before he could control himself. "I pushed before and almost ruined the best thing to ever come into my life," he admitted. "I won't make the same mistake twice. If it's darkness you want, my darling, it's darkness you'll have. But mark my words, you'll come to me in sunshine one day."

He flicked off the lights and the shuttered office grew dim and dusky. The last vestiges of Meredith's timidity fled then, and she answered Archer's hunger with one even more devouring. They loved one another in the traditional way, his body covering hers, hers cushioning and bearing his glorious weight. But the heat of their love animated the act with a power that both transcended and glorified their every physical movement.

As Meredith lay against the thick, soft carpet in glowing fulfillment beneath Archer, he buried his head against her neck. She felt several wrenching shudders in his chest pressed against her own. Her hands soothed over his back and she felt a wetness trickle down her neck. Was it sweat or could it have been . . . not a tear?

"Archer?" she asked.

But his only answer was to roll onto his back and hold her to his chest even more tightly, pressing her head into the crook of his neck. After a few minutes had passed, he said in a thick voice, "Let's not talk. Don't tell me how long it will be before this can happen again. Let's not even say good-bye. When you're ready, when you have to, just leave. I'll be waiting for you when you return."

Meredith lay for a long, still moment on Archer's chest and let the tidal surge of his heartbeat fill her mind and block out all thoughts, especially ones of the inevitable parting that each beat of his heart brought one second nearer. For just a few minutes, she wanted to be absolutely with him. Someday, she promised herself, it will never have to end.

Archer shifted beneath her and they both rose. They looked at each other and Meredith knew that he was right; there was nothing else they could say. Not now.

In silence they dressed and parted.

The night of the New Year had already begun. Meredith was grateful for the darkness. She couldn't have borne facing a blinding bright sun. She felt as if an automaton had replaced her, sitting behind the wheel driving her home. She'd been eviscerated, hollowed out, the real Meredith Tolliver left back on the carpeted floor of Hanson Development.

And that feeling, she told her wilted self sternly, is exactly why you must keep on driving. She repeated the words she'd told Archer again in her mind, that she would come to him only as an equal partner. She had to build her inner strength before she could mesh with him. Meredith beat that thought through her mind like a chant to ward off the overwhelming urge she was battling to simply turn around and return to Archer's arms.

At midnight that evening she was watching the televised clock in Times Square blink in the New Year. Thor was asleep on her lap and she tried to remember a time when she'd felt lonelier. She knew one existed but couldn't immediately recall it. After seeing the year that had changed her life laid to rest, she toasted the new one with a mug of herbal tea and went to bed.

But sleep did not come. Instead, all the thoughts she'd tried to drown out listening to the oceanic beat of Archer's pulse swam up to the surface of her consciousness. They bore only one message and it was: "Meredith Tolliver, you are a fool."

Fool? she demanded of herself. She'd been convinced that, heartbreakingly hard as it was, the course she was following was at least wise, was the rational thing to do. But the instincts she'd overridden when she'd left Archer all disagreed. It wasn't strength she was seeking, it was safety. A love as powerful as the one she bore for Archer Hanson was a terrifying, uncontrollable thing and it scared her. Scared her into rationalizing that she needed time alone to fortify herself.

Coward, the instincts she'd attempted to deny mocked her. There was no denying them now as Meredith lay alone with only herself and the truth. Finally facing that truth was like seeing all the jumbled pieces of a puzzle she'd been attempting to work blindfolded fall into place. No corner of her mind remained askew. The picture was perfect. What she had to do, wanted desperately to do, was clear. She felt positively buoyant as the weight she'd been shouldering for so long was released. Great stone masses were transformed into piles of feathers.

Her plan firm in her mind, Meredith set the alarm, rolled over, and for the first time in months, slept soundly.

She was up before the alarm went off, scurrying to the window to check the weather. Thank God, the warm spell was continuing. She showered, taking extra care to shave her legs right up to the tops of her thighs, and dressed quickly in the precise outfit she'd decided on the night before. She glimpsed herself in the mirror when she'd finished, pleased with how elegant her taupe boots looked with the emerald green cape Archer had given her skimming their tops.

A silvery dawn moon, like a New Year's reveler surprised by morning, still hung over the volcanic cones of the West Mesa. The field that had been the site of the Fiesta was populated now only by Archer, Cloud Waltzer III, some of the familiar faces from Solar Concepts, and a couple of TV news crews. A shiver of nervousness nudged away Meredith's jubilance. She parked back away from the center of activity and wrapped the cape more tightly around her as if trying to draw courage from its velvety warm folds. What had seemed the perfect plan last night now appeared somewhat flawed. For a second or two she wondered what on earth she thought she was doing. The answer beat through her with a revivifying strength: She was reclaiming her life.

Fortified, she marched over to the edge of the crowd. Archer was too preoccupied to notice her approach as he made the last-minute checks, assuring himself that all vital equipment, like a lighter for the auxiliary propane system, was on board.

Phil, her neighbor, did spot her. The blast of the propane burner covered his greeting as he caught sight of Meredith. Archer's back was to Meredith and his attention was absorbed by the flame he was carefully directing into the upright envelope. After spending weeks developing it, he didn't want the least flicker of flame overheating it. Meredith hurried over to Phil, and with nervous apprehension squeezing her voice, she told him her plan, at least the part of it that involved him.

"Sure," he agreed eagerly as she hesitantly asked if, just this once, she could replace him on the flight. Phil had immediately sensed that something far more important than a lighthearted lark was at stake.

The sun was streaking slanted rays over the Sandias when Archer, still monitoring the flame roaring above his head, called out, "Climb in, Phil, we're lifting off."

Rather than straddling the rim, Meredith hopped up onto it, steadying herself with one hand and keeping the cape pulled tightly about her with the other, then swung her legs into the basket.

Feeling a body land behind him, Archer ordered, "Let her go," and the hands keeping the straining balloon earthbound released their hold. They bobbed up like a ball that had been held underwater.

Archer turned off the burner and finally looked around. In that second, Meredith felt as she had on her first balloon ride. She felt she had made an inexorable error. The surprised delight she'd expected to see wasn't anywhere in evidence.

"What are you doing here?" Archer demanded angrily.

Stunned by his reaction, Meredith couldn't force out her reply fast enough.

"I told you that I wouldn't be played like a yo-yo," he informed her with a menacing heat.

"That's not why I'm—" Meredith began, but Archer cut her off.

"We're landing," he informed her bluntly, reaching a hand up toward the rip panel cord. The blond hairs along his arm glinted in the sunlight. Meredith's own hand went up to stop his.

"Don't," she pleaded with him. Then, in a stronger, surer voice, she asked again. "Don't."

They continued to ascend. Behind Archer, Meredith watched the peaks of the Sandias, gulleyed with early morning sunshine, come into view, then vanish as they gained altitude. Soon there was nothing but boundless sky behind him. In a distant corner of her mind, she thought that this was the way Archer should always be framed—a heroic figure with a spirit from another, bolder time, sailing through a sun-drenched sky.

Archer's hand stopped, but Meredith knew it was

only a momentary reprieve. He was not a man used to being pushed and she had already forced him farther than any other human had before. She had to bring them both back from the brink of the abyss she'd led them to, and quickly.

"You said that one day I would come to you in sunshine," she said, her voice quavery and uncertain now that the moment of the ultimate test of her courage had arrived. With trembling hands, she parted the folds of the cloak. "That day has come."

Archer's mouth fell open into a slack hole of amazement. Sunlight played over the naked curves of Meredith's body, gilding its ivory delicacy with a golden patina. A smile that started at the soles of his feet crept across the length of Archer's face, sealing his mouth into a seam of growing joy. He would have scooped her into his arms then and there, but something stopped him. He had to know if she was sure. He couldn't, wouldn't allow himself, to be plunged anew into the desolation she'd left him in yesterday. He stood motionless. This time had to be for always. For always, or never.

Meredith saw the testing question in his eyes. She pulled the cloak back farther. The cool air and Archer's hot gaze teased the crowns of her breasts into wakefulness. She slid the voluptuous, deep green fabric over them. It swished about her waist, the juncture of her thighs. Volumes of understanding passed between her and Archer as her fingers unknotted the bow at her throat. The cape fell to the wicker floor. This time was for always.

Archer opened his arms to her and she stepped into them, stepped into the life they would share together.

"Does this mean you still want me?" she asked, hugging herself to his warmth.

"'Want' does not even begin to cover the territory," Archer answered, a laugh building deep in his chest. He knelt to retrieve the cloak. "I do this with the greatest reluctance and concern for your health," he said, wrapping it around her shoulders.

As the cleansing laughter of delight and fulfillment rumbled through him, Archer held Meredith away from him to gaze into her face. "Never stop surprising me."

As she reached up to capture that enrapturing Viking mouth with her own, Meredith whispered, "Never stop, period. Just never stop."

Cloud Waltzer III, warmed by the sun and dancing on merry zephyrs of wind, rose through a cloudless sky, bearing her passengers forward into their future.